MW00883403

To Eclair, for everything.

Chapter One
The Position

Maybourne House
Cavendish Square, London, 1810

Patience was one of several virtues with which Jane Althea Smith, known to all London as the enigmatic mystic Mistress Althea, was not blessed.

The others were, in no particular order: humility, a convivial personality, and a forgiving nature. She had been informed many times that she also lacked a general sense of optimism and the docility common to most females.

She was not particularly honest, either.

However, *that,* she would argue, was a matter of survival.

When her very life, or the wellbeing of any one in need, depended on forgoing with honesty, Althea had always found herself helpless to resist. Besides, lying was harmless when the ones being deceived could afford it, and those were the only sort of people she dealt with dishonestly.

This philosophy had made her the most talked about woman in London. Exclusively in hushed voices, of course. The famed Mistress Althea had taken the town by storm in the last year, if only behind closed doors.

Speaking of which, she was getting cold.

Althea rapped on the front door of Maybourne House. Again.

Good god, she hated waiting. There was nothing worth doing that could not be attended to promptly.

That was one virtue she did have, Althea mused, staring up at the enormous white stone edifice before her. She was always on time.

If only the same could be said of her clients.

She raised her hand to knock once more when, blessedly, the door opened.

"Mistress Althea," the gaunt butler intoned with a half bow. "Apologies for the delay."

Strange how as Mistress Althea she warranted an apology. If the man knew who and what she really was, he'd likely never have bothered to apologize.

But then, she'd never been allowed through the front door, either.

"Thank you-" she said, pausing for the butler's name.

"Goggins, m'am," the man said. He was very old but carried himself like a top shelf domestic. Althea wondered how he came to work for this family. What little she knew of them, she did not think they could find, let alone afford, a man like Goggins. Perhaps he was a holdover from the family's glory days, now many decades and two generations past. Goggins was certainly old enough for that.

"Thank you, Goggins," she said with a smile. Despite the elite affectations of the character she presented, Althea had always believed in being kind to household staff. Unless they gave her a reason to not be, but that was rare. The servants knew everything, after all, and in Althea's life, as everywhere if one were clever enough, knowledge was power.

The butler gestured Althea inside, and gently shut the heavy door behind her. She gave him her black cloak and even blacker reticule, then took in the house while he arranged her things in a closet near the door.

One could tell a lot about someone by their house. Althea had been in so many grand houses that she barely blinked an eye at a marble floor or an ornate gilt bannister. The Earl of Maybourne came from a very old, well-respected family, but if rumors were true- and they often were- there was little money in the ancient coffers. So Althea had expected the house to be respectable but perhaps shabby- either that, or a grand attempt to pretend riches, with faux grandeur to distract the eye.

This house was none of those things. The floor was some sort of pale grey stone she could not name, elegant and timeless and only improved by wear. An elegant dark wooden staircase ran along one wall to a broad landing, its mahogany railing polished and gleaming. The walls were simple, paneled white, giving precedence to the family portraits and beautiful landscapes adorning them. It was not flashy in the least, but the quality and care put into the place were obvious.

Unease rippled through Althea.

This was a house she could imagine being happy in, which was odd, as she'd been in more of the *ton's* massive estates and grand townhomes than she could count, and she had never felt that way before. There was an ease to this place, a simple, quiet luxury far more potent than any gold or marble could offer.

Her eyes wandered up to the paneled ceiling, painted to look like a spring sky of robin's egg blue with gentle swirling clouds. A hopeful gesture in London, and just as elegantly rendered as the rest of the entryway.

Then she saw it- a flaw.

In the very center of the ceiling above the entryway, which was even higher than the rest of the ceiling, as if above the entrance to the house was a

tower of light straight to the heavens. But instead of a
window or the sun itself, Althea looked up and saw a
round hole and several scuff marks directly over her
head in the very center of the elevated ceiling, where a
chandelier should be. Except there was no chandelier-
just a dark, jagged hole in the gentle blue sky.

The hairs on Althea's neck prickled and a sense of
foreboding flooded her. The hole was strangely
disturbing and definitely out of place, but there was
nothing unnerving about it. It should make her feel
better. This old house was merely that, an old house,
and the Earl was obviously struggling if he could not
afford to patch up so glaring a flaw.

Althea smiled inwardly, pushing away her unease.
A desperate man was just the sort she preferred,
because desperation made one vulnerable to belief,
and belief was the secret to Althea's success. As long
as the Earl could pay her fee, she didn't care if his
whole beautiful ceiling fell down.

"This way, m'am," the butler, Goggins, said,
stepping up beside her and gesturing down a long
hallway to the side of the staircase. "His lordship will
meet you in the rose salon."

Althea followed Goggins down the hall. The first
open door emptied into a light-filled breakfast room.
The next door led to a parlor done all in shades of

blue. The third door Goggins passed was shut, a sinister-looking metal latch bolting it shut from the outside.

A chill ran down Althea's spine. The house was beautiful and calming and strange and unsettling all at once. As if something very wonderful had been slowly taken over by darker forces. She did not ask Goggins about the latch.

The rose salon looked out over the rear garden of the house and was more of a pale brownish salon, really. The once pink furnishings had, like Goggins, seen better days, though the room itself was as elegant as the entryway with pale walls, a polished floor of light wood, and an elegant fireplace of the same light wood.

Althea sat on a worn pale pink settee and, once Goggins had left to call for some tea and cakes and do whatever other things butlers did in aristocratic households, she took a closer look at her surroundings. The room was old, and not in the current fashion, but beautifully made. She could tell from the floors to the moulding that a lot of care, and money, had gone into this house, once upon a time.

The fireplace again caught her eye and she rose despite herself to get a closer look.

There were little carvings all over the mantle and

down its pale, natural wood sides. At the top there was clearly the design of shooting stars and radiant suns. The stars swirled around the suns like waves dancing past precious stones. It was odd, and beautiful.

It was also carved with great attention to the natural patterns in the wood itself, the design cascading down on either side until it reached the height of Althea's knees. There, the sky, both day and night, met flames. Not only the flames of whatever would be inside the grate, which was strangely unlit for such a chilly day, but flames carved into the wood itself, so artfully they almost appeared to be moving.

No that wasn't it- they *were* moving.

Althea blinked.

The flames stopped moving.

Good, she thought. There was no place in her life for anything that was not practical, tangible, directly in front of her, and entirely *real*.

The door opened.

"Mistress Althea! Praise the heavens you are here! This house will be the ruin of us all!"

A petite blond woman old enough to be Althea's mother came swooshing in on a cloud of scarves and feathers and made straight for Althea.

"Lady Maybourne?" Althea asked, immediately

assuming the air of distant authority and mystery for which Mistress Althea was renowned. All thoughts of her personal fascination with the fireplace and its dancing wooden flames were shoved down and saved to consider at a later, possibly nonexistent, time.

"How did you know?" the woman asked, looking at Althea in wonder. "You really are gifted with psychic powers, aren't you, child?"

"It's not a difficult guess, mother," a dry voice said from across the room. A tall, blonde man with an arrogant expression walked in. He had his mother's watery blue eyes, but where hers were cloudy, his were clear as ice. Althea felt herself go on edge. Some men one knew to trust immediately, others had the opposite effect. This one, unsettlingly, fell somewhere in between.

"And you must be the Earl of Maybourne," Althea said, delivering a curtsy at the exact height warranted by an earl.

Charles Ridgely, Earl of Maybourne, inclined his head. "Mistress Althea. Please, do sit." He gestured back to the settee where she had been moments before, and she returned to it. The Earl's mother gripped her hand as if it were a lifeline and sat beside her, hope and belief pouring from her.

This was going to be a complicated job. Althea

could sense it already. And given the state of the place she had half a mind to decline it purely out of concern that her fee may go unpaid.

Fortunately, there were ways to ensure such things.

She straightened her straightened her back. She was unusually tall for a woman, and even sitting could evoke a powerful presence. "First things first, before we begin, before you tell me what you know and before I begin to tell you what I sense in this house- and believe me, my lord, my lady, I do not wish to frighten you, but from the moment I entered this house, I sensed a dark and dangerous presence here- before we touch the other side with even the smallest brush of our living selves-" at this she gently squeezed Lady Maybourne's hand with the slightest of movements, making the old woman jump and laugh nervously- "I must tell you my rules."

The Earl, who'd seated himself on the settee across from Althea and his mother, raised a thin, blonde brow. "Rules?"

"Call me Althea, please" she said with a warm smile that, on principle, never reached her eyes. "And yes, rules. First, I must go about my business as I see fit. I will take your requests into consideration, but the spirit world does not operate as we do and there are forces here only I can understand after a lifetime of hard-won experience and natural gifts. This must be respected."

The Earl shrugged. "Fine."

That was easy enough. "Second, if at any time I give you or any member of the household instructions that seem odd or unusual, you must heed them. The sooner I have succeeded in my task, which may of course require means sensible only to the forces that lie beyond our plane of existence, the sooner I shall be gone and the household set back to rights."

The Earl nodded his consent.

This was much easier than usual. Althea felt her suspicions deepen.

"And third, my payment must be paid in half now, with the rest once the job is done."

"Half up front? Charles is that-"

"Quiet mother," the Earl said, leveling Althea with his steady, cool gaze. "Mistress Althea, your terms are acceptable. Mother, I think there has been a delay with the tea."

"I saw the maid on the way here, I expect any moment now it will-"

"Please go check on the tea, mother. I am sure our guest will find it difficult to resolve our little dilemma without proper refreshment."

Lady Maybourne recognized her dismissal and

released Althea's hand, giving a little curtsy before taking her leave. As soon as the door snapped shut behind her, the Earl turned his full attention on Althea.

The effect was jarring. The Earl was a forbidding man, young but accustomed to obedience. Althea had met many such men, but this one made her nervous. She couldn't say why. Nothing made her nervous. It wasn't just the Earl, though. There was something about this house that was not quite right. It felt so alluringly lovely, and yet wrong. Appealing, but… she didn't know the word… *sinister* felt melodramatic, but that was the only one that came to mind. For the second time in as many minutes, she considered declining the job.

"A thousand pounds," the Earl said point blank, and any thought of saying no to the job vacated Althea's mind. She had never been paid a fee half so high for a single assignment.

She would have worried she'd heard him wrong, but she had excellent hearing and there was something about Maybourne's stern confidence that told her he knew exactly what he was offering.

"Five hundred now," she confirmed smoothly, as if his offer hadn't floored her.

"And five hundred in a week," he confirmed.

"A week?" That was odd. She was happy to finish the job quickly, but Mistress Althea's credibility rested not on following her own interests, but in fulfilling the expectations of clients, clients who did not believe spirits worked on given schedules. Althea, of course, knew spirits could work on any schedule, if the numbers were right and the numbers were more than right in this case. But as it was all a game, she must play her part. "My lord, the spirits are unpredictable, if they are entrenched it may be-"

"Althea, or whatever your real name is, let me be frank," the Earl said, leaning back and for the first time looking tired and, Althea thought, human. "I know spirits are not real. You know spirits are not real. I know you know spirits are not real and now you know I know it. Fair enough?"

She gave him a look. "I convene with the spirits every day, my lord. I cannot say I know any such thing."

He knew what she meant was *"I literally cannot say I know any such thing or else my entire livelihood is blown, you bastard."*

Maybourne smiled, and gave another of his short nods. "Very good. Then we are in accord. I need you to convince my sister there is no ghost in this house. Or, at the very least, that the ghost she insists is in this house, has gone. That will then satisfy my mother, as well, who has not personally voiced an acquaintanceship with any spirits, but as you can see is a deeply impressionable woman and wholeheartedly believes my sister's allegations of a spirit in this house."

Althea gave him one of his own nods, an understanding look passing between them.

"Brilliant," the Earl continued. "You see, I have a problem. Several problems, in fact."

"I am sorry to hear it, my lord," Althea said, more curious than sorry. She'd never known an Earl to have any real problems. Any hiccup in their lives was readily smoothed over with money, just as this Earl was proposing to use Althea. Althea had seen real problems, and superstitious drama had never been one of them.

"You, Mistress, can solve my problems."

The assertion was flattering and merely confirmed Althea's suspicion that whatever the Earl was referring to, it was not what Althea considered a real problem.

Maybourne continued. "Despite my best efforts these last five years since since my father's death, the estate is in decline. Rapid decline."

That, Althea thought, explained the state of the

house. Even now she could see dust in the corners of the room, where no dust should be while an Earl was in residence. She could no longer worry about being paid, however, as even five hundred pounds up front was a kingly payment.

The Earl was still talking. "I tried to keep to the country in an effort to curb expenses, but now that my sister is of age she has demanded a London Season."

"Young ladies often do," Althea noted.

"Indeed," his lordship agreed. "But you see, I can only afford the one season."

"Is that a problem?"

"One of them. Yes. You see, it has to be good. She must marry, and soon. I cannot afford a second season, and if she does not marry well, I may not be able to afford anything else, either."

Ah. That was it. His sister marries a man with money, the rest of the family's problems are solved and they could keep all their grand houses and extensive staff and fine clothes. Just as Althea suspected, this was a quandary of the wealthy and titled variety, not the starving and destitute sort.

"That should not be too difficult. I have heard the rumors that your sister is a beauty, even a diamond of the first water, if a little rustic," Althea said, hoping such an observation was not too forward. Then again, where Jane Smith cared for manners, Mistress Althea cared nothing for societal rules. It was part of her enigma.

"You have heard correctly. It has been two months and she has already had two dukes, one earl, four marquesses and lord knows too many poets sniffing around her skirts."

"Do not tell me she has fallen for a poet, my lord."

"Worse," Maybourne said with a grimace, "she has fallen for a ghost."

Althea's anxiety vanished. Whatever she'd thought this job would be, this wasn't it. She had never dealt with such a peculiar circumstance, but the thrill of a new challenge had always excited her.

"I see why you did not simply summon a matchmaker," she said.

Maybourne looked more exhausted than ever. "Believe me, if it were that simple, I would have. I tried. My mother's dearest friend is the biggest busybody in town and has introduced a veritable parade of suitors but Charlotte will have none of them."

Althea nodded. She already knew what was happening here. All her cases always came back to the people involved and their own very earthly wants and needs and fears. Spirits had nothing to do with it.

How could they?

Spirits did not exist.

What did exist, however, were spirited young women. Althea already knew that Miss Charlotte Ridgely, sister to the Earl of Maybourne, was either exceedingly dim or very, very clever.

Althea put her money on the latter. There was nothing like originality to gain power, and power meant control. Althea already saw that the young woman in this household was the one with the power, at least for now. There was some reason Charlotte did not wish to marry and she had concocted a very creative albeit melodramatic way around it.

Althea flashed a genuine smile at the Earl, letting it reach her black eyes. Not too broad, just an upturn of her full, red lips, all still very mysterious, but she knew it gave the effect of a flame alight in the darkness. Her mother's eyes had also been dark, nearly black, set in a long, pale face just like Althea's, and anyone who thought such coloring was anything but an asset was a fool.

The smiled worked. The Earl's mouth fell open a little, despite himself. She felt the hope coming off him in waves. "So you'll do it then? You'll convince my sister and my mother the ghost is gone?" he asked.

"Of course," she said, confidence deepening her

smile. "It will be my pleasure."

Chapter Two
The Family

"Excellent," the Earl said, obviously pleased. "When can you start?"

Typically, Althea would make a show of considering her options, alluding to other more demanding clients, playing up the severity of the haunting or the possession or whatever it was she was being asked to remedy, but the Earl held no pretenses that the services she was offering- or the precipitating ethereal force that warranted them- were real. She was not going to outright admit any of this to him, but the freedom was refreshing. The money, a sum four times higher than her normal rate, was even more encouraging. She had no need for pretense.

"Now," she said.

"Fantastic." The Earl reached into his pocket and pulled out a bank note for the sum of five hundred pounds.

Althea fought to keep her pale, slender hand from shaking as she took it from him. Just before he released the cool, crisp paper, the Earl's eyes met hers. She saw cool calculation in his gaze, and something softer, a little desperate even.

Good.

She gave him a curt nod and he released the note into her palm.

The door opened then and Lady Maybourne appeared. She was followed closely by a footman and a maid carrying the tea service and a tray with a selection of cakes, all of which were placed on the table between the settees.

"This looks lovely," Althea said, tucking the note worth a small fortune into her pocket of her skirts.

"You do eat sweets, I hope?" Lady Maybourne asked nervously.

"I love them," Althea replied.

She meant it. She'd always had a sweet tooth and no matter how many wealthy households she entered she still marveled at the excess. Though there were only three of them, enough cakes and sweetmeats filled the tray to feed a dozen people. Althea took one, only one- a small tart. Temptation and indulgence were two vices she had never had the luxury to allow herself, even as her mouth watered to try everything on the platter.

But there was no room for excess. She had to remain focused at all times on her goal: financial freedom. Mistress Althea could not last forever, and before the ruse was found out by someone more concerned with fraud than the antics of the spirit world, she needed to be long gone from London.

She also needed to be rich.

"Has my son explained the nature of our troubles to you?" Lady Maybourne asked as she poured them each a cup of tea and sat down beside her son.

"He has," Althea confirmed, declining both sugar and milk in hers. She found that even such minor indulgences clouded her focus. The dowager noticed the unusual preparation, but said nothing.

"More importantly, mother, Mistress Althea has agreed to assist us. She feels quite confident that she can rid the house of this troublesome spirit and return Charlotte's attentions to more pressing concerns."

The older woman could not have looked more relieved if she had just been informed that rumors of an immediate French invasion were false.

"Thank goodness," she sighed, putting four lumps of sugar in her own tea. "It has been dreadful ever since we arrived. And that's without the day-to-day troubles. Pots clanging, paintings falling, door slamming themselves shut."

"Don't be dramatic, Mother," the Earl chided. Althea noticed he had not touched his tea, which held a single dollop of cream.

"You saw it too, Charles, when that painting swung out front the wall right across the hall on the third floor."

The Earl sipped his tea, saying nothing.

His mother persisted. "Don't put on airs for Mistress Althea, this is nothing to her! And she has agreed to help us. She should know everything!"

The Earl shifted uncomfortably in his seat and Althea wondered why he had not mentioned the other strange events. Obviously his mother was as convinced of the spirit as he had claimed, but his failure to mention these other occurrences was curious. He took another sip of his tea, but did not deny that he had also witnessed the phenomena his mother described.

"You're quite right, Lady Maybourne," Althea said assuringly. "I should know absolutely everything unusual that has happened since you have been in the house. Spirits often manifest in the obvious ways you just perfectly described, but they can make themselves known in more subtle, insidious ways as well."

"Insidious?" Lady Maybourne's eyes widened in concern.

Althea nodded solemnly. "*Very*. I once- no, no, I won't worry you with the details of other cases I have seen, suffice it to say only that the sooner I can set to work here the better an outcome we can all expect."

Lady Maybourne set her cup and saucer down on

the table nervously, her imagination running wild with what Althea alluded to but refused to described. Perfect. "Yes, yes, I can see time is of the essence here, certainly."

Althea glanced at the Earl, expecting him to roll his eyes, but he did not appear remotely skeptical now. He was watching his mother, genuine concern in his cool features. The hairs on Althea's neck prickled with that sense of foreboding again. There was definitely more going on here than she had been told.

"Then let us begin." Althea set down her now empty cup and straightened her spine, gathering her professional aura around herself. "Before anything else, before I spend another moment in this house, I must test its energy. One must know the texture, so to speak, of the presence one is communing with, its spectral environment and resonance. Reaching out to obtain this information also informs the spirit of your own presence and intention to communicate with it."

"You mean to do this now?" Lady Maybourne asked, eyes as wide as the saucer she clutched in her bony hands. "Is it dangerous?"

Althea paused just long enough before answering solemnly. "It can be. If the spirit is strong, it may also glean my intention to not only speak with it, but drive it out. If that happens, and there will be no doubt in your mind if that is happening, you and your son must leave the room at once."

Mistress Althea nodded with all the fearful conviction of a penitent at the altar. Althea was pleased to see the Earl was back to looking skeptical, his facade stony and revealing nothing.

"Please close your eyes. It is rare, but it has also happened that spiritual emanations may present suddenly."

Both the Ridgelys shut their eyes. This was going to be too easy.

Althea remained seated, but lifted her arms wide and up towards the ceiling. She began a rhythmless, continuous hum. After a moment she began to sway, her own eyes closed now, she knew the more transported she appeared the more convinced- and satisfied- her customers would be.

On cue, she gave little gasp. Lady Maybourne jumped as if startled. Althea continued her humming.

After a minute or so, she lowered her voice and spoke the words she had said a thousand times before.

"Oh spirits of this place, spirits of this house! Between this world and the next you lie, ever present, never to die, unholy friends and vicious fiends, we seek your wisdom, knowledge gleaned. Join us here, we have no fear, for we hold ourselves open to mysteries beyond."

Althea's voice was increasingly ragged, as she uttered the last line, it rose in volume with every word until the final cry shuddered through the room. "I entreat thee, now! Show thyself, share thyself, bring thyself… forth!"

Althea's eyes flew open on cue, just in time to watch the tea tray fly across the room and crash into the wall beside the fireplace. At the very same moment a bloodcurdling scream came from upstairs.

Althea quickly gathered herself.

The Earl's eyes were open now and he was looking at Althea as though deeply impressed. She couldn't tell him nothing like this had ever happened before. Obviously his mother had been so moved by the dramatic end of Althea's spell she had kicked the little table on which the tea tray sat and sent the thing flying. As for the scream….

The sound of footsteps thundering down the stairs in the hall reached them. Heavy, frantic steps, echoing through the house like a herd of elephants were stampeding. As the sound got closer, Althea knew the rose salon had to be their destination. Bracing herself, she looked to the door.

It flew open and crashed into the wall, rattling the

paintings.

"Charlotte! Where are your manners?" Lady Maybourne said in a weak voice. She was obviously shaken, as Althea had suspected.

"Mother, *who is that?*"

Althea blinked. She was not looking at a herd of elephants, nor even a ghostly apparition. She was looking at the loveliest young woman she had ever seen.

Loveliest- and angriest. The girl was in her late teens, just entering the full promise of womanhood, already possessed of slight curves on her fashionably petite and frail figure. Pale blonde hair fell in perfect ringlets around a sweet, heart-shaped face that was pale in rage. Bright blue eyes, so like her brother's, narrowed on Althea just as rosebud lips pursed in keen assessment.

This was the noted debutante Miss Charlotte Ridgely, the young woman Althea was being paid an outrageous sum to save from her own manipulative imagination. The girl was good, too. She must have been listening to the conversation from somewhere upstairs. A loose floorboard, perhaps. It was obvious she was the source of the scream, at just the perfect moment to add credence to her own charade.

Clever young lady.

Althea dipped her head, just slightly. "I am Mistress Althea," she said, before the dowager or the Earl could speak. Althea knew instinctively that if she were to succeed here she needed to take charge from the beginning. This girl was no fool.

But then neither was Althea.

"Oh, I've heard of you," Miss Ridgely scoffed. "Really, Mother? She's a fraud! Occultists and mystics don't *do* anything. It's a lot of hogwash. Benedict told me so."

At the words, Lady Maybourne paled. She was obviously going to be of little help here. Fortunately, the Earl, who like any gentleman stood the moment his sister entered, was at hand.

"Actually, Char, it was my idea," he said, not unkindly. "And she is not a fraud, obviously, as her first attempt to commune with the apparition resulted not only in our tea service decorating the carpet, but clearly gave you reason to come downstairs. Isn't that so?"

Charlotte trembled in anger. "No! I- I heard she was here and wanted to see her myself, to tell her we don't need her so-called services, but I was too busy fixing my hair to come down until just now."

"And what, you saw your reflection when you were finished and screamed? Come now, Char. We all know you're a better liar than that."

Althea watched the girl flinch and knew the words cut deeply.

"I beg to differ, Lord Maybourne." Althea broke in, also standing. She was unusually tall for a woman, and while she did not match the Earl's considerable height, she knew she made an impression. Char's eyes widened a little at the sight of her. Althea knew what she saw. She was all black eyes and black hair and sharp cheekbones, pale and gaunt, a creature of the darkness. Wholly unlike the delicate rose-faced blonde that was Charlotte, who looked to be the very vision of life and vitality.

"It is obvious your sister is a terrible liar and is deeply moved, both by her own youthful spirit and that which she had befriended. Obviously she is lying about what happened just now upstairs, but bullying her into submission will not out the truth."

The Earl, obviously well-versed in deception himself, made a perfect show of looking affronted by Althea's words. No one spoke to a man of his station in such a manner, especially not a lowborn woman of questionable repute.

"Fine," he said curtly, "you ask my sister what happened."

"I think we all know what happened," Althea said,

much to everyone's surprise.

"We- we do?" Lady Maybourne asked.

"Yes," Althea responded, pure confidence. "The girl is frightened, but that is understandable. I made contact with the spirit, just as I told you I would, and the spirit, obviously being the suspicious sort, left Miss Maybourne's company abruptly, causing her to scream, and then manifested in this very room, invisible to us yet, causing the tea tray to go flying. He is at this very moment listening to every word we speak."

There. She'd both defended Charlotte and corroborated her elaborate fiction, setting her up for later disillusionment, *and* she had given Lady Maybourne an excuse for why her foot would fly forward and kick the table, upending the tray. For her part, Althea had just earned a little bit of both ladies' trust and goodwill, and, if the look of assessing satisfaction on the Earl's face was any measure, a bit of his approval as well.

"How did you know that?" Charlotte asked breathlessly, sitting in the armchair between the settees. "How *could* you have known Benedict was with me just now? He said you were a fake."

Althea gave her her most charming smile. "My darling girl, was there not a time you thought ghosts were falsehoods as well?"

Charlotte's delicate rosebud of a mouth snapped shut. The girl was very convincing. Althea would have to be doubly so to persuade her to give up her fiction.

"Is the ghost here now? In this room?" Lady Maybourne asked in a hushed voice.

"He is not," Althea replied, hoping the girl would not contradict her. Charlotte, for her part, merely sat on the sofa with her brother and looked at Althea as if she were some strange sort of undersea creature.

"Oh thank heavens," Lady Maybourne sighed. "Though I must say I am terribly curious-"

"What are you here for, really?" Charlotte asked Althea bluntly.

"She's here to help you communicate with the spirit," the Earl of Maybourne said.

At the very same moment his mother said, "She wants to guide the spirit to the next world. To help him."

Charlotte's eyes narrowed. "Which is it? I don't need 'help' speaking with him and he has assured me he cannot go anywhere but here. He is trapped in limbo. He has already tried everything he could think to get out of it, to move on. It's impossible."

"A ghost cannot free themselves alone," replied Althea. "They are too close to their predicament, you see. It requires a knowledgeable and skilled outside force to open the portals through which they must travel."

"So you want to take him from me, is that it?"

This was dangerous ground. She needed the girl's trust before she could go any further, whether her endgame would be pretending to remove the spirit- or simply convincing the girl to drop the charade. "Only if he wishes it," Althea said smoothly. She caught Lord Maybourne sending her a slight nod from over his sister's shoulder. She was on the right track.

"He won't talk to you."

Althea smiled at Charlotte with what she hoped was sisterly understanding. "Why wouldn't he? Doesn't he want help?"

The younger woman straightened defiantly and Althea could see the generations of aristocratic breeding in her. The effect was not flattering. The younger woman spoke, "He does not. He is content with his lot, especially now that we are in residence. He wishes only for my continued company."

Althea saw the Earl's mouth open to protest, but she spoke first. "Then I shall be all the more interested in communicating with him, through your assistance, perhaps. This ghost of yours sounds like an unusual spirit, and one does find even the most fantastic apparitions dull after a while."

"He is anything but dull," Charlotte said with a blush. The thought flickered in Althea's mind that rather than a brilliant manipulator, the girl might be genuinely mad. Perhaps she really did fancy herself in love with an invisible specter. *That* would be financially improvident. The Earl would not relish the revelation that his sister was so unwell.

Fortunately Althea had always found that where there was a will, there was a way. She had a will to earn this commission, ergo, she would find a way. Neither madness, nor genius, nor any other obstacle would stop her.

At that moment the door opened.

"We'll need another tea service, I'm afraid," Lady Maybourne said loudly. When no one answered, Althea looked up, a motion soon echoed by the others.

There was no one there.

"*Ben*," Charlotte said with a roll of her eyes. "He's trying to give you a hint, Mistress Althea. He wants you to leave."

"If that is the case, I am afraid he'll have to tell me himself."

"Is he here? Is he spirit amongst us?" Lady Maybourne squeaked in excitement or trepidation, it was impossible to tell.

"Not so much a spirit," a man's low voice spoke from beyond the open door, causing the occupants of the rose salon to jump in shock, "as a solicitor. Apologies for the disappointment."

As the words settled in the room an older gentleman stepped inside. Middling height and build, he had brown hair shot through with silver and carried himself like a man of great consideration.

"Wilkes!" Lord Maybourne exclaimed, standing to greet the unexpected guest. "You near scared us half to death, opening the door like that."

The newcomer, Wilkes, blinked. "The door was opened when I arrived."

Maybourne laughed nervously, and Althea felt that frisson of unease shoot through her again. Something was definitely wrong in this house.

"Naturally, naturally," Maybourne said, clapping a hand on the other man's shoulder in a distinctly goodnatured gesture. The Earl did not notice Wilkes flinch at the contact, but Althea did.

"And who is this lovely creature?" Wilkes asked, his gaze settling on Althea.

That was laying it on a bit thick, she thought. Charlotte Ridgely, an obvious diamond of the first water, was seated mere feet away from her. No one in their right mind would consider Althea even worth notice in such company.

"May I introduce Mistress Althea?" Maybourne guided Wilkes over to Althea, who stood to greet him. "Mistress Althea, this is Mr. Rupert Wilkes, the family solicitor and general ombudsman."

"A pleasure, Mr. Wilkes," Althea said with a dip of her head.

"Likewise, Mistress. It is an unexpected delight to meet you, having heard such tales of your unearthly skill. All discreetly, of course."

Althea raised a single dark brow. "Of course. Yet I am surprised to find you are familiar with my work. I did not think my reputation had much traction in the circles which you no doubt enjoy."

"My line of work requires me to be familiar many things," Wilkes said silkily and Althea decided she did not like him. She had spent so many years dealing in deceit, she could recognize others in the trade.

"Wilkes was the one who recommended you," Maybourne said brightly. He was obviously very optimistic about Althea's chances for saving his family fortune. She found her own confidence wavering.

All her instincts were telling her that this was a bigger job than she had been told, and more dangerous, too. There was more going on here, and increasingly she felt the only reward awaiting her was trouble.

She had made an art of avoiding trouble. She could just leave…. come up with a mystical reason for going… tell the Earl the deal was off….

But what if he threatened to out her in retribution? He was a powerful peer, and every day she kept Mistress Althea alive and working was a day she courted prosecution for fraud. Even if Maybourne was not a threat, Wilkes might be. She saw immediately that the older gentleman knew she was a fraud just as well as his employer. They could have her arrested, or, if the mood suited them, force her to complete the job.

They could even force her to do it for free.

Well, they could try. She would run, and figure it out. She spoke French and Italian. She could convince anybody anywhere of anything. It was one of her few gifts.

But if she stayed? If she complied with their wishes and completed the job?

They would pay her. She didn't trust Wilkes, but she trusted the Earl to be forthright. He was too far above the likes of her or Wilkes to deal dishonorably, she saw it in everything from the way he carried himself to the way he watched his sister from the corner of his eye, wary of any misstep.

Althea felt the knot in her chest ease a little.

One last job, *this job*, and she would be free. Rich, and free.

"Mistress Althea?" Maybourne's voice broke through her thoughts, and she realized she had been so lost in thought she had missed the conversation entirely.

"Apologies," she said, "transmissions come and go, at times I must attune to them. You were saying?"

Maybourne allowed the excuse even as Althea heard Charlotte make a sound suspiciously like a snort. "I was saying that we are honored that you have accepted our invitation," said the Earl, "not merely for the compliment of your presence but for the hope it offers us in this…. predicament. It seems Wilkes was correct in his judgment, as always."

"I felt certain you could assist the family," Wilkes concurred smoothly. "It was difficult to obtain your information, as I am certain you know, but I managed. I like to keep my ear to the ground."

She fixed the solicitor with a haughty stare. "And the ground told you I was the best at this sort of thing?"

The man met her gaze. "It did. Every shadow in London whispers your name. Tells tales of the miracles you've performed for any number of high profile citizens and peers of the realm. Quite remarkable, if the stories are true."

"Why shouldn't they be? I keep my client list discreet, but I cannot help if they spread the word of my successes for me. My successes, after all, are really those of my clients."

"Quite so," Wilkes dipped his head, his eyes not leaving Althea's. "Communicating with the spirit world must be perilous enough without the additional fear of His Majesty's laws."

Althea raised a single, thin black brow and gave him her most imperious look. "I break no laws, sir. I offer only my skills in translating the wishes of the dead for the living, and vice versa. Some would argue it is a godly endeavor."

"And some would say such talk is blasphemous."

Lady Maybourne made an affronted sound as her son stepped in. "Come now, Wilkes," the Earl chided. "You convinced me to bring our guest into this matter. Don't scare her off with your ominous legal ruminations."

Wilkes checked himself, and gave Althea a little bow. "Of course. I meant no offense, Mistress. I am merely in awe of such a gift as yours."

"No offense taken, sir. I am both a godly woman," Althea said, uttering a blatant lie, and following it with a truth, "and a person of science. The truth of our existence lies between the two. Magic and other such superstitions have nothing to do with it."

Even the Earl registered surprise at that.

"You are not a superstitious woman?" Lady Maybourne asked fretfully. Althea felt everyone's eyes on her, Miss Ridgely's being the sharpest.

"I do not know the rules that guide the spirit realm, Lady Maybourne, only that there may come a day when they are widely understood and accepted. Even now, electrifying machines defy our comprehension of the world and would they too not have been considered magic mere decades ago?"

"True enough," Wilkes admitted. "You are obviously a woman of substance and education, beyond your more esoteric gifts. You apprenticed with the famous Madame Veira, did you not?"

An alarm rang in Althea's head. She had tried to distance herself from that bit of her past for years now. This man was good. Which was, potentially, very bad. Althea knew her employment depended on word of mouth but she tried her best to keep as many pieces of her story private as possible. She preferred to be the one who revealed her secrets, and it was unnerving that this stranger should already have so many.

"I am familiar with Madame Veira. She counseled me when I was just beginning to understand the nature of this work."

Wilkes kept his tone mild even as his eyes glinted with cunning. "They say the King himself once summoned her in secret to communicate with his dead wife."

"I know nothing of that," Althea replied simply. It was a lie. She knew all about that. She'd been raised on the story. It was one of Madame Veira's favorites. George II was near death and Veira only a young, untried woman new to understanding her powers in this field, when she was summoned to the palace. As Veira told it, the long-deceased queen was eager to speak to her beloved, to counsel him in patience in life and assure of him untold joys in death. Althea had often asked how Madame Veira had found the courage to confront the king with such a story, but Althea's mentor had always insisted it was all true. Althea had decided long ago to commit to her own fabrications with such conviction. She'd known from a young age that a lack of confidence, any wavering of consistency, meant prison, or worse.

She pushed away the thought. She was not going to prison. This was her final job. She had five hundred quid on her person with another five hundred coming, all she had to do was what the Earl asked of her. It should not matter that his solicitor seemed cunning at best, devious at worst. She did not know what this man Wilkes wanted from her. He'd arranged to have her hired and yet seemed openly hostile to her presence. She didn't know what to make of it, and once again she wondered if she was a fool to accept this job.

One thousand pounds… five hundred now…

The Earl, reading her silence as disinterest, cleared his throat. "Mistress Althea, perhaps you would like to be shown to your quarters? I have business with Wilkes this morning, but I can have the housekeeper give you a tour of the house and see you settled into your rooms."

Althea thought he must have misspoke. *Rooms* with an 's'? She would no doubt be staying in a broom closet or in the attic with the other servants. She did not mind. The free meals more than made up for such accommodations and as this job would only last a week, as per instruction…

She did want a moment to collect her thoughts, however. This was going to be a difficult assignment. She could already tell.

"A tour would be most appreciated. I must feel the energies of the house, the sooner the better."

"Excellent. I shall ring for the housekeeper."

Chapter Three
The Visitor

Althea had been inside the homes of many peers in her career as a highly sought mystic, but as she followed Mrs. Hooper through the first floor of Maybourne house, she had no doubts that this was the finest of them all.

Granted, in subtle, unobtrusive ways. It was not the largest, nor the oldest, nor the most expensive house. *That* title went to the home of a viscount she had relieved of a demon in the servants' stairwell. That estate had been practically solid gold there was so much fine gilt plate on the furnishings. The effect had been gaudy and off-putting.

Maybourne House was anything but that. It was a little shabby and it was obvious when one looked carefully that the family was having some financial difficulties. The carpets were very fine but a little too worn, though the frayed bits were thoughtfully concealed. The upholstery was all done in colors that had not been in style for decades, but were tasteful enough that they still sufficed, even if they did not dazzle. If one got close enough, one could see how the drapes were battered by the sun and dust collected in neglected corners.

None of it mattered.

The house was quietly stunning. The thought and detail that had gone into every element of the design and construction of this place was evident. The fabrics may be unfashionable colors, but they were obviously the finest one could import from Turkey or Egypt or even further abroad and must have cost a fortune when they were first procured.

The carpets were battered, but they still retained their original dignity. The edges were plush when Althea's boots sank into them, the threads fine and tight. The place must have befit an empress when it was first built, in quality if not in size.

The notion tugged at Althea's heartstrings. A passion for fine things had always been her secret shame. That, and sweets. She had an easier time both obtaining sweets and, paradoxically, eschewing them. Perhaps because they were so readily acquired.

But there was little value in appreciating finery. No room for caring about such trivial things in a life such as hers. When everything could crumble around her at any moment, everything she'd worked so hard for snatched away, what did it matter if she used the finest silver or secondhand pewter?

Her mother had suffered the same affliction, and it had cost her her life. Madame Veira had treasured fine things and watched as it was all taken away from her, leaving her destitute. No good came of coveting wealth, Althea knew that. She also knew that wealth was a woman's ticket to freedom. Her money would be spent on a cozy cottage far from anyone who knew her. There would be no extravagance, only comfort and safety.

Those were priceless.

Which was why Althea wished she could ignore the beauty of Maybourne house. It was obvious great care and expense had gone into its construction. She did not notice to see the fanciful design of the tiles on the second story landing, a mosaic depicting a fantastical island surrounded by a swirling sea. She tried desperately not to recognize the craftsmanship in the bannister, carved ever so subtly to mimic the undulations of the waves, with tiny abstract shells carved in the wood at the base of each support. The bronze sconces on the walls molded into the shape of bursting suns.

She did not want her heart to be lifted by the beauty of such a strange, wondrous old house, but it was no good. She couldn't help herself. It was magnificent, even with the dust and wear of the years marking its age and mild neglect.

"Mrs. Hooper," she interrupted the older woman's

lengthy explanation of the family's dining schedule and preferences, "who designed this house?"

Mrs. Hooper stopped halfway up the stairs to the third floor and looked back at Althea. "The house, Miss?"

"Yes. It's unusual, isn't it?" Althea waited expectantly.

A shadow flickered over the woman's weathered face. "I can't say as I've noticed," Mrs. Hooper hedged and continued up the stairs, ignoring Althea's original question. Goggins, passing them on his way down the stairs, shot the housekeeper a hard look. That uneasy feeling washed over Althea yet again. Perhaps she should try and finish this job in less than a week.

Mrs. Hooper's tour, such as it was, continued across up to the third floor and down another hall. Mrs. Hooper was mostly concerned with listing which rooms they passed- as if Althea could possibly remember so many when all of whom looked exactly the same from this side of a closed door- and rattling off the identities of the Maybourne family members in the many portraits on the walls.

As Althea looked into one pair of icy blue eyes after another, she wondered who this ghost of Charlotte's was supposed to be. An ancestor? Inspired by one of these ominous portraits? Or a long forgotten stableboy, charming and young and forever out of reach?

Althea needed to speak to the girl alone and learn as much as she could of the matter. First, however, she would seek out some of the staff. There was no doubt the entire house knew about Charlotte's game, and while interviewing the girl herself was essential, the more Althea knew before that conversation about the ruse and Charlotte herself, the better.

"Mrs. Hooper," Althea said again, as they paused outside yet another door.

"Yes, m'am?" Mrs. Hooper's owlish eyes rested on Althea, blinking.

"I do not wish to upset you, but given the purpose of my time here at Maybourne House, I must ask. Have you seen any spirits?"

"No, m'am." Mrs. Hooper jumped back into her explanation of how often the guest rooms were dusted and aired out, despite never being used.

Althea interrupted her. "Are you sure? You have not seen anything unusual? Nothing of the sort Miss Charlotte has claimed?"

Mrs. Hooper broke off. "I have not. Believe me, if a handsome strange man appeared at my bedside in the dead of night to make me giggle and carry on, I would know it, and I wouldn't stop him, neither." She winked conspiratorially, the gesture taking Althea by surprise. There was always more to the household help than they initially let on.

"Is that what Charlotte has said is happening?" Althea asked.

"Something of the sort, though she hasn't explained it all to us," Mrs. Hooper replied thoughtfully. "She did say he was handsome."

"Then what do you mean about the giggling in the dead of night?"

Mrs. Hooper's milky face blushed crimson. "I hear her, m'am. When I'm doing my rounds sometimes. I can't sleep at night, so I walk the house. Never seen no ghost meself, but I can hear her chatting away and laughing like a maid at May Day."

Althea marked another notch in the column labeled 'Charlotte is Mad.'

"And do you ever hear who she is talking to? Another voice?"

Mrs. Hooper shook her head. "Oh no, m'am. Just Miss Charlotte, too low for me to make out the words. Not that I'm prying, mind you."

The housekeeper seemed to realize this conversation was edging on greater intimacy than she should allow. "That's all though. No other funny business. Sometimes fires put themselves out or dishware falls off a table, but that's not spirits. I'm a god-fearing woman, m'am, I don't harbor superstitions."

Althea was of a mind that superstitions took many forms, and considering oneself god-fearing could be one of them, however, she said nothing. The only other people she had ever met who harbored her level of skepticism lived hard, cruel lives. In her experience, people either gave the weight of their hopes to a higher power, or they turned their backs on assistance, divine or otherwise. Althea had long been in the latter camp. She could only rely on herself.

Curiosity got the better of her, and she summoned her professional persona. "Do the fires often go out? Do dishes regularly move across tables?"

"Sometimes, m'am." Mrs. Hooper dropped her gaze to examine a pattern in the wood of the door. "Often, really."

Althea's brow furrowed. Perhaps the entire house was suffering from some minor delusion, some latent mold or fumes in the house? There was, as ever, a practical explanation for these phenomena, it was simply a matter of finding it.

"What do you think is causing it?"

Mrs. Hooper turned abruptly and continued down the hall. "I haven't the faintest idea, m'am. I keep my eyes down and my nose in my own business."

The woman's tone was not accusatory, but Althea sensed it was an admonishment all the same.

"I am here to help the family, Mrs. Hooper."

"All the same, if I were you I'd take care. Of myself, and the girl too. Not right in the head, that one." Mrs. Hooper realized only too late what she had said. A pale, work-worn hand flew to her mouth. "Begging your pardon! Here are your rooms, Mistress."

This last bit came out in a hurry, and before Althea could say another word the older woman had unlocked the door before them and scampered away.

Apparently, Althea was going to be given a proper guest's room after all. At the end of the hall, likely small and simple, but it was a sign of their esteem- and expectations- that they should give her a room on one of the family floors.

The door swung open with a slight creak as Althea opened it.

She froze.

This could not be right.

It wasn't a bedroom. It was another sitting room, nearly the size of the rose salon but done in a series of rich, dark greens. The effect was lovely, but it did nothing to-

"Hello, m'am," a pert voice said behind her.

Althea spun around. A maid was looking up at her expectantly.

"I'm Henrietta, but you may call me Hen. I see to this part of the house. If you need anything at all, just ring for me," she gestured to a bell pull near the fireplace.

"Thank you, Hen, but I'm afraid there's been a mistake."

The young woman could not have look more dismayed if a ghost had in fact appeared. "A mistake, m'am?"

"Yes," Althea said kindly, "Mrs. Hooper was rather flustered and forgot to show me to my bedchamber. Would you be so kind as to take me there?"

Hen's brow furrowed, before smoothing into a comforting expression often reserved for small children or elderly relatives. "But of course, m'am. Right this way."

To Althea's surprise the girl did not lead her back to the hall. Instead, she strode across the sitting room to a door Althea had paid no heed to on the other side. Hen opened it wide.

Beyond the doorway was the most opulent bedchamber Althea had ever seen.

A massive four poster bed took up nearly the entire room, even up to the high, paneled, dark wood ceiling. The draperies were dark green like the sitting room but rendered in velvet. The coverlet and bedding appeared to be silk, all done in the same series of luscious forest shades.

Althea's mouth fell open.

"Is something the matter, m'am?"

"This is- this is mine?"

"Yes, m'am. The Earl thought it best you should have this room. He is very pleased you're here, if you don't mind my saying so."

Althea nodded absently. Her mind was still trying to wrap itself around this change in fortune.

That familiar inconvenient part of her that loved luxury and beauty was dancing a jig.

Ah well, in for a penny, in for a pound. It would hurt to leave such a place after the week was up, but she would be a fool not to take advantage of good fortune when it knocked down her door, wouldn't she?

Althea was no fool.

"It's perfect. Thank you, Hen."

"Of course, m'am," the girl gave a curtsy and left the room.

Althea stepped gingerly into the bedchamber. The carpets here were not worn. They were so fine and plush they felt like new. She sank into them and felt guilty for wearing her boots. Carpets like these demanded silk slippers….

Or bare feet.

In fact, the entire room was made for bare skin and sensual enjoyment. She could see it now as the took it in more carefully. This was a space designed for pleasure. And sin.

The portrait above the green marble mantle confirmed her theory. Old and stately, it was the most erotic portrait Althea had ever seen.

A young woman, dressed in a style of the last century, bosom bared, lay curved back over a silk settee not unlike the one in the sitting room mere feet away. The young woman's eyes rolled back in ecstasy as not one but three gentleman pleasured her in a variety of ways even Althea had not fathomed, for all her years circulating socially in the demimonde. In the background of the scene there was a flowering garden with a waterfall and, inexplicably, a faintly rendered string quartet. Whether the lovers were themselves performing or the music was entirely in the young woman's head was left up to the viewer.

Althea gaped.

She was no prudish miss. One could not grow up in the circumstances she had and not know the ways of the world, of men and women and sex. But this-

this was the base and carnal elevated to *art*. For all its flagrant excess it was the most beautiful painting she had ever seen.

The sound of something crashing to the floor behind her shattered her thoughts.

Althea spun around in the direction of the noise, only to see a candlestick- thankfully unlit- had fallen from the little table beside the bed. The window was closed, so a breeze hadn't done it. Obviously one of the maids had not placed it securely back in its place when she finished tidying up this morning.

In a moment, Althea placed the candlestick back on the table and sat on the bed to further admire the room. It was magnificent. The wallpaper was even a work of art. It was delicate, but notably masculine, depicting illustrations of far off adventures on the high seas, with a profusion of sea nymphs and mermaids interspersed. To her surprise, even some of the pirates and sailors depicted were women. All beautiful, of course, as whoever was responsible for the design had a clearly prodigious imagination. Whatever fantastical impulses had gone into the rest of the house, the architect had outdone himself in this room.

And this was only a guest room. Althea could scarcely imagine what the Earl's chamber looked like.

With a sigh she leaned back, melting into the soft down of the bed linens. She stared up at the underside of the canopy, all thick, draped damask with careful gold tassels on the edges. She felt like a princess.

No, that wasn't right. The colors were too strong, the fabrics too heavy.

She felt like a queen.

"Well, Jane Smith of Covent Garden, you've outdone yourself this time," she murmured quietly to herself.

As if in relief, her body slumped. Exhaustion, undeniable and overwhelming, enveloped her. Perhaps she should close her eyes for just a moment. She would be expected at dinner, after all, and she would need to be sharp and observant to make the most of it. This was a job. She could not forget it, no matter how enticing the strange, old house itself might be. The sooner she understood what was really going on with Miss Charlotte Ridgely, the sooner she would be paid in full, and the sooner she would be free to live the life she truly wanted. A vision of a small cottage in a quiet glen, a house filled with books and the sound of a merrily blazing fire, filled her mind. She had never felt safe in all her life, but soon, so very soon, this vision of peace and comfort would be hers.

Althea's eyes eased shut and she knew no more.

* * *

The sense that someone was watching her woke her some time later. It was one of her least favorite ways to be awakened, but she had learned not to let on immediately that she had broken her slumber. She kept her eyes closed, her breathing slow and steady. Did the Earl of Maybourne not trust her after all? Had he sent someone to spy on her… or worse?

Althea listened.

The house was quiet, though it was hard to tell what was going on in the rest of it as the hall lay on the other side of the sitting room, and even though the door between the bedchamber and that space was still open, it was a sizable distance. Sizable enough that the fire in the sitting room had done nothing to warm the bedchamber. It was freezing cold. Of course, the drafts were terrible old houses and this one was both very old and absolutely massive. Who had ever heard of a guest room with its own sitting room? She felt like a queen indeed.

Then she heard it. A small tapping sound. *Tap. Tap. Tap.*

Not mice. Something larger, and more concentrated.

A branch on the window?

Tap.

No. The sound was not coming from the window. It was coming from somewhere closer.

Somewhere much too close.

Tap.

The foot of the bed.

She sat up, eyes wide, hand immediately reaching for the little blade she kept tucked in her stocking, even when she slept. Old habits died hard.

It was hard to argue the habit was unwarranted when there was, indeed, a man at the foot of the bed, watching her. She inhaled sharply.

"Who are you? What do you want?"

"I think the question, dear lady, is who are *you* and what do *you* want?"

"I am not the one lurking a woman's bedchamber as she sleeps, sir. I insist you leave, at once."

"A woman's bedchamber?" the man laughed and Althea thought there was something odd about him. His movements were wrong somehow, but she couldn't say why.

"Yes. It's mine."

"*Yours*? Hardly! Dear god, look around you. Does this look like a female's boudoir? *Your* boudoir? You're dressed half like a nun and half like a reaper."

He gestured to the heavy, dark drapes and wallpaper of seafaring escapades, the pornographic art on the walls, and her, in full Mistress Althea attire, covered from toe to chin in black.

"His lordship assigned me this room."

The man smirked, the expression cold and his eyes hollow. There was something very odd about him indeed, if only she could light the candle on the nightstand to see him clearly...

"It is not his lordship's to assign. Didn't you wonder why the best suite in the house hasn't been occupied for nearly eighty years?"

Althea blinked. "No. I mean, I had no idea. Why should I?"

The man gave a brittle laugh. "Why should you indeed. I thought you were special, Miss Smith."

His use of her real name sent a chill through her, unrelated to the plummeting temperature of the room. Had he been listening earlier? Watching her? Fear pooled in her belly. "I don't know what you mean."

The man's smirk deepened. "I thought you knew things about the unseen. Other worlds. Spirits."

"I do," she said, hating the waver in her voice.

"Ghosts?"

He moved then around the post at the corner of the bed, rounding it towards her. Panic rising in her gut, Althea leaned over and fumbled with the matches beside the candlestick.

The man did not pause. In fact, his movements were eerily fluid, as though he floated on water. A primitive knell of warning rang in Althea's chest and she struck a match.

It fizzled.

The man laughed. He was almost looming over her now, only feet away. "There is no need to be afraid, Miss Smith. Not yet."

"Who are you?"

"If you don't already know, I suppose it doesn't matter, because if you're half as intelligent as you pretend to be you will leave this place tomorrow. Is that understood?"

"I have a job to do here. I'm not leaving until I finish it."

"And just what is that job, precisely? Convince poor Charlotte that ghosts aren't real?"

"Amongst other things," Althea hedged, fumbling with a second match.

"I'm afraid you aren't going to be able to do that," the man said simply.

The next match caught, and light flooded Althea's vision. She put it to the candle, ready to explain to him that she would do precisely that and more, if needed. She was a survivor, a woman of her word who always got her man.

Except, as she turned back to tell him all that and demand he leave at once, he was gone.

Unease crept up her spine.

She was alone.

The man had vanished. The only indication he had been there at all was the lingering scent of pine needles and good brandy.

Althea blew out the candle and curled back into the bed, wondering for the first time if perhaps in this job she had finally reached her limits.

Chapter Four
The Suitors

Althea's slumber was deep and host to many strange, unsettling dreams she could not remember when she awoke at dawn. Her body was accustomed to a working woman's hours, though she knew the schedule was anathema to peers like the Earl of Maybourne and his family. They would likely not rouse until nearly noon.

Althea found such indolence both dull and wasteful, but then, she did not have many positive opinions of the *ton*. In her experience, aristocrats were all spoiled, soft, and out of touch. Fortunately, she was none of those things, and thus had the advantage in her dealings with them.

Althea's stomach grumbled and realized she'd slept through dinner. She decided to dress and then go to the kitchens. The best part of waking early in a house like this was that the cook was always awake first, and that meant fresh bread, hot from the oven.

Althea's mouth watered at the thought and she dragged herself out of the comfortable bed to the wash basin against the wall. A gilt mirror rose above the little washing table. Althea grimaced at what it revealed. Her long, delicate face was paler than usual.

Her high cheekbones only emphasized the shadows under her eyes, which were darker than usual. Her black hair, the color of a raven's wing, was a tangled mess. The thick waves were always a challenge to subdue, but as there would be no one but the servants about at this hour, she decided a simple chignon would suit for the morning.

She sighed and sat on the bench at the dressing table. The bread would have to wait a moment. A silver brush rested in a drawer beneath the basin, waiting for her. It was worth more than some of her friends made in a month. She picked it up with a sigh and set to work.

With every pull of the brush, memories of the night before returned. The details were hazy, but she'd had the most unsettling dream. It had been alarmingly lifelike, but jarringly surreal. She'd seen a man at the foot of her bed. He was displeased with her presence here. She remembered he had been handsome, but odd, faintly glowed, like a god in the moonlight.

She blinked. The curtains had been drawn, so there had been no moonlight. There'd been no fire, either. The room had been freezing cold. The man could not have glowed. How had she seen him so clearly?

Her heart jumped at the thought before she remembered it had all been a dream. Lifelike, yes, but an illusion all the same. The man could have just as easily been a talking horse or a singing teapot.

Althea examined her work in the mirror and, satisfied with her work, threw on a simple morning gown of light grey cambric and made for the sitting room and the hall beyond.

A soft scratch at the door stopped her short. "Come in."

Hen opened the door with her hip and entered with a tray of coffee and scones. The moment she entered the room her face paled and she looked nervously around the quiet, darkened space. Remembering her manners she asked, "Good morning, Mistress. I was hoping to bring this up before you woke, apologies for the disturbance."

The edge in Hen's voice and her faint stammer as she said 'disturbance' awoke in Althea a deeper suspicion that the man last night had not been a dream after all. Hen set the tray down on a table by the window and pulled back the drapes.

"I trust you slept well?" Hen asked, obviously trusting no such thing.

Althea shrugged and answered blandly, " I slept like the dead."

She picked up a scone and took a bite as Hen blanched. *Interesting*, Althea thought.

She set the scone down "Tell me, Hen, who was the young man they put up to it last night? A footman? A stablehand?"

"I- I don't know what you're talking about, Mistress," the girl stammered, spilling coffee everywhere as she attempted to pour some for Althea.

"You're a bright girl, Hen. I'm sure if you give it a little thought you'll know exactly what I am referring to, and whom. It's only that he startled me, looming over my bed in the darkness and demanding I leave. It was quite unsettling."

Hen was as pale as the fine white china she shakily returned to the tray, spilled coffee now pooling across the silver.

"You saw him then?" she whispered so quietly Althea barely heard her.

"I did," Althea responded matter-of-factly, alighting on one of the chairs beside the table. "Just as he obviously hoped I would. Now, who was he? A friend of Miss Ridgely's?"

"I- I suppose he is that, Mistress, but-" Hen shook her head and backed up slowly towards the door. "Oh, no, if he doesn't want you here, you'd best leave. He's kind enough at first, but he don't stay that way when if he don't wish to and this is his house, really, no matter what the toffs say about it."

"Is the Earl indebted to him, then? That might explain a great deal."

"No- it's, oh Mistress, I can't say more, even now as the sun is rising," Hen said glancing nervously towards the grey dawn visible through the windows. "I shouldn't said nuffin'. Only we're worried, we are, about Miss Ridgely-"

"So Miss Ridgely is the one who put him up to it?"

Hen shook her head, taking another step back. The floorboard beneath her creaked and she jumped so hard even Althea startled.

"What is wrong, Hen? Is he a bad man?"

Hen kept moving backwards, and was nearly to the door. "He's not bad, Mistress," she said in a hushed voice, "but he's not a man, neither. I- I shouldn't-enjoy your breakfast, Mistress."

With that, the girl slipped out the door, leaving Althea to ponder her strange behavior.

Miss Ridgely was obviously behind this. The girl was a charming creature, but it appeared she had enraptured the entire household into her schemes. Even more intriguing, she had hired a man to rather convincingly portray the ghost she claimed to love. That was obviously who the young man last night had meant to portray. It should have unsettled Althea to learn the nocturnal visitor had not been a dream, but it didn't. It was impressive. He must have opened a window to create the chill, but she wondered how he'd achieved the glowing effect. Perhaps as part of her work on this case she would find out.

Althea took a thoughtful bite of her scone. This job would be interesting, if nothing else.

An envelope on the tray caught her eye, directly in the path of the spilled coffee. Althea rescued it and tore it open.

Firm, looping handwriting greeted her. She smiled and read on.

Dearest, as you did not appear for supper last night I assume you've taken the assignment and this shall find you ensconced in the Earl's household. I hope your task goes smoothly and without trouble. There is more than enough of that about lately. Let me know if you need any advice and I shall see you when it is done. - N.

Althea was quick to pen a response in her own spidery, florid script.

My darling N., The Earl's case is an unusual one. They've gone so far as to create a spirit out of a footman to scare me off. I am well equipped to handle such attempts, however, and have no doubt the true nature of this house's secrets will be revealed to me in due course. There is no light like the truth, as well you know. With love, Althea

By the time she'd finished her correspondence and

most of the scones and coffee, the unease that had followed Althea since the night before was nothing by a memory. All that remained before her was to learn as much as she could about the household, and Miss Ridgely, in particular.

The following day and a half were uneventful. Althea assured the Earl she could finish within a week, but she would need to come up with a strategy before any steps could be taken. He'd agreed and allowed her free reign to explore the house and interview the staff. Unfortunately none were as forthcoming as Hen had been that first morning and Hen herself remained scarce, seeing to her duties only when Althea was not in her rooms. It was obvious the girl was avoiding Althea, but that was not surprising.

It was evident by the end of the first day that no one wanted Althea to know anything about this supposed ghost- most especially Miss Ridgely.

Charlotte Ridgely was a closed book and a rude one, at that. She flatly refused to speak to Althea, or even acknowledge she was present in the house. Althea dined with the family in the evenings, and though she initially made several attempts to draw the girl into conversation, Charlotte pretended not to hear her, finally leaving the table despite the admonishments of her brother and mother.

She had not dined with them since.

Lady Maybourne was deeply apologetic, while the Earl had used the behavior as fodder for his argument that something needed to be done.

The family's situation was obviously dire. Mr. Wilkes visited nearly every day, giving Althea a gracious hello, then closeting himself up with the Earl in the study. Althea, who had excellent hearing, had caught snippets of their conversation as she passed down the hallway.

It seemed the Maybourne estate was in the sort of financial freefall only an excellent marriage could turn around.

This impression was confirmed on the afternoon of her third day at Maybourne House, as she sat with Lady Maybourne in the blue parlor. Althea was reading a book on reported spectral visitations of the Middle Ages, while the Countess sewed the likeness of a terrier onto a handkerchief.

Somewhere down the hall a door slammed loudly enough that both women jumped.

"Your otherworldly guest?" Althea asked.

Lady Maybourne's brow furrowed in concerned. "My son, I'm afraid. Charles is in a wretched mood. His most recent investment was reported lost at sea somewhere off Gibraltar this morning. He'd been hoping his share of a rather lucrative tea shipment from the Indies would turn things around, but then, it seems we have the luck of-"

Lady Maybourne paused.

"The devil?" Althea asked.

The older woman touched the small silver cross she wore around her neck. "I try not to say such things in this house. This place has always been… listening. It's part of why we decamped to the country when Charles was born, you know."

"The spirit was present even then?" Althea asked, curious.

Lady Maybourne nodded solemnly. "Oh yes. My husband didn't believe me, of course, but I knew it from our first night here. He bought the house, you see, not long after our marriage. He'd gambled away the family's old London home without telling me, and found this place for a steal. Terrible with money, my Henry was."

"It's a beautiful house," Althea said, "I imagine it was a sound investment."

"It was a shambles," Lady Maybourne looked around sadly to the places where paint was chipping on the ornately painted ceiling. "It's better now, but not by as much as it ought to be."

"Who owned it before your husband? Seems a pity to let such a place go."

Lady Maybourne shrugged. "I couldn't say. It's not that old, you know. Built within the last century, and obviously at great expense. I think some bankers owned it, or a trust, or something. Anyway, it wasn't occupied when my Henry found it. It had been empty for decades, minus a skeleton staff just to keep it occupied. The neighbors funded that, just to keep it from being vandalized."

"How very sad. I wonder who built it? It must have been so grand, and to let it languish… what a dreadful waste."

Lady Maybourne gave Althea a dark look. "A waste? Oh no, my dear. Surely you of all people can sense it?"

Althea did not waver. "Naturally. But I cannot reveal my own thoughts on the matter, Countess," she said smoothly. "Until my work here is done it is for the best of both the residents of Maybourne House and its resident spirit that I keep my impressions to myself. Please continue, however. Your knowledge of the house may prove invaluable in my ability to free its ghost."

"She cannot reveal her thoughts, mother, because she is a sham." Miss Ridgely snapped, sweeping into the parlor with her head held high. She alighted on the sofa beside her mother and shot Althea a smug look.

"If she were the real thing, she would already know who built the house."

"Careful of your tone, dear," her mother chided.

"My tone is appropriate for the circumstances," Charlotte sniffed.

"And just what, precisely, are the circumstances, Miss Ridgely?" Althea asked, implacable.

The younger woman straightened. "The house was designed and built by Lord Benedict Aston, the fifteenth Duke of Stafford, about eighty years ago. Shortly before his untimely death due to a wretched family curse. This house was his tragically short life's crowning achievement and would be considered one of the best houses in England if he had lived long enough to see it properly established."

Althea's brows raised. "I had no idea you harbored a passion for architectural history," she said drily at the same time the Lady Maybourne gasped, "A curse?"

Charlotte ignored her mother.

"I have the best tutor." She leveled Althea with a cold, even stare. "I'm surprised you didn't already know, however. After all, he is the ghost haunting this house."

Althea marveled at the girl's imagination and leapt at her chance to finally make some headway with the girl.

"Whenever I have spoken to Benedict, the house never came up. What is the matter, child? Didn't he tell you?"

"You- spoke- to Ben?" Charlotte asked, pale.

"Is something the matter? Didn't he tell you?" Althea asked.

"No," Charlotte replied with surprising venom, "he didn't."

Althea blinked. Charlotte was jealous.

Which meant either she, for whatever reason, was going to double down on her fiction about the ghost. Or, if she were in fact mad, she actually believed Althea had spoken to the ghost and did not like it.

Either way, Althea was making progress.

"Interesting," Althea tilted her head to the side. She was treading a fine line. She did not want to antagonize the girl. It was essential she befriend Charlotte enough to learn how to convince her to drop her story. "Ben spoke so highly of you. He told me you share everything."

Charlotte looked positively murderous, with all the misplaced passions of a sheltered young woman for her first love. "He doesn't like you at all. He wants you out of here, and so do I."

Lady Maybourne placed a hand on her daughter's knee. "Charlotte, darling, calm yourself. Mistress Althea means no ill will. We should be delighted that she's made contact with your Ben!"

"He *is* my Ben," Charlotte grumbled, resembling a petulant child more than ever. "And he doesn't want to leave this house. She won't be able to make him."

"If he doesn't want to leave, "Althea cut in before Lady Maybourne could, "then I shan't make him. I simply wish to help him. All spirits need help. If they didn't, they would have already passed on to the next world. Has Ben told you what is keeping him here?"

"A curse." The voice was calm, masculine, and strangely familiar.

"What was that?" Althea asked.

Charlotte blinked. "I didn't say anything. I don't want to talk about it any more, I won't give you any ammunition to use against him."

Althea glanced around the room. "I thought you said it was a curse."

"You did say something about a curse, didn't you, Char?"

Charlotte crossed her arms and glared at Althea. "Yes, but Ben won't tell me anything more about it, and even if he did, I wouldn't tell *you*."

An amused chuckle sounded close by. "It was a witch's curse, and not just any witch, either. You'd be shocked if I told you who she was."

The voice- was dry, clear, and directly behind Althea. She spun around to look at the rest of the room.

It was empty.

"Are you alright?" Lady Maybourne sounded genuinely concerned.

"You said it was a witch's curse."

Charlotte looked at Althea as if she was mad. "No I didn't."

Althea raised a hand to her temple. Perhaps the frustrations of the last few days were wearing on her. "You didn't say anything about a witch? Just now?"

"No dear," Lady Maybourne said gently, worry in her kind eyes, "we didn't."

"I think perhaps I need to lie down," Althea said, rising. "The spirits can be chaotic in their communications sometimes, and my defenses are not always as strong as they should be. This house is so full of energy."

The words were practiced nonsense, but for the first time in her life, Althea wondered if maybe they were closer to the truth than she wanted them to be.

She'd marked her place in her book and was preparing to stand when the parlor door opened.

Goggins entered with a small silver tray holding three parchment cards. He extended the tray to the Countess. "Guests, m'am."

Lady Maybourne looked at each card in turn, then gave Goggins a broad smile. "Let them in, Goggins! Let them in! Do not keep the gentlemen waiting!"

"Gentlemen?" Charlotte asked suspiciously.

"Yes, gentlemen! And they are here to see you! It's Lord Thacker, Mr. Grimsby, and Lord Leslie! We met them at Lady Phillips' ball last week, do you not recall?"

"Suitors?" Althea asked, settling herself back into her seat. She wanted to see how Charlotte interacted with living gentlemen. It was important research, after all.

Charlotte shot her another dark look.

"Very fine suitors!" Lady Maybourne exclaimed, beaming. "Oh, yes, do stay Mistress Althea. I'm certain some good company will clear your mind in no time."

"I'm not," the dry, male voice said over Althea's shoulder.

She spun around again.

Nothing.

"I'd be delighted," she muttered, turning back around and shaking off the feeling that something unusual was happening. She'd been sleeping poorly again, and that could do a host of unwanted things to ones peace of mind. After this social visit she would go upstairs and take a nap and set everything back to rights.

The Countess was busy ringing for more tea and cakes, but Charlotte was watching Althea, her eyes narrowed with suspicion. Fortunately at that moment three very different gentlemen swept through the door.

"Lady Maybourne!" the first, a rosy-faced, blonde man of large proportions declared. "A pleasure! Just to think, we should all descend upon you at once. Quite unplanned, I assure you. Quite unplanned."

"Lord Thacker," Lady Maybourne beamed, extending a hand in greeting. "We adore surprises, and especially a trio of such handsome, amiable ones!"

"You're too kind," the second man, a nervous looking fellow with dark, thin hair replied.

"Mr. Grimsby," the Countess indulgently smiled at him, then turned to the third man. Her smile widened so much Althea thought she might injure herself. "And Lord Leslie! My, this *is* a treat!"

The third man, tall, broad, and classically

handsome, with curling blonde locks and warm chocolate eyes, bowed over the Countess' hand. "The pleasure, I assure you, is ours. When one wishes for good company, one must only be grateful to find it in excess."

"Yes, indeed, and here we have it in spades!" tittered Lady Maybourne, beaming up at him. It was painfully obvious who her favorite was. Lord Leslie looked like Charlotte's male counterpart, the golden Adonis to her delicate blonde nymph. None of this was lost on Althea, or, apparently, Lady Maybourne.

Charlotte, for her part, remained notably impassive.

"And who is this English rose?" Mr. Grimsby asked rather painfully.

Althea blinked and realized a moment later the man was referring to *her*. Everyone turned towards her, awkwardly aware she was as far removed from an 'English rose' as it was possible to be. That is, unless that rose were, perhaps, plucked and dried.

Dressed in a high necked gown of a red so dark it was nearly black, Althea knew she looked more like a creature of the shadows than any sunny lady of Mayfair. Her hair was too dark, her eyes too black, and even her skin too pale, but not in the fashionable way that often included a hint of pink. No, hers was pale with the vaguest hit of olive beneath, as though some ancestor from Italy had spent too long in a cave.

"That's Mistress Althea," Charlotte snapped and Althea decided she did not like her very much.

"She is?" Lord Thacker asked, glancing from Althea to the Lady Maybourne and back, "You are?"

"I am Mistress Althea," Althea replied in her most mysterious voice, raising a single, slender bejeweled hand for the gentlemen to bow over.

They approached and pressed their lips to her long, thin fingers in turn, their narrow lips lightly brushing her profusion of gold and silver rings.

"May I ask what precipitates such fascinating, and dare I say, exotic, company?" Lord Leslie asked, stepping back and looking to his hostess.

Lady Maybourne stumbled for a suitable response.

Althea, the professional, saved her.

"The servants have been seeing a spectral presence in the kitchens. The Countess thought it best to call me in to calm the household."

Lord Grimsby nodded seriously. "Can't be too careful."

"How terribly exciting," Lord Leslie said, a gleam in his eyes telling Althea he did not believe a word of her claims.

Which was just as well. She had no use for the

nonbelievers, even if she was one of them.

"Yes, we are honored to have her here," Lady Maybourne explained. "The household has been so unsettled by the, er, spectral presence. In the kitchens."

"I imagine so. The working classes can be so sensitive to such occurrences." Lord Leslie gave Althea an assessing glance. Besides being the best looking of the three visiting gentlemen, he was obviously also the smartest. Althea wondered that such a man had not turned Charlotte's head already.

Why was she so set on inventing a ghostly beau and avoiding the obviously viable option before her?

It was an absurd mystery which obviously had more to do with stubborn, spoiled debutantes than anything supernatural, but Althea needed to find the answers. Quickly.

The servants appeared then with more tea and cakes and arranged the chairs so the three gentlemen could sit, which they did. Althea wondered in passing how the upper classes didn't outgrow their fine clothes every month, considering the amount of sweets they seemed to consume. This was not the first household in which she'd noticed the trend.

Sighing, she took a cake for herself. After all, she was soon to be out of this line of work.

Lady Maybourne poured the tea for her guests, as Mr. Grimsby nervously glanced at Althea.

"It's an honor to meet you in person, Mistress."

Althea inclined her head and continued to chew her cake.

Mr. Grimsby continued, eyes strangely vacant. "A friend of my cousin told me you helped his sister communicate with her dead son last year. Such a precious boy he was, and you brought her such joy. She wasn't sure he was happy, of course, but now she knows he is."

Something like guilt twisted in Althea's gut. She remembered that job well. The poor woman was barely Althea's age and utterly bereft. Althea had nearly refused payment, but the woman's relief at learning her small child was no longer in pain stopped her. She could not let the woman know it was all a lie, a careful product of theatrics and planned noises, a well-timed vase falling and Althea's own keen observations about the family.

Lord Thacker's pudgy, pink face brightened. "You know I saw a ghost once. As a boy. It jumped down at me when I was in the stables one night, a terrible specter of a man with no head."

Lady Maybourne paled. "Lord Thacker, such imagery! Charlotte is-"

"I am fine, mother," Charlotte cut her off. "I'm not afraid of ghosts."

Althea did not miss the glare Charlotte threw her way at the words. No, she did not like Charlotte Ridgely, and the feeling was very obviously reciprocated.

"A -apologies," Lord Thacker stammered, "I simply wondered, after all that-"

"Was it a barn owl?" Lord Leslie interposed. "I once had a similar experience with a particularly large one at my stable in Kent."

Lord Thacker's round face grew a deeper shade of fuchsia. "I have seen many a barn owl, Leslie, and this was no bird. My question, however, concerns the ladies at hand."

"I'm sure they've seen a barn owl, as well," Lord Grimsby muttered and Althea recognized the faint scent of opium about him. "England's got hundreds."

Lord Thacker's color deepened. "Thousands, I'm sure, Grimsby. But if you'll please, I simply wish to ask what the spirit in the kitchens here is *doing*? I have always been fascinated by the unseen, or, perhaps one should say, the undead."

"The spirit in the kitchens?" Lady Maybourne blinked.

"Yes, the one Mistress Althea is allegedly here to

dispel," Lord Leslie said, taking a sip of his tea. Althea recognized a fellow skeptic in him. Such a man could be dangerous to her work, or, perhaps, useful, if he were let on to the plan.

She tucked the thought away for later and said, "I take it you are not a believer, Lord Leslie."

"I am not," he confirmed. "No offense, Mistress."

"None taken." She inclined her head. "In due course we shall learn that the truth of our corporeal existence is far more complicated than we on this plane imagine."

"Do you really believe that? That one day we shall all either know ghosts to be real, if not be one ourselves?"

"Something like that," she replied, "yes."

"Liar."

"Why would I lie about such a thing?" she asked, looking at the three men before her, only realizing belatedly that none of them had spoken.

"I don't know," Lord Leslie said blankly, "why would you?"

"Probably money."

Althea glanced from one man to the other, unsure which had said that. "I don't do it for money," she said unsteadily, "so much as the profound satisfaction of helping both the living, and the restless from beyond, find peace."

"But you do expect payment."

Althea knew for a fact now that none of the three men before her had spoken. She'd been watching. Which meant..

"That's very good of you," Lord Thacker said, casting a worried glance from Althea to Lady Mayboune. "Very good. Can't be pleasant being stuck in limbo, trapped between this world and the next, unseen and unknown for all eternity. You're doing excellent work, Mistress, I'm sure." His smile was tight and Althea knew he humoring her.

"God, the man is a cad, isn't he?" the low, dry voice said, now coming from across the room. "I think we'd all be better off if he went on his way, don't you?"

Althea watched as a candlestick on the table near the door rose a foot into the air, turned slightly, as though being examined, and then set itself back down.

Althea jumped, her tea cup nearly upsetting the saucer she held,. It was obvious she had overtaxed herself the last few days. The pressure of this, her final, most important, most lucrative job, was weighing on her.

That's all it was. A simple hallucination brought on by stress. Common enough, and readily cured by a good night's undisturbed sleep.

"Are you all right?" Lord Grimsby blinked his bleary eyes.

Althea took a deep breath. "Yes, thank you. There are… disturbances, in the house. But do not worry, they are harmless and discernible only to me."

The disembodied voice chucked, deep and mocking. "Harmless and discernible only to you, eh?" The voice was closer now. "Well, if that's how you want to play it. I hate to disappoint a woman."

Suddenly the air behind Lady Maybourne and Charlotte *moved*. None of the others noticed. They continued their conversation unawares that some sort of hole in the space between the sofa and the door was opening up, twisting, convulsing-

No, that wasn't right. It shuddered. Shadows drew up from the corners of the room and undulated, coalescing from nothingness into *something*, the air itself moving light and darkness and taking form.

The form of a tall, sharply handsome, slightly transparent young man. Althea immediately recognized him as the figure who had awoken her on her first night in the house.

He had not been a dream.

He had been real.

Or, at least, as real as one could be when one was a-

"Ghost," she breathed.

Althea watched in mute horror as the man threw her a wicked grin. "Indeed," he said then winked. "Let's have some fun, shall we?"

Chapter Five

The Tempest

The porcelain cup and saucer the woman called herself Mistress Althea was holding fell to the floor with a satisfying crash.

"Oh," Ben chided, catching her dark eyes with his own, "we can do better than that."

It was time he did something about her presence here. The woman was nothing but trouble and trouble was the last thing he needed. The situation was dire enough without her charade complicating matters. Worse, she was distracting Charlotte and it was obvious tensions between the two women were mounting. The Earl could not be imposed upon for help, so it was left to Ben, and whatever resources he could have.

A body was not amongst them, but there was no reason that should hinder him.

It would be easy enough to chase the woman out. She was already half terrified. All Ben needed was to add a dash of confusion, a hearty dollop of embarrassment, a few witnesses, and a *scene*. It was evident the famed mystic did not actually believe in spirits, and Ben had little doubt a hint of proof would go a long way. He would send her running, afraid of losing her credibility as much as the spirits themselves.

Ben grinned to himself. He could no longer taste food or know a woman's touch, but he could absolutely savor the guilty pleasure of wreaking havoc. In life he'd abhorred chaos, but in death he had found it one of his only pleasures. It was odd the ways death could change a man.

One thing that had never faltered, however, was the fact that Ben always, *always*, got his way. He would not be denied, and just now, his only desire, was that Mistress Althea *leave*.

The obnoxious Lord Leslie could leave too, now that Ben thought on it. Leslie was clearly in Wilkes' pocket and Ben had ascertained some time ago that Wilkes was not a man to be trusted. Neither, then, was Leslie. Which was just as well because the cocky blonde Lord was clearly set on wedding Charlotte and that was not going to happen.

Fortunately, both these annoyances could be dispersed with one single, spectral tantrum. *Perfect*, Ben thought. He had always, both in life and death, adored efficiency.

"Did you say something, dear?" Charlotte's mother asked Althea.

"I think she said 'ghost'," That was the awkward,

red-faced Lord Thacker.

"Ghost?" somebody else echoed, but Ben was no longer listening.

He was moving.

Summoning only a fraction of the force he was capable of, he directed his attention to a tall, narrow display cabinet full of china on the far side of the room. Althea was watching him, her black eyes narrowed- everything was happening very quickly, Ben knew, but since his death he most often felt time moved like molasses in January, so it was all very slow and obvious to him- and tilted her head slightly. She knew he was about to do something bad.

Which he was.

Ben raised a single, shimmering hand and watched as Althea's red lips parted, whether to warn the others or to stop him, he would never know.

Because with a flick of his wrist, purely for dramatic effect, he sent the cupboard crashing to the floor in an explosion of sound and splintering wood.

Pandemonium ensued. The three gentlemen leapt to their feet, tea and cakes spilling everywhere, as Lady Maybourne began screaming.

"Ben. Ben, stop it!" Charlotte shouted in the direction of the cupboard. She could not see him- he could at least control who he was visible to in this form- and she looked like a right fool.

Nearly everyone rose to their feet as the butler and Lord Maybourne both ran into the room. Everyone except Mistress Althea. She remained seated, back to the toppled cupboard, dark eyes steady on Ben, as if unimpressed. As if in challenge.

Whatever initial shock he had created in her was gone, or at least immediately concealed.

Ben clenched his jaw. He needed to get this woman out of his house, before she ruined everything. If she did not think she was afraid of ghosts, he would make certain she learned her mistake.

Black eyes locked on his, apart from the pandemonium of everyone else in the room, she quirked a single eyebrow as if to say, "Is that all you've got?"

It wasn't.

He raised a brow in return- a trick he had practiced as a boy in front of the mirror lifetimes ago in hopes of one day being a renowned rake, which was, all things considered, a rather pitiful aspiration- and gave her *more*.

With another slight flick of his wrists- both this time, as if directing a phantom orchestra- Ben flipped the cupboard and its contents again over with a loud bang. The little party which had drawn closer to

examine the fallen display leapt back, just as Ben
waggled his fingers with a flourish and the contents of
the cupboard flew upwards.

Plates, platters, tea cups, and several large
porcelain punch bowls shot into the air and hovered
there, spinning.

"Hell and damnation, what is this?" Lord Leslie
exclaimed, scrambling back.

Lady Mayboune fainted and was caught just in
time by the usually unflappable butler, who watched
his employer with wide eyes. The Earl remained still,
his face ashen, body stiff, as if he could will it all away.

The scrawny, unhealthy-looking suitor- Mr.
Grimsby- was giggling nervously, while Leslie was
breathing hard, fists clenching and unclenching, eyes
locked on the suspended china.

Charlotte was shouting "Stop it Ben!" at the
floating dishware.

Ben leaned against the wall on the other side of the
room, watching Mistress Althea.

She turned to him, then threw a glance over her
shoulder at the floating china, and looked back to him,
unmoved. Another challenge.

"You're not afraid of ghosts?" Ben asked, making
his voice deeper and more terrifying, like the
screaming echoes of a thousand souls.

Althea shrugged. "Not particularly. I don't believe in them."

Ben wanted to maintain his composure. He really did. He ought to have the upper hand. He desperately wished this impertinent, blasphemous con woman would get out of his house and take that damnable prig Leslie with her.

But her stubborn disbelief brought back to him every moment he could remember in the last eighty years or so when he had tried to reach out to the living and failed. When a long-ago friend screamed in horror and ran. An old lover cried the steps of his townhouse and could neither see nor hear him. A child new to the neighborhood, lonely and curious, sought quiet in the house- only to flee in terror when Ben attempted to reach out. It had happened too many times. Disbelief had caused him untold frustration, pain and loneliness. He wanted to control it, to *prove* that he was still here, still desiring of human contact and company, but he had no control whatsoever. It was as though the more he sought some agency over his supernatural predicament, the further any hope of it became. It was agony. It was torture. It was unbearable.

And Althea's cool disregard was the final straw in several decades worth of frustration, obsolesce, and utter despair.

Ben snapped.

The china went flying. It shot around the room as a small cyclone twisted into being. The force of spiraling wind ripped up the carpets, the drapes, even the wall sconces in a spiral, twisting funnel. The fire that had been merrily crackling a moment before went clean out and ash began spewing as the hearth vomited its contents all over the room, filling the air with a violent maelstrom of ash, debris, and various hurtling objects.

China smashed into the walls with a shattering crash, the doors slammed shut and locked themselves, and everyone was screaming, ducking for cover.

Everyone except Althea.

Eyes still on hers, Ben felt himself growing, becoming part of the storm that raged around them.

"Get out of my house!" he shouted at her, his voice like a thousand ancient gods of war, shaking the foundations of the house he loved so much, the house he was trying so hard to protect.

The only sign Althea was moved at all was the way her hands clenched in her lap, her knuckles an even paler white.

"No." Her full, pink lips mouthed the word as ash and a porcelain punch ladle flew past her face.

At the fringes of Ben's consciousness, he noticed

the Lord Leslie shielding Charlotte, who was weeping and cursing, still talking to the overturned china cabinet. Mr. Grimsby was laying on the floor, blinking up at the storm with vacant eyes. Lord Thacker had plastered himself to one corner of the room, where it appeared he had wet himself. The butler, Goggins, was still supporting Lady Maybourne, who gained consciousness only to yelp in terror and lose it again.

Althea never flinched.

Energy draining, Ben gave a yell of frustration that caused a second cupboard- this one full of silver- to crash to the floor, narrowly missing Leslie, who was now fending off an attacking tea cup.

The yell turned into a cry that faded and just as Ben felt the last of his energy seeping, he looked once more to Althea.

"You will leave," he said, meaning both Althea *and* Leslie, but there wasn't time to explain, to yell or scream or *make them obey*… there wasn't energy… he felt his form dissipating… with the last of his powers he gave a frustrated snarl and was gone.

The cacophony ended as quickly as it had begun.

The moment the ghost, who was obviously Charlotte's paramour Ben, disappeared, everything fell to the floor and was silent.

There was a long moment of disbelief, and then everyone turned to Althea.

"What. Was. That." Maybourne growled through gritted teeth, ash covering his perfectly tailored coat of dark superfine and once impeccably polished Hessian boots.

"Proof that I am desperately needed here, just as I thought," Althea said, rising to gain control of the situation. She was rattled to her core, but her only route to success was to conceal that fact. "The spirit is getting increasingly restless. Someone could have been injured, or worse."

"I'm injured!" Lord Thacker cried, holding up his hand. A small cut, no more than an inch long and barely bleeding, slashed across his knuckles.

"Then you see the danger here," Althea pronounced, looking at the ashen faces- both in coloring and literally ash-covered- around her. "He must be escorted to the world beyond."

"No!" Charlotte cried, but her mother, who was still being supported by Goggins, reached out swatted her arm to shush her.

"I think perhaps this is out of our purview," Lord Leslie said smoothly. He gave a sniff and looked around the room, disdain and something like fury in his own pale face. "Obviously if you need any assistance with this… *mishap*, Maybourne, I shall be happy to help. Personally I think the place ought to be torn down."

"No!" Charlotte cried again. "If you destroy the house, you'll destroy Ben!"

"Who is Ben?" Mr. Grimsby asked, rising to his feet on shaking legs.

"No one," Althea snapped before Charlotte could speak. The last thing these suitors needed was to think the girl who lived in the haunted house was mad as well. The Earl cast her a grateful look. "Just a beloved footman. He loves the house."

Charlotte caught her mother's eye and shut her mouth, suddenly aware of herself. She sniffed and nodded.

"We do care a great deal for our staff," the Earl covered smoothly. Althea saw the suitors move past Charlotte's outburst, all except Lord Leslie, whose handsome face had taken on a calculating look, as if he guessed who Ben was. Althea wondered what the man would make of it. She wondered what *she* was going to make of it, when she had time to process her thoughts. Ghosts were real. And, if Charlotte was telling the truth about the house, this particular ghost was tied to it.

Interesting.

"I think it best if we take our leave," Lord Leslie said, breaking the line of Althea's thoughts. She only vaguely nodded her farewell as he offered his goodbyes to the family and walked out. The other two men, neither of whom offered any assistance and both of whom now eyed Charlotte as though she'd grown an extra head, made their exits as well.

Althea doubted they would continue their pursuit of Charlotte's hand. She was beautiful, but impoverished, and if there was any chance her dowry might include a haunted house and terrifying brushes with the supernatural, Althea doubted any reasonable man of *ton* would want her. She knew all too well that men of that class were selfish, driven by greed and bettering their own reputations to the detriment of anything, or anyone, else.

"Mistress Althea!" the Earl of Maybourne said sharply, rounding on her, "My study. Immediately."

He strode from the room. Althea followed at a reasonable distance.

Just before she reached the door to the hall she heard Charlotte call after her in a shaking, triumphant voice, "I told you he doesn't want to leave. You'll go first, mark my words!"

Lady Maybourne's sharp rebuke was the last thing Althea heard before she shut the parlor door behind her with a snap.

Up the stairs and to the right, she entered Maybourne's study.

"Close the door," he said. She obliged.

With a heavy sigh, the Earl sank his lean frame into the armchair behind his desk. "That was overdoing it a bit, don't you think?"

Althea blinked.

"It was very well done, obviously. *Very* well done," he poured a finger of scotch from the decanter on his desk into two glasses, offering one to Althea. "The damages shall be docked from your pay, of course, but I have to admit, I am impressed."

Althea's mind reeled as she sat in the chair opposite his.

He still thought ghosts were a fabrication? After all that? If she were capable of such theatrics she would be running a sold out show in the grandest theater in London, not pandering to the sentiments of superstitious aristocrats.

But he was docking her pay?

Fury coursed throughs her. She could not let that petulant *ghost* ruin her work. Defeating him *was* her work, and that fact remained even now that he was real.

Pushing aside her roiling feelings about the

afternoon's events, Althea centered her mind on what was most important: completing the job.

"The last few days showed me that matters were more advanced with your sister than I thought, my lord," she said, careful not to admit either that she was a fraud, or, as it turned out, the ghost was not. "I did not anticipate the other gentlemen to be in attendance this morning, but I think it worked to our advantage."

"You mean to *your* advantage. After word of this gets out your business is going to quadruple. But then, I doubt that's a coincidence. You obviously know your trade well."

Althea flushed. She took pride in her work, even if she could not take credit for this unexpected turn of events. She could not, however, reveal the truth nor the fact that whatever came of this job, it was going to be her last. She had no desire for more work, and, if anything, she was ready for her reputation to fade away. It would be difficult to retire if anyone cared enough to come looking for her. She already knew she would have to change her name the moment she left London. Mistress Althea belonged to the city, to its ignorant, selfish upper classes and their petty whims. She would soon leave it all behind, no matter how in demand her reputation made her.

Still, Lord Maybourne's praise flattered her. She

was only human, after all, and she had worked since she was fourteen to build the career she was now so eager to be rid of.

Althea met her employer's clear blue eyes. "I do not pursue my work with an eye only to my own aggrandizement, Maybourne," she said, her tone sharp. "I have a gift. I did not ask for it nor do I revel in it, it simply is. That I may use this gift to help others is my only objective."

He raised his glass with a wry smile twisting the corners his thin lips. He did not believe her for a second. "That, and the money."

She was best served by being what her employers wanted her to be- the genuine thing, or, as the case may be, a savvy fraud. She could not outright confirm her ruse, but she knew to push too hard against the truth would only undermine her rapport with the Earl. Althea dipped her head and raised her own glass in salute. "One must survive."

"Indeed."

They both drank.

Maybourne's face grew serious. "Those men were the only suitors Charlotte has yet entertained this season. To lose them is a terrible blow. Worse, I think, than you realize."

A shot of guilt went through Althea, even though

she knew it was not her fault. Blame lay squarely on the ghost- *Ben*- but she could not explain that to Maybourne. Not yet. Perhaps not ever. The only thing that mattered now was that she rid the house of the ghost, or, barring that possibility- after all, she had never *really* done any such thing before- rid Charlotte of her fascination with him. Whether the Earl believed it or not was irrelevant, so long as she delivered his desired outcome.

"It was an unfortunate coinciding of events," Althea replied carefully. "I think, however, Charlotte has faith in my credibility now. She will be much more malleable to my persuasions."

"I hope so," Maybourne stared thoughtfully into the crackling fireplace against the far wall. "You've certainly made the spirit convincing in its desire to remain here. I heard a ghostly shout of 'get out' quite clearly. I don't know how you managed it, but it did seem directed *at you*. Seems to me an odd tack."

Althea swallowed to buy herself a moment. "If Charlotte truly believes this spirit exists, it only makes sense it would desire me to leave, just as she does. Even if she does not believe in the ghost" - Althea's mind raced to tie together what Maybourne believed and the shocking truth- "and it is all a ploy of hers to avoid the marriage mart, the more real I make it seem, the better chance I stand of convincing her to end the charade. If I can convince others, or seem to, it will make it all there more difficult for her to argue when the ghost then reveals future intentions. To seek peace, after all, for instance."

"Or denounce my sister's interest?"

"Sad, but possible, yes."

This was getting too complicated. Althea would need time alone to think and figure everything out, but for now she needed only to get Maybourne off her back. Whatever she could say to appease him, she would. She could decide what to do about a *real* ghost later.

Maybourne nodded at her words. "Several possibilities of attack. Wise, Madam Althea, very wise. My sister is stubborn and spoiled. I'll admit to some fault in that, but I never thought she would jeopardize her future this way."

"Marriage is a fearful thing to a young woman. It is her entire future at stake. I am not surprised she might balk at the prospect."

Maybourne's brow furrowed. "I suppose you're right. She's been raised to know her duty, and she seemed so excited when we first came to Town, but duty is not always easy, is it?"

Althea knew it wasn't a question, and the words

were meant for himself as much as for her. She said nothing.

The Earl sighed. "Perhaps from now on we work to *attract* young men, not repel them, yes?"

"As you wish."

The corners of Maybourne's mouth twitched. "Though if I'm honest, Lord Leslie is the only one of the bunch I'd consider for her. The other two are no great loss."

"I wouldn't know, sir," Althea replied, a dutiful employee. She did not give a damn who Charlotte Ridgely married.

Maybourne glanced at her. "I suppose you wouldn't, wouldn't you," he murmured and Althea did not bother to decipher his tone. "At any rate, well done today. You had me half convinced the bloody ghost was real."

"Did I?" Althea asked, and she thought she heard a low, faint male chuckle somewhere in the shadows behind the Earl. She ignored it.

"You really are as masterful as the rumors claimed. It's no easy feat, in our age of superior knowledge and scientific enlightenment, to make the dark superstitions of a less informed age come to life."

Althea's stomach fluttered. She would have wholeheartedly agreed with him a few hours ago, but now she did not know what she thought. "The dead have always been with us, my lord. It is merely the ways in which we perceive them that alter, not their presence amongst us."

Maybourne raised his glass salute and downed the rest of its contents. "Spoken like a true professional."

"And you speak as a most cynical unbeliever, my lord."

"I am certainly that. But the more interesting question is, do *you* believe, Mistress Althea?" his crystal blue eyes shimmered in the firelight.

Althea answered with words she had spoken a thousand times in the fifteen years, but for the first time since she was a child, she meant them. "Of course I believe, Maybourne. I would be foolish not to."

Maybourne nodded. "Fair enough. By the way, my mother is hosting a little dinner tomorrow night. I hope you'll attend. We are discreet people, of course, but I do not want you to think we are hiding your visit with us."

"You're not worried your friends will condemn your hosting a notorious occultist? Dealing with the supernatural can be dangerous you know. At the very least, there could be a prison sentence for dealing in lies."

A muscle in the Earl's jaw twitched. "I know the

laws. You're not claiming to practice magic and neither am I. Our friends are discreet people, and I'm not quite so staid as you seem to believe, Mistress Althea."

Althea's brows rose. "Do you harbor some hidden interest in alchemy, my lord? You would not be the first."

Maybourne did not smile. "I only mean that my business is my own concern as is the company I keep. My friends know this, and if anything they would enjoy the opportunity to speak to a such an icon of the shadows as yourself."

"An icon of the shadows," Althea murmured. "May I borrow that?"

"Of course," the Earl grinned, the effect rendering him almost boyish. "Good afternoon, Mistress."

And with that, Althea was dismissed.

That night she could not sleep. She had excused herself from dinner, pleading a headache, and spent the evening pacing her rooms.

Now it was nearly midnight. She had given up the pacing and instead sat in the armchair before the fireplace in her sitting room, no longer impressed by the grandness of her accommodations.

She had a single focus now, and it was not the

beauty of Maybourne house nor its attendant furnishings.

It was its resident spirit.

One she had to remove, or, at the very least, discourage from entertaining Charlotte Ridgeley's attentions. If such a thing were possible. Althea honestly had no idea.

The task had been complicated enough when the ghost was only a figment of Charlotte's imagination, but what had happened today in the parlor was no fantasy.

Althea's mind reeled. She was certain that her previous jobs were fakes. She had been faking it all, at least. Nothing even close to today's events had ever happened to her before. Once a teenage boy had thrown a sheet over himself and wandered the garden moaning, but she had seen through that immediately.

This was different.

This was… *real*.

She rubbed her aching temple with one hand and closed her eyes against the flickering of the fire in the grate. There was no use letting her mind wander into the past, to all the jobs where she'd lied and faked and pandered. All that mattered now was the hard, cold fact that the ghost haunting Maybourne house, and Charlotte Ridgeley's affection for him, were real.

And now she had to actually do what she'd promised the Earl- or fail.

Failure meant no money, at best, but more likely arrest ,along with far worse possibilities. She could not fail.

A sigh escaped her lips, heavy and weary.

"Sleepless, are we?"

Althea eyes flew open. She did not need to see who spoke, however. She knew who it was, recognized the smug, smooth, low voice. She glanced to the armchair across from her, where the faint figure of a darkly handsome man sat.

Ben.

The ghost.

"How long have you been watching me?"

He examined the long fingers of his large, veiny and transparent hand. She was surprised to see that even in death calluses marked his palms and fingertips, paler even in this translucent state. Charlotte had once claimed he was a duke, but these were not the hands of a duke but a day laborer.

Ben didn't bother too look at her. "Don't flatter yourself. I have other matters to attend to, you know. This is a large house."

Some intuition told Althea he was lying, that he *had* been watching her for some time. But she let him have his conceit, and changed tack. "Other matters? Like piecing yourself back together after that little tantrum downstairs?"

Althea didn't know why, but she was not afraid of him. Even during the objectively terrifying spectacle in the parlor, she had not cowered. Her heart had raced, but she had remained steadfast.

It had been his eyes, locked on hers. Though he had no corporeal form and obviously offered her only ill will, she had trusted his intentions. *Him.* Ben was clearly trying to scare her, but she knew on some bizarre, instinctive level that he would not actually harm her and that he was, for all that he was a phantom, he was also trustworthy. A man of honor. She could rely on such a man, even if that meant she believed when he said he wanted her gone.

Besides, she had seen far worse treatment from living men than she had from the dead.

"Little tantrum?" he asked in that silky voice that lilted ever so slightly with the ingrained arrogance of the upper classes. His eyebrow quirked up, just as it had earlier.

It made him look like the worst sort of rake.

The loose linen shirt he wore, open nearly to his waist, did nothing to hinder the effect.

If Althea loathed the rich, she despised its most

indolent and luxuriant participants even more. Rakes and libertines were the worst of the lot. Lords given to drink and gamble more than they tended to their tenants or responsibilities. They took everything and gave nothing in return, believing authority and pleasure their automatic due.

The easy grace and power with which this man, this *ghost*, carried himself, reeked of exactly the most despicable sort of entitled roué.

Her tone was light, but firm. "You behaved precisely like a child who wasn't getting what he wanted. I would say that is a tantrum, wouldn't you?"

"Well, it got your pay docked, and Charlotte is never going to be on your side now, so I think I actually got exactly what I wanted."

"Hardly. You want me to leave, yet I'm still here."

He tipped his head towards her, acknowledging the hit, his ghostly pale dark hair falling forward. It was overlong, grown to a length not popular for generations. His clothing, what little he had of it, also spoke of an earlier time. Fleetingly, Althea wondered what his life had been like, when and how precisely he had lived. How long he had been like this, trapped between worlds.

"For now," he replied simply. "I'm beginning to think I don't mind your presence here."

"You want me to stay in Maybourne House?"

He raised a single, strong, slender finger and wagged it once. "No. I'm afraid I don't want you to stay long, but I think I *am* due some entertainment."

"Do I entertain you?"

"You intrigue me."

A voice in Althea's mind reminded her she was sitting having a perfectly reasonable conversation with a half-embodied largely translucent man who had been dead for far longer than she had been alive.

She brushed the thought aside. It wasn't helpful, and Althea was, above all things, practical.

These were the cards she had been dealt, and all she could control now was how she played her hand.

"I intrigue a lot of people," she said with a smile that did not reach her eyes. "It's my job."

"And yet you shall not be successful in this one I'm afraid. I will not leave this house." His tone broached no argument.

Althea thought for a moment, tapping her fingers on the armrest of her chair. "Will you pretend to? I don't really care either way, so long as you set Miss Ridgely free."

"Can't do that," he said, rising to float in front of the fire. The flickering light of the flames danced through his body, making him appear to flicker, too.

He stared at the burning logs.

"Why not? What use do you have for a silly, selfish chit of a girl?"

Ben shot Althea a sideways glance. "If I didn't know any better I'd say I just heard a bit of jealousy."

Althea scoffed. "Jealous? Of Charlotte Ridgely? Why on earth would I envy an spoiled little piece of muslin like that?"

Ben smiled wickedly. "You *are* jealous. And why shouldn't you be? She has a comfortable life she did nothing to earn, and you have to fight for everything you have in a line of work that could see you imprisoned, or worse. She has a family who loves her, and you, I'd bet my once very impressive fortune, do not. She is a perfect English rose in the peak of her blossom, and you-"

"I what?" Althea's voice was steel.

"You are a creature of the darkness, Mistress Althea. I suspect that was the case long before you chose that moniker."

He was right. About all of it. Althea watched him with stony eyes.

"How did you land on it by the way? Quite a leap for Jane Smith."

"Althea is my middle name. "

Both his eyebrows rose. "Interesting. I would have

thought you'd distance yourself fully from, well, whatever it is you're trying to escape."

"The best lies hold a kernel of truth, didn't you know?"

His smile turned wicked.

"Smart girl," he said, looking at her with new appreciation. "Yes, I think I'll let you stay on a while."

"You act as though you have a choice."

He shrugged, firelight shifting and dancing through him. "You're right. I cannot make you leave. I cannot do much. Which is why I need Charlotte and I will not let her go. Sadly, I assume this means you won't be getting paid."

A knell of unease rang in Althea's gut. Everything was different now that the ghost was real. Everything except her need for that money, and, she knew, if she bailed, the Earl of Maybourne would turn her in for fraud. The damage downstairs from today's disaster made that inevitable.

She had no choice. The ghost had to leave, or at the very least, leave Charlotte alone.

"What is the girl to you? No offense but a man in your position can't have much use for a pretty face, or, well, anything else Miss Ridgely has to offer."

"She is a beauty isn't she?" Ben sighed. "There are many things a man misses when he's dead. The feel of a woman. Her softness. Her warmth. Her *musk*."

"If you keep talking like that, you will succeed in driving me out," Althea grimaced. "Don't dodge the question. Why Charlotte?"

"Just as you have your reasons for being here, *Althea*, I have mine," Ben murmured with a yawn, stretching his flickering arms. He floated away from the fire, towards the shadows near the door. "I think that's enough getting to know one another for now, don't you? I can't overindulge in your company, I might get bored, and then where would we be?"

"Have I entertained you satisfactorily so far?" Althea asked drily.

"Better than you can imagine. Sweet dreams, dear lady."

With that, he was gone, vanished into thin air. Only the faint scent of pine and fine brandy lingered.

Curious, Althea thought, of all the day's revelations, the most surprising was that ghosts had a scent. At least his was pleasant.

Some minutes later she was curled into the massive four poster, drifting into sleep. Nestled into the plush bedding, Althea's mind floated towards the figure of a tall, handsome gentleman whose mocking smile made her want to open his ridiculously open shirt even more. She had the distinct sense he would not mind if she did.

Althea remembered none of her dreams the following morning.

Chapter Six
The Secrets

The following morning Althea breakfasted quick
and early. A boiled egg, fresh bread, and some coffee,
no cream or sugar. She dined in the kitchens with the
staff and cook, who had given up protesting the
arrangement. The family was never awake so early,
she told them, and she would not tolerate the effort of
a full breakfast being made on her behalf alone. She
knew it grated on their pride, but she also knew they
were grateful for the reprieve and the company. She
told them stories of other homes she'd stayed in, other
peers she had assisted- never names, of course, but she
knew some of the staff were clever and well-connected
enough to guess some of her previous clients. She
didn't mind. She never told the stories that should be
kept truly confidential, and sharing her experiences
heightened the chances that the staff at Maybourne
house might share their own one day.

As soon as she'd finished breakfast, Althea made
for the library on the second floor. She poured over
dusty tomes for an hour, then another, then another.
The dull light of a rainy English dawn gave way to the
slightly less dull light of a rainy English morning. It
appeared most of the books in the library hadn't been

touched in years, decades even. She doubted the collection belonged to the Ridgeleys at all, but rather to one of the mysterious prior owners of the house.

Finally, she found what she was searching for.

A heavy, leather-bound volume of family history. It was not for Ridgely family history, but that of the Dukes of Stafford.

Charlotte had claimed Ben was the fifteenth Duke of Stafford. It was a title Althea had never heard of before, which was surprising, as there were few dukes in the world and most of them were either notorious or renowned. Or just very rich and powerful.

Anticipation fluttered in Althea's stomach as she sat down at the table in the center of the room and opened the book onto its dusty wooden expanse. If she knew more about who Ben had been, she might uncover a way to convince him to cooperate with her plans.

The book's bindings were heavy as she settled them open, and its stiff, yellowed pages creaked when she pried them apart. But the information was there. Her heart picked up in pace as she read.

The Staffords were an old family, having come over with William the Conqueror in 1066 and thus earning their illustrious title. Court favorites of both the Yorks and later the Tudors- an intriguing feat- they seemed to lose favor during the reign of Henry VIII. That was not surprising given the descriptions of their deaths, which implied they were at best an unruly lot, and at, worst, monstrously awful.

Althea believed luck was what one made of it, but even she began to notice an uncommon amount of misfortune in the Stafford line. The Dukes of Stafford had a gruesome past, and in more recent centuries nearly all of them died young and in unusual circumstances.

One Duke had poisoned himself with a draught meant for his mistress. Another had been drunkenly writing a blackmail letter when he passed out, fell forward and got his own quill through his eye. A third had, even worse, been murdered by his own cook, with whom he had been having an affair, after said cook had caught him buggering both a footman and his own, legitimate wife, in the larder.

It appeared all of Althea's suspicions as to the quality of Ben's background were correct.

He was one of a long line of entitled, self-serving, aristocratic profligates.

Which made the steady warmth of his otherworldly gaze all the more unnerving.

"Finding anything useful?"

Althea glanced up to see Goggins in the doorway.

"This is an unusual book. It's the most thoroughly detailed family history I think I've ever read. I don't even have a family letter older than I am, I'm the first who could read."

"Some of us chart our successes on parchment and vellum, others in a grandchild's smile. I think we both know which is more valuable." The butler walked to the side of her chair and glanced down at the heavy leather volume before her.

"Ah," he said knowingly, "I thought you might find that."

"It has been added to over time, like a log book."

"Yes," Goggins nodded, "My predecessor informed me of it when I first took up employment here. Each Duke would record the history and death of the previous one, which became all the more valuable as there were so many and they died so often."

"They do seem to have died young."

"Indeed, far too young. But then the curse knew what it was about."

Althea stilled. Until yesterday afternoon the mention of a curse would have meant as much to her as a reference to unicorns or flying carriages. Impossible. Silly, even.

After Ben's alarming display, however, she could not dismiss such things. That mention of it came from the serious, stoic Goggins was only more troubling.

"What do you know about this curse? Miss Ridgely mentioned one yesterday."

Goggins glanced towards the door, as if to ensure no one was about, then sat in the chair opposite Althea, a graceful move his employers would never witness. But Althea was not upper class, she was Goggins' equal, and she was not offended that he treated her as such. Rather, she was grateful.

The butler leaned in and spoke in a hushed voice.

"What did Miss Ridgely say about the curse?"

Althea shook her head. "Not much. Only that it is the reason the ghost is here, but she did not know the details."

A shadow passed over Goggins lined, angular face. "I do not know much myself. I came to Maybourne house fifty years ago, when I was young and they needed a footman. No one else would take the job, and I was desperate."

"Who was living here then?"

"No one. It was owned by an investor who had purchased it when the Stafford line died out, and he rented it to wealthy families for the season. A small number of us stayed on to maintain the place. I was one of them."

Althea watched him carefully, a sense of

foreboding rising.

"It was still called Stafford house then, and the butler, my predecessor, had served under the Stafford family. He was here when- when the fifteenth Earl of Stafford passed."

"You mean Benedict? From yesterday?"

Goggins' face was ashen. "Yes. I've never seen him as active as he was yesterday afternoon. I've witnessed objects moving, felt the odd chill, encountered enough in these last five decades to believe there was a spirit here, but yesterday..."

The butler looked frightened, and Althea wondered if perhaps her lack of fear was in error. There was more to this house, and Ben, than she had given credit to thus far. Something darker.

"What do you know of the curse? Of Benedict's death?"

Goggins' voice lowered further. "Very little. None of the staff who had been here spoke of it much. It was some sort of sudden tragedy, in the formal salon, from what I heard. The sitting room, they called it ironically, but it was really the grand receiving room for the family."

"Is that the bolted door downstairs?"

"Yes. I have never even been inside. The Earl of Maybourne, when he took up residence, tried to enter once. It was impossible to budge the door, even when we managed to remove the bolts."

"Aren't there windows from the outside?"

"Blocked off from the inside. We tried that too, but to no avail. One of the footmen quit over it, said he had a bad feeling about the whole thing. The Earl gave up and has not spoken of it since."

Althea pondered that a moment. "How did the Ridgely family come to own this place?"

"The investor sold it off for a pittance after a decade of trying to let it out for more than a week. No one would stay here longer than that, you see, except the three of us who maintained the place long term. Myself, Cook, and Mrs. Hooper."

"You never had any trouble?"

"I wouldn't say that," Goggins hedged, then pivoted. "The house is worth a fortune. It truly is one of the finest in London in quality and design. Yet until the Earl moved in a few months ago no one could stand it. Even the previous Earls of Maybourne barely used it. They paid so little for the they kept it as an investment, and generally leased other quarters while in Town. Besides, they could not sell it even when they tried."

"*Did* they try? I know the Earl is struggling now and could doubtless use the coin."

Goggins gave a brief nod. "Between you and me, he's tried. Maybourne prefers the country, so they don't really need the place, but they do need the funds. The current Earl is the first in a long line of that family to have any sense. The rest were gamblers. That solicitor, Mr. Wilkes, is here almost every day trying to help the Earl come up with a plan. It's taking everything they've got to stay here for the season and marry Miss Ridgely off. She's their only hope."

Althea took this in. The family was just as desperate as she'd guessed, and they were willing to pay her a small fortune to ensure the Charlotte married well. The only thing standing in their way was Ben, and the only thing that, apparently, could help them, was her.

She swallowed, a knot twisting in her chest.

Ben seemed set on keeping Charlotte's attentions for himself and seeing her unwed. *But why? And what could Althea do about it?*

"Can you help them, Mistress Althea?" Goggins' voice was soft, the kindest she'd heard from the staunch butler. She met his clear grey eyes.

"I don't think I have a choice," she said.

Goggins gave a short nod, as if satisfied, then rose. He was nearly to the door when Althea remembered something else Charlotte had said, something important that only the insanity of the day before could have driven from her mind.

"Did the fifteenth Earl of Stafford really build this place?"

A sad smile tugged at Goggin's narrow lips. "Yes, Mistress. This house was built by the fifteenth Duke of Stafford, Benedict Lionel Aston. Our resident ghost. His death in is in that book, listed only as a construction incident. This home was both his crowning achievement and his untimely end."

With that, the butler slipped out the door and was gone.

That afternoon Althea left Maybourne house for the first time since her arrival. In light of recent revelations, she decided some fresh air and time to think were in order.

She hired a coach and took a rattling, noisy ride to the edges of Covent Garden. Narrow, dirty, and crowded, the twisting streets of the Garden could not be any less like the boulevards of Mayfair.

The hired hack pulled up at the address she had given, in front of an old narrow home made of brick and smoke stains. Stepping over a puddle of indiscernible filth, Althea stepped up to the battered, scratched door of the place and knocked three times slowly and three times quickly.

It took a moment, but soon she heard the jangling of locks being unlocked.

When the door opened, Althea's face broke into its first genuine smile in days at the sight of the old woman standing before her.

"Nora," she said, wrapping the woman known to the wide world as Madame Veira in a warm embrace.

Ancient, her once black hair and brown skin paled with age, Nora's eyes still glittered with ferocity and life.

"My darling girl," the old woman said. "What a surprise! Did you finish the job so soon?"

"Not yet," Althea said, following Nora's welcoming gesture and stooping to enter the low, narrow house. A delicate staircase ran up one wall to the upper stories, and a long hall led to the lower rooms and the back of the house. Nora had lived here for forty years, renting the extra rooms out to the less fortunate and keeping little for herself.

"It's not going well then?" It was not a question.

"I've never had a job like this."

Althea had followed her friend to the very back of the house to the kitchen, where water was already boiling. Together- Althea knew where everything was with long-earned ease- they prepared a pot of tea and sat at the low table in the center of the small space.

"Is the Earl troubling you?"

"No. It's not that."

"What then? You look pale. You should be happy. This is your last job, if you still insist on retiring."

The words carried more weight than Althea could afford to dwell on. If she finished this job, if she earned the fortune the Earl of Maybourne was willing to pay her even with the sum deducted for yesterday's incident, Althea could buy a place in the country big enough for both of them. Nora still rented this place, even after all this time. A series of blackmailers and poor luck had drained much of her savings and she'd never been able to buy a home of her own as she'd long wished for.

Althea wished for more for her friend, and for herself. Nora had taken Althea and her mother in when they'd been left destitute. She'd given Althea a trade, a way out other than working on her back. Pandering the occult was arguably less risky than prostitution, if more difficult. It certainly paid better, and lasted longer, and gave Althea opportunities she never would have had otherwise. Nora had given her everything.

Althea wanted to give her something in return.

She took a small bag out of the satchel she carried

and slid it across the table to Nora.

"Until this job is done," she said, meeting the older woman's eyes.

Nora looked down at the stack of gold coins. Althea had cashed the first bank note, and while she'd securely stashed away most of it, she wanted Nora to have some now. A comfort, and a promise. "Your mother raised you too well, child," Nora said, blinking back tears. "She would be so proud of you."

The words shouldn't have brought the sting of tears to Althea's own eyes, but they did. Nora had taken Althea and her mother in all those years ago, when her mother had fled the brothel in which Althea had been born. That her mother had died only a few years later of fever was neither woman's fault, and Althea was fortunate that the childless Nora had stepped in to raise her.

And teach her what she knew of the living, the dead, and the ways in which hope could be offered for lucrative gain. She had always been there, the one constant in Althea's life. Her only sense of safety, of home.

Althea could not let her down. Covent Garden was no place for an old woman, even one as worldly and savvy as Nora. She deserved quiet, and peace, and that cottage in the countryside Althea would provide for them both.

She just had to finish this job.

"There is a complication, Nora," Althea said, not meeting her friend's eyes. She could have written a letter, but this conversation was too strange, too delicate, too *dangerous* to risk having it intercepted.

Nora's brows rose. "If it's not the Earl, then who is it? You've dealt with nonbelievers before."

"The problem is not a lack of belief. It's... too much."

Nora's brow furrowed now. "I should think that would make things easier. You could charge more, even."

Althea took a deep breath. "The ghost is real, Nora."

There was a long pause, and Althea braced herself for censure. Nora was a practical woman, the most down to earth and sensible Althea had ever met. She had seen it all and knew everything. There was no way she would credence this development. She'd spent her life following in her own mother's footsteps, one of a long line of women who had capitalized on the superstitions of others. Nora had always told her there were mysteries in the world that could not be explained, but every job Althea shadowed her on as a child, assisted with and learned from, had been a ruse.

There had never been any proof that ghosts were real.

Althea hoped Nora wouldn't think she was going mad, now that Althea understood that reality was far more complicated than she'd realized.

Nora's lips quirked up at the edges. "I was wondering when that would happen."

Althea's eyes shot up to hers. "You believe me?"

"Of course I do."

Relief washed over her. Althea had not realized what it would mean to have someone, particularly the person who meant the most to her, believe her.

She barely believed it herself, and yet Nora was regarding her with a steady gaze, as though she had just announced dinner was ready, not that the fabric of their understanding of reality was missing a massive, important piece. The revelation of Ben's existence was fantastic. It completely rattled everything Althea knew about the world and her place in it, and yet Nora appeared wholly unfazed.

"What's he like?"

"Excuse me?"

Nora took a sip of her tea and gestured to Althea to speak up. "This ghost of yours. What's he like?"

"How did you know it was a he?"

"Lucky guess," Nora's grin was mischievous. "Come now, what killed him? That's the trick to helping them along."

Althea shook her head. "I don't know yet, but *you* know something about *real* ghosts?"

Nora chuckled. "My darling girl, you don't think my entire career was all smoke and mirrors, do you?"

Althea blinked, speechless.

"Sometimes the spirits were genuine and other times the client only needed to believe they were. I never brought you on the real jobs with me because spirits can be unpredictable and I would not risk your safety."

The world around Althea reeled. "But you didn't tell me."

Regret fluttered across Nora's wrinkled face. "I knew one day you'd come across a genuine spirit and then I would have to help you, but they became increasingly rare as the years went on, and part of me hoped you'd never have to face one."

"Ben doesn't seem that bad. Stubborn, perhaps, but not dangerous."

Something dark flashed in Nora's cloudy eyes. "Let us hope you are correct."

"He seems to enjoy my company, even though he wanted me gone at first."

"Interesting. Sometimes the kinder spirits are grateful for assistance."

Althea pondered that. "If he needs assistance, it does not seem to be mine. He has befriended the Earl's sister. She thinks she's in love with him now and refuses to entertain any living suitors."

"Is she daft? Or merely scheming?"

"Neither," Althea shrugged. "She won't say much to me. She loathes me. But I have gathered that her affection for Ben is genuine. I don't know what he thinks of her, only that he doesn't seem to love her, but he does seem set on keeping her attentions himself."

"Interesting." Nora sipped her tea.

Althea continued. "The Earl doesn't believe in any of it, even though Ben made quite a show yesterday throwing things about."

"They do that."

Althea laughed. "Apparently. Maybourne thinks it was one of my tricks. He knows I'm a fraud, but that's why he hired me. He needs me to convince his sister to drop this charade. Now that the ghost is real I don't know what to do."

"A sticky wicket, my girl. And the ghost won't help you?"

"He wants to stay in the house, and he seems to think Charlotte will help him achieve that."

After a long pause, Nora spoke. "You must get closer to the ghost, if the girl won't speak to you.

Learn what you can about how he died, what he left unfinished. Sometimes it is something physical, an act or a building or a letter left unsent. Sometimes it is a matter of the inner life. Sometimes, I'm afraid, there is nothing one can do."

"I do know he built the house he's trapped in, and that he is cursed."

Nora's face darkened and she set her teacup down with shaking hands. "A curse is involved?"

Althea nodded. "Is that bad?"

Nora took a death breath. "That depends. Usually, yes. It is merely a matter of *how* bad. A soul trapped in limbo by a curse does not operate the way a usual spirit would. The curse dictates the terms of imprisonment, if the soul can leave, and where it can go if it does."

An ominous feeling settled in Althea's gut. "How does one undo a curse?"

For the first time in all the years Althea had known her, the woman known as Madame Veira, most famed of occultists, looked afraid. "All curses can be undone. It is part of what makes them binding- there must be a way to counteract or complete it. But you'd need to learn the exact wording of the curse, and it is likely you will not be able to do it, anyway."

"What do you mean?"

"The curse is often the burden of the one who bears it. If this spirit of yours, Ben, does not wish to undo his curse, then he will be forever as he is now. Bound to the house, the place of his death."

A memory flashed through Althea's mind. Lord Leslie telling Maybourne it would be better to tear the house down, to be rid of the ghost that way. "What if something happens to the house?"

"If he is tied to the land, nothing. If it is the house itself that binds his soul, then he would go… elsewhere."

Fear rippled through Althea. "Elsewhere?"

"A place between life and death, not limbo, but another place. Like being pushed through a door that leads to nothing. Or that is how my mother described it."

Althea shivered. "That sounds terrible. Maybe that is what Ben is trying to avoid. Perhaps he can't break his curse, but he doesn't want to go *elsewhere* either."

"Who would? It is a fate worse than death."

Althea stared at the knotted, battered surface of the kitchen table.

"What is he like? This Ben?"

"A Duke." Althea did not know why that was the first thought that entered her mind. Ben seemed to be many things. Stubborn, disagreeable, entitled- a Duke, then. But he was also observant. There was a gentleness in the way he spoke to her, a humor in his conversation and the way he described the world, that made Althea not quite hate him.

He was a Duke, and he couldn't help that, but maybe death had given him a perspective not shared by others of his ilk. Perhaps he wasn't all that bad.

The realization was half-formed and unsettled her. She pushed it aside to consider later. She had never liked any member of the aristocracy and she wasn't sure she was ready to, even if they were long deceased and possibly, just maybe, a little less odious than most.

Nora's brows rose. "A Duke? No wonder he is set in his ways. You have your hands full."

"I do," Althea mused. "But it's a challenge. *He* is a challenge. All these years I didn't believe in anything but money. I don't know what to believe any more."

Something like regret shone in Nora's face. "I'm sorry I lied to you about the spirits, and I am sorry you thought it was only about the money. It has always been a means for survival, for all the women of my family who could avoid the gallows and the pyres, but it is about helping people, too. Both the living and the dead."

A thought, strange and ridiculous, entered Althea's mind. "Are you a witch? Are you- do witches exist? Is that where curses come from?"

"I am not a witch, nor were my foremothers. We are gifted with keener sight than most, but there is nothing magical about it. Spirits chose to whom they appear, I merely know the ways to encourage them to do so."

"Oh."

"But witches do exist. I've never met one, and I never wish to. They're rare, mostly long dead or in hiding now. But in the olden days they were more common. You're correct in guessing they are the source of curses. Those few blessed with true magic may wield it, but I know little of their kind."

Althea decided that once she got her cottage in the country she was going to curl up in bed for a month straight just to make sense of everything she'd learned in the last week. It was too much. Ghosts and witches walked, or floated, among them. It was the nineteenth century for heaven's sakes, not the Dark Ages. Such things shouldn't be real.

But they were.

And for now, at least, they were her problem.

Nora watched the thoughts play over Althea's face. "When you've been around as long as I have, Althea, the only thing you know for certain is that we never really know what life is about, nor all the mysteries it contains, and that is for the best. We do no need to know everything. Life is much better for the unknowns it offers."

"Doesn't that frighten you?"

Nora smiled, her wrinkles crinkling deeper. The familiar expression settled Althea's mind. "I think it's wonderful. Wouldn't you be bored to tears if you knew everything there was to know?"

Althea thought on that as she finished her tea, feeling like herself for the first time in days. Feeling like she was on the edge of something new, something big, and, no matter what Nora said, something a little frightening.

Chapter Seven
The Book

"I hate her."

Ben fought the urge to disappear and go down to the kitchens, maybe knock some pans around just for fun. Instead, he took a deep breath. "Charlotte, your brother has hired her. She is a professional, and-"

"A professional *fraud*. You told me yourself she wasn't a genuine mystic. You said nobody can control spirits and you only speak to whom you wished." At that the young woman preened, clearly pleased that he so often wished to speak to *her*.

Except, he didn't. At first he'd enjoyed his chats with Charlotte. She'd been lonely and afraid those first weeks in London. Girlish excitement at finally experiencing a Season had quickly soured into dismay when she'd realized all her suitors were either old or awful, and sometimes both. Many were also dull or ugly, two absolute sins to a young woman fresh from the schoolroom raised on notions of romance.

Oh, Charlotte Ridgely had been raised to anticipate a proper, practical marriage- but she had also learned to hope for something *better*.

Ben was a cad to capitalize on that hope.

Not that he'd originally intended to. He'd only

found her intriguing, at first. He'd been bored out of his mind and she was young and vivacious and happy to speak to him. She'd only screamed once, the first time he'd appeared to her, and had quickly decided that living a real life gothic romance was terribly exciting.

Charlotte didn't know Ben had no romantic feelings for her. She couldn't. The more she got to know him, the more he got to know her family, the more he realized he needed her.

The house was in trouble. Ben spent most of his time eavesdropping on the Earl and his solicitor, Wilkes. The Earl needed money, and Charlotte's marriage would ensure it. The house was to be her dowry- the only remaining un-entailed asset in the family coffers. Wilkes seemed delighted and was continually pushing the Earl on the matter, and on securing Lord Leslie, his nephew, as Charlotte's future husband.

The whole thing stank of deceit. Wilkes was up to something and the Earl was too desperate to realize it. Leslie was a cad of the first order, and Charlotte was their pawn.

"You're being very quiet." Charlotte continued her embroidery as she watched him, his faint form hovering in the armchair across from her. "What are you thinking about?"

"The future," Ben mumbled. A future he felt slipping increasingly out of his control. He'd carefully orchestrated everything in his life and had largely managed to do so in death. The house still stood, the servants obeyed him, and the occupants largely respected him. Not Maybourne, but the man's mother and sister certainly held Ben in high regard.

All of that, managed without even a body, and yet it wasn't enough.

"Our future?" Charlotte asked.

Ben hated the question, hated himself for inspiring it in her. Their interactions had been wholly chaste. He had done nothing to encourage her romantic notions except fail to put a stop to them. Which was, admittedly, *something*, but he had not whispered sweet nothings in her ear or told her naughty tales or even remotely discussed sex.

Charlotte was naive. She had only the faintest notions about lovemaking, and all of them came from her family's horses in the country. Which, Ben hadn't told her, was only the most base form of fucking and completely unrelated to love.

The afternoon she'd shared her insights on the matter with him he'd nearly given her up there and then. She was seventeen, and a rustic, isolated seventeen at that. He had no business letting her talk to him about such things even if all he did was sit and nod, which he had.

It was somehow worse when she talked about *them*. *Their* future indeed. Ha! There was no future for them- he was dead and far too old for her, anyway. It didn't matter that he'd only been in his twenty-fourth year when he died. That had been eighty-five years ago. He had lifetimes of experience and she was only beginning to have one.

"You're not going to marry Leslie, are you?" He pivoted, asking the question that weighed most heavily on him.

Charlotte set down her embroidery and Ben saw she was working on a detailed portrait of a small lapdog.

"Leslie? Of course not. I know he's my brother's favorite, especially since the Marquess of Bancroft gave up on me." She sighed, the sound too heavy for such a delicate creature. "But Bancroft was nearly sixty and Leslie, well, Leslie isn't you, Ben."

Guilt soured Ben's stomach at the same time triumph coursed through him. He did not know how long he could keep this up, but until he found another way to save the house, he had to try.

At least, for now, he was succeeding.

* * *

Althea did not return to Maybourne House until well after dark. After visiting Nora she'd gone to several bookshops to find anything she could on the expulsion of spirits. She almost regretted it. She liked Ben. He was an entitled peer and far too observant, but he did not treat her like either a servant or a freak.

She would be sad to cast him out, if it came to that. She wasn't sure what her options were. If Nora was correct, casting Ben from the house could send him *elsewhere,* which sounded dreadful. Althea did not wish that on any soul.

But perhaps that wasn't where he would go. She did not know how curses worked, or ghosts, or any of it, but she knew no one would question her if she scoured London for answers. After all, she was Mistress Althea, and everyone assumed she already had them.

Four bookshops, one church, an apothecary, and a black market astrologer's office later and Althea was no better off than she'd started, only hungrier.

Maybourne House was quiet when she entered and she ducked silently into the kitchens. Cook had left a covered plate of roast pork, boiled potatoes, and cheese for her with a poorly scribbled note that read: "For our favorite guest, A."

The sight filled Althea's heart nearly as much as the meal filled her belly.

Carefully, Althea cleaned off the dishes as best she could and crept up the stairs towards her rooms. The massive four poster bed called to her, a siren song of lush comfort she knew would only last a few more days.

Three more. She had three days to figure out how to convince Ben to cast Charlotte Ridgely aside, or, if that failed, to cast Ben out of the house.

Althea gave a heavy sigh as she reached the door to her private sitting room and opened it. She wasn't even going to bother to bathe tonight. She was too tired, she would deal with it in the morning.

She would deal with it *all* in the morning.

All that mattered was that glorious, grand bed waiting for her in the next roo-

"Where have you been?"

Ben knew he shouldn't care. He didn't, really. It was just he had little else to do. The Earl had gone out for the day, he'd tolerated Charlotte as long as he could, and Althea was far more interesting, anyway.

But she had disappeared. Which was fine, she could do that. She could leave and go anywhere she pleased at any time, out in the world, away from the house.

Ben could not. That was just the the way of things.

It was not his fault he couldn't leave the house.
That there was no one worthwhile to bother. That he, a
Duke who'd attended Eton and Oxford and traveled
the world and built the damn house, had been to
reduced to naming 'bothering' as one of his top
hobbies.

Neither was it his fault that he could not stop
thinking about Althea.

After all, he really didn't care where she had been
all day.

So he asked again.

"Running errands? Visiting friends? Visiting
lovers?"

Althea glanced at him with tired eyes. "More than
one? Impressive."

"You look tired enough for it."

She grimaced and waved a hand at his half-visible
body. "All this and charm, too? It's a good thing you
can't seem to leave the house, the ladies of London
wouldn't know what to do with themselves."

Ben glowered in response. She irked him, but he
couldn't remember the last time he'd been so
delighted to hear what someone would say next.

Althea set her reticule down on the credenza just

inside the door and dropped into the chair by the fireplace to look at him. "You know, I didn't take you for a busybody."

"Charlotte was tiresome today. I desired a respite from her company. Ever since you arrived she demands constant reassurance that I'm not going to leave her. She wants me to drive you out."

Althea did not glance up from taking her boots off. "What a waste of time."

"Completely. Assuming you mean mine, of course."

Althea laughed and the sound warmed him. Metaphorically.

Althea set her boots by the cold hearth and leaned back in her chair, lit only by the candelabra she'd carried in from below stairs. "Who did you talk to before Charlotte arrived? From what Goggins tells me you chased off any other possible friends."

"I hardly consider Charlotte a friend."

Althea's eyes brightened. "What is she then? Do you return her affections?"

Ben should lie. He really should. Althea was a danger to him, to Charlotte, to the whole blasted thing. He had a rule to never trust anyone, and she was the top of the list of people he should apply it to. He should not tell her anything.

"No," he answered honestly. "Miss Ridgely is merely useful to me."

Althea said nothing, but picked some invisible lint off her dark grey skirts. God, the woman wore drab clothing. Dramatic in cut and fabric, certainly. Lots of lace and starched satin, but always up to her neck and always in the darkest colors possible.

Ben had a sudden vision of her in deep red with a plunging neckline and decided to change the subject. "What *did* Goggins tell you?"

"Oh, many things. But it seems the house has always had *some* living people in it."

"You mean servants," he said automatically. Looking at her face, he immediately wished he could take the words back.

"Are servants not people, *Your Grace*?"

She addressed him as if his title were something dirty. If Ben had any blood, or veins for that matter, he knew his face would be reddening. "Of course they are," he snapped. "But they have little interest in talking to me and generally nothing new to say. It's always household gossip or telling me about the massive spider they found under the stove that was so large it took two footmen to kill it."

"That's all servants talk about?" Althea snorted. "I find that hard to believe."

Ben ran his ghostly hand through his ghostly hair, which didn't move. "Fine. It was just the once, and it was a kitchen maid. And to be fair, I was trying to frighten her."

"Why?"

"Why what?"

"Why were you trying to frighten her? You seem rather desperate for friendship to me."

The words hit too near the mark, and Ben decided he didn't like this vein of conversation. "There's no point in explaining what it's like to be dead, Mistress Althea. But don't worry, you'll find out soon enough."

Her single brow rose again, an irritating gesture he couldn't help but like. A little. "Is that a threat?" she asked.

Ben grinned. "Possibly. Or maybe it's just the nature of things."

"Does everyone who dies become a ghost?"

Ben scoffed, wishing all of a sudden he could have a glass of brandy. God, he missed brandy. "I have no idea. I'm the only one I've ever met."

Althea thought on that a moment. "Will you tell me about the curse?" she said abruptly.

Ben blanched a paler shade of pale. "Absolutely not. Will you tell me where you were today?"

"Absolutely not. Why don't you go bother

Charlotte with your overreaching questions?"

Ben groaned. He was enjoying talking to Althea as though things were normal. She had not even blinked when she entered her rooms and he was waiting for her. It made him feel almost human. Almost… alive.

He liked it.

He did not, however, like talking about Charlotte Ridgely.

"I'd rather not," he answered drily.

"If you dislike her so much, why did you seduce her?"

He snorted, floating into the chair opposite Althea, keenly aware that he was only visible today from the waist up. He'd been feeling drained lately, and he knew why. Worry over the house, *his* future, was wearing on him.

Which was the reason he needed Charlotte Ridgely's good will.

"Because I don't want her to marry," he said simply.

Althea's eyes narrowed. "Why do you care if she marries?"

"Because I know who she is going to marry, and if she does, it's bad for me. Very bad."

"You can't possibly know who she is going to marry and I don't understand what the problem will be for you if- no *when*- she does."

"It's better if you don't understand. After all, your purpose here is to get rid of me, isn't it?"

"My purpose here is to get Charlotte Ridgely married."

"Then we are at cross purposes."

They stared at each other a long moment, and Ben marveled again that Althea took his existence in stride. She treated him as though she saw a ghost every day, which, for all her professional reputation, he knew she did not. She was a curious creature. A fraudulent mystic, but a legitimate woman of substance.

Much better company than Charlotte Ridgely.

Still, he could not trust either of them. Althea or Charlotte. No one except himself, just as it had always been.

It didn't matter if he told Althea the truth. She wanted to help the Earl of Maybourne marry his sister off, and neither of them knew what Ben did.

The Ridgelys were being conned.

Not by Althea, though he supposed technically, perhaps, that was also true, but by someone whose lies were far more dangerous, to the Ridgeleys and to Ben. Wilkes was desperate to get his hands on Charlotte and the house- not directly, as her brother would never go for that- but his every conversation with Maybourne confirmed Ben's suspicions that Wilkes was no good. Ben hadn't yet uncovered the details, but he knew if Wilkes got ahold of the house, through Leslie or by other means, Ben would no longer be safe. Wilkes had no scruples whatsoever and was greedy, too. Ben had caught him stealing more than one piece of family silver when Maybourne wasn't looking.

"Who is Charlotte going to marry?" Althea asked, "Surely if she wanted to marry anyone she would not be so wound up about you."

"Oh, she doesn't want to marry him."

Ben could tell Althea's patience was wearing thin, so he added, "Have you had much interaction with Wilkes, the family solicitor?"

"No, but I met him."

Ben nodded.

"Perhaps start there, if you want to know more. And stay away from Leslie."

Althea sighed. "Are you a ghost or a sphinx? Why won't you just tell me what's really going on in this house?"

"Because I don't trust you," he said, his voice more heated than he liked. But it was true. He liked Althea, more than he should, probably, but he didn't trust her. He couldn't trust her or anyone. Didn't she understand?

"Fair enough. But don't you want help? Perhaps I can assist you in- in whatever it is you need."

Ben snorted. "Are you trying to uncover whatever unfinished business my lingering bodiless soul yearns to set to rights so I may finally rest in peace?"

She had the decency to look abashed. "Possibly."

"Well don't waste your time. I don't have any. I'm not that kind of spirit, if that kind even exists. There's nothing I can do to move on to the next world. My only options lie between worlds, and this existence are preferable to the Void."

Althea paled. "The Void?"

"That's what I call it. I sense it, sometimes. It's not death- it is something between life and death, like where I am now. But it's- it's nothing. If I ever leave here, I go there."

To Ben's surprise, Althea took this revelation in stride. "Nonsense. Of course ghosts can move into the afterlife. I don't know if it's the one they talk about in church on Sundays, but even you admit you're stuck between two worlds. This one, and the next. If ghosts couldn't move on to the next world, *this* world would be full of them."

"And how do you know it's not?"

She paused, lips pursed. "You know as well as I do

there are not ghosts everywhere, even if there may be more than I realized."

"I don't have the answers, Althea. I don't think anyone does. But I know my case is unlike most. I did not die of hideous trauma or injustice, there was no lingering bit of business or care that snagged my soul and caught it, trapped it, here on its way to the next place. My essence lingers because of a curse. A curse that will never let me move on. The only place I can go is farther in between, more deeply… cursed. Into the Void.

She nodded and murmured something that sounded like *elsewhere*.

"What's that?"

She cleared her throat. "So now you expect me to believe in curses, too? What, did you anger a witch in the woods one moonless night? Step on her newts? Steal her broom?"

Ben gave her a hard look. "It doesn't matter. All that matters is that the curse traps me between this world and the next, and I cannot move on. Ever. But this house- this house keeps me from losing myself. Does that make sense?"

Althea fixed him with a steady stare. "I think so. Keep going."

"It took me a long time to figure it out, but I've

learned some things these last eighty-five years. Namely, I am tied to this house. I cannot leave it, even for a moment. I poured so much of my life into the building of this place that it has saved me, somehow. I can feel the darkness at times, pulling at me, pulling me closer to madness, to the Void, but the house stops me. As if I am anchored to it, and thus, to this lingering excuse of an existence. As long as this house stands, I may be a ghost, but I am also myself."

"And if something happens to this house?"

Darkness washed across Ben's face. "Then I fall into the abyss."

Silence then, broken only by the crackle and pop of the fire in the grate.

A weight felt as though it had lifted off Ben's chest. He couldn't say why, exactly. It made no difference to tell her these things, but somehow he felt lighter for it.

It felt good.

Which troubled him.

"You look exhausted," he said, changing the subject again.

A smile played on her full, red lips. "Flattery won't win me over, Your Grace."

"Call me Ben."

The words were out before he could stop them, and then he did not wish to. The look on her face, the sudden, vulnerable surprise of this simple intimacy, caught something in his chest. She was a beautiful woman, all angles and fine, striking drama, but that look on her pale, unusual face stripped away all the years of hard work and bitterness. She looked young and almost innocent.

Then, in a flash, it was gone.

"I have had a long day. If you don't mind, I think I'll go to my bed."

"You mean *my* bed." That was on purpose.

The way Althea's lips fell open slightly sent a thrill through Ben.

"Excuse me?"

He waved towards the door that led into the bedroom. "You've been sleeping in my bed. This whole suite was mine."

A thoughtful look washed over her. "You said something about that didn't you? That first night. It's not a woman's room…"

"Well, many women have enjoyed it, but no."

She wrinkled her nose. "Spare me the details. Certainly the obscene art makes a little more sense now."

Ben grinned. "Do you like it?"

She rose from her armchair and turned towards the bedroom. "It's fine."

Ben floated after her. "I had that painting commissioned you know. The male models were strangers, but the lady was my favorite mistress."

"I asked you to spare me."

"Fine. I'll spare you if you give me your honest opinion of it."

They were standing in front of the painting above the mantle now, the young woman driven to eternal ecstasy by her three lovers.

Ben swore Althea was blushing. Finally, she answered. "It is the most beautiful painting I've ever seen."

The words were quiet and rang with truth.

Ben smiled. "I have a present for you."

She shot him a wary glance.

"Don't worry, it's nothing macabre. I'm a ghost, not a fiend. It's in the drawer of the table there, on the left side of the bed."

Suspicion rippled off Althea as she went where he indicated and pulled opened the drawer. She gasped just as, without a sound, Ben disappeared. It was a cheap move, evaporating in the middle of a conversation, but there were a few benefits to being a ghost and that was one of them.

He transported himself to the kitchens, where he hovered invisibly on the ceiling watching a footman sneak in and steal some muffins. It wasn't interesting, but it took his mind off the woman upstairs.

The woman with the black, knowing eyes who made him feel at ease even though she was the last person he ought to trust.

It was a riddle. *She* was a riddle.

Ben had always enjoyed riddles.

He simply wasn't sure how he felt about this one.

Althea was at a loss for words. She'd spent her life in the shadowy underworld of London, on the fringes of polite Society. She counted among her friends madams and whores, lesbians and widows. She also spent a lot of time in bookshops of all stripes, including the several she'd rummaged through today.

None of that prepared her for what was in the drawer.

A book, bound in fine leather with gilt lettering in an alphabet she'd never seen before, filled with the most beautiful drawings she'd ever seen. Each of them more erotic than the last.

She flipped through the first few pages then her head flew up as she turned back to Ben.

But he was gone.

"Cad," she murmured, before tucking the book back in its drawer.

He wanted to her to look at it. To enjoy it.

She wasn't going to. Not because she had any prudishness over such things- to the contrary, she enjoyed the pleasures of the flesh when the right time and partner appeared- but because *he* wanted her to.

Ben had seduced Charlotte Ridgely into obeying his every wish, but Althea was no unworldly debutante. She was not going to fall under his spell.

She was going to defeat him, one way or another.

Chapter Eight
The Dinner

Lady Maybourne's dinner party the following evening commenced promptly at the stroke of nine. It was an intimate affair for only a small group of the family's close associates. Lady Maybourne and her two children were delighted to host their guest of honor, the illustrious Mistress Althea, who appeared in the full dramatic, otherworldly regalia Mayfair whispered about in the darkest corners of ballrooms where scandal flirted with superstition and sin. Many knew of her, few admitted to knowing her, and fewer still were daring enough to admit their acquaintance with her publicly. That the Ridgelys did so, even for a small number of close friends, was unusual.

Althea wondered that they were not afraid to harm Charlotte's chances on the marriage mart by being open about her presence at the house, but then, Ben's tantrum was unlikely to remain a secret and better to control the narrative than be controlled by it, she supposed. The Earl was an intelligent man.

Not one to disappoint, Althea wore her most striking black gauze veil and longest black lace gloves with a dress of midnight silk that shimmered faintly, as though it had swallowed the stars themselves. Her raven black hair was pulled half back, the curls set faint and wild by a subdued but helpful Hen.

The ensemble was unusual and wanton, given the tight, fashionable curls most women wore. Althea's hair had never tolerated that sort of management. A loose wave was the most she could do, but she had found it served her well. Combined with her large, dark, kohl-rimmed eyes and red lip stain, the effect was striking. She looked otherworldly, even dangerous. Precisely as she intended.

As she entered the blue parlor before dinner, she'd hoped maybe she *was* a little dangerous. Just enough to keep the wolves at bay. She would do anything to protect her future and those she cared about, and this costume was armor in that battle as much as it was a professional asset. Hen had already told her Wilkes would be attending the dinner, and if Ben's suspicions were true, he was not a man to be trusted. He might well turn her in for fraud even if she pleased the Earl. *That* was not a danger she cared to court.

So she would present the danger first.

The effect was swift and certain. From the moment she entered the room, the last of the evening's guest list to do so, Althea felt her presence ripple across the gathered peers like a silent, ominous wave.

"It's her," a man breathed from somewhere near

the fireplace. She did not bother to see who it was, because at the same moment Lord Maybourne strode up to her and gave her a little bow.

"Mistress Althea. You are a vision this evening." She could have sworn he said *vision* with a gleam in his eye, an allusion to her perceived abilities. *A joke. Surprising.* But as he extended his arm to her, the Earl's face was so aristocratically passive it was hard to imagine the starched young lord capable of such a thing as a joke.

Which was well enough. Althea was here tonight not to enjoy herself, but to work.

Maybourne escorted her about the room, making introductions. The Countess sat in rapt conversation with Lord and Lady Benwillow, an elderly couple so ancient and shriveled they would barely reach Althea's elbows when standing. Charlotte was near the fireplace speaking to a ruddy-faced middle-aged man and his sister, introduced to Althea as 'Mr. Firth and his spinster sister Miss Firth."

Althea met Miss Firth's cool brown eyes with frank kindness, but found only disdain there. The woman obviously knew who she was and had no interest in cultivating her acquaintance. Althea did not flinch, however. She was used to the majority of society viewing her poorly. It was part of her job- if she was widely accepted everywhere, she would not hold the cache that made her so valuable, and her rates so exorbitant.

Finally the Earl of Maybourne brought her to the final two men in the group. Mr. Wilkes, the solicitor, and much to Althea's surprise, Lord Leslie.

"Mistress Althea," Wilkes bowed. "The most fascinating member of our little party."

Althea gave him a tight-lipped smile. If Ben was correct, Wilkes had answers for her. But she could not trust him- or Ben, for that matter, who was just as likely leading her on a wild goose chase away from her true aims. All the same, she was going to keep a close eye on Wilkes and speak to him privately if the opportunity arose.

The older man continued, "And you've met my nephew, I hear."

"You nephew?" Althea asked.

"He means me," Lord Leslie raised Althea's gloved hand to his lips, giving no indication he recalled the bizarre events of two days prior. He had not, apparently, breathed a word of it to anyone. "Wilkes is my uncle, on my mother's side."

"I had not realized," Althea said, her mind racing to piece this new information together. Did Ben know? He must have. He'd already linked the two together.

Whatever Ben was upset about involved both of these men. Althea was not surprised. Both of them felt wrong to her, as if they were hiding something.

Not that she could blame them- she was hiding things, too.

All introductions made, Althea sidled graciously away from Wilkes and Lord Leslie to chat with the other guests for the hour or so before dinner. Lord and Lady Benwillow were the most intrigued with her, but were so hard of hearing the conversation was stilted and difficult. All the same, it was obvious the couple was beloved by Lady Maybourne so Althea did her best to entertain them with acceptable stories of her exploits.

As she wound tale after tale, all of them entirely fabricated, she swore she could hear a wry, judgmental chuckle every so often coming from the fireplace.

Althea did not bother to look, lest she see Ben's handsome, condescending face flickering in the flames. After their strange conversation the night before Althea had spent the entire day trying not to think about him.

It hadn't worked.

Finally, the dinner bell rang. The Earl of Maybourne escorted her into the dining room, where she was seated between Lord Benwillow and, to her dismay, Lord Leslie. She had avoided Lord Leslie in the parlor, subtly remaining engrossed in conversation with the other guests. She was not eager to face his impressions of Ben's display. This cost her the opportunity of speaking with Mr. Wilkes, and potentially sleuthing what he knew of the pending suitor Ben had alluded to, but she had already thought to call on Mr. Wilkes privately in a day or so.

The gentleman in question was seated too far along the table to be a useful now at any rate, as he was ensconced at the far end where Lady Maybourne held court.

Althea sighed and dug into the first course, directing her conversation briefly at Lord Benwillow, which involved a lot of shouting.

"ARE YOU COMING TO THE BALL?" Lord Benwillow yelled in Althea's ear during the second course.

"Which ball is that?" she replied loudly enough she thought Nora could hear her in Covent Garden.

"LADY MAYBOURNE'S MASQUERADE. SHE IS HOSTING ONE IN A FORTNIGHT. FOR MISS RIDGELY. A BALL."

Althea took an unseemly large gulp of her wine. "I did not know it was happening. It is for Miss

Ridgely?"

Whether it was the use of her name that caught Charlotte's interest or she had already been listening in, Althea didn't know, but the young woman chimed in from across Lord Leslie. "It's for my birthday. But I'm sure you'll be gone by then."

If this seemed rude, no one commented on it.

"A masquerade ball for your birthday? What a fantastic occasion. I'm sure you will be the most stunning creature in attendance." Lord Leslie's obvious flattery caught his uncle's attention, causing the old man to give Leslie a calculating look. From what little Althea had heard this evening, Leslie had been laying it on a bit thick. If Ben was right, Wilkes was desperate for Leslie- *his nephew*- to marry Charlotte. It all made sense now, and the stakes were high for the shifty solicitor, who kept casting wary glances at Althea.

She ignored them.

"Of course I'll be the most desirable woman there," Charlotte preened. "It will be my birthday, after all."

"And perhaps you will have even more exciting news to celebrate by then," Wilkes said across the table.

Charlotte's face fell. "One cause to celebrate is more than enough. Besides, I've always wanted to attend a masquerade."

"ARE YOU COMING TO THE BALL?" Lord
Benwillow asked again on Althea's other side.

She gave the older gentleman a kind smile and a
loud, well-enunciated reply. "I am afraid not, my lord.
But it promises to be an excellent time."

Ben was grateful he could no longer weep, because
Lady Maybourne's dinner party was boring him to
tears. Perched atop the central chandelier hanging
over the dining table, he kept himself unseen and
unfelt by the gathering of middling aristocrats making
small talk and drinking his port. It was *his* port, after
all. Maybourne had found the extensive collection of
bottles Ben had long ago locked up in a massive,
hidden cellar below the kitchens.

The scent of those bottles of beautifully-aged wine
was no doubt luscious, and it pained Benedict that he
could not enjoy neither the smell or the booze.

It was a pity only some of his senses remained in
the afterlife. Sight and sound were strong, but smell
was long gone. Touch and taste had disappeared, too,
as if only the most basic abilities were allowed in this
cursed existence. Not for the first time, he wondered if
this was part of whatever cosmic penance he was
paying. The curse that gave him this half-life was sort

of a living hell, and he had long conjectured that meant all aspects of it were somehow a punishment. He could see and hear the living world, just enough to never forget he was still amongst it, but he could take no part or pleasure in it.

Music, at times, came close to an indulgence, but it was so rare anyone came to the house who could play or sing decently this fact was only a tease. Charlotte Ridgely was atrocious at the pianoforte, for all she had not one but two music tutors, and her singing voice was worse than her playing. Cook could carry a tune, but most of her songs were so broken up by various cursings and mutterings about ingredients they were hardly worth listening to.

That left him with only the pleasures of conversation and visual beauty to enjoy. The conversation of the assembly dining beneath him this evening was hardly pleasurable. It was the insipid small talk of middling gentry, and Mistress Althea, who was far and away the most interesting member of the group, seemed largely inclined to listen to the others and participate only when directly drawn in.

At least Ben had eavesdropped in the parlor before dinner and enjoyed her rambling tales of spiritual divining and automatic writing, close encounters with all manners of ghouls and poltergeists. They were all hogwash, but she had done a marvelous job of entertaining her audience. She had one tale in particular about hunting down a hobgoblin at a lord's country estate that been downright hilarious.

Even Ben had felt... something.

Which was unusual. For decades his primary emotions had oscillated consistently between vaguely numb and dully bored. Anticipation, humor, delight... only now did he realize he'd forgotten those sensations. If he had a heart, it would hurt at the notion, but he did not, and so he merely took these facts as they came to him.

He was enjoying Althea's presence far too much. Even the presence of the one living person he truly despised could not ruin his interest in the evening.

"Say something, woman," Ben hissed from his high perch, only to himself and only because no one knew he was there. "Your lips were built for sin, I want you to *use* them."

His little private joke was spoiled, however, because the moment he voiced the thought, Althea looked straight up at him. *Through* him. As though she *could* hear him- the notion sent a jolt through him. A jolt of alarm and something far more delicious he didn't stop to consider.

Whether she heard him or not, however, the

universe was kind enough to oblige him anyway.

"So what precisely brings you to our oh so very fair corner of Mayfair?"

Mr. Firth, pleased with his double use of the word *fair* and obviously thinking himself a clever sort of man, turned his attention on Althea, who had focused solely on eating and listening for the last fifteen minutes.

For Althea's part, she would rather no one speak to her the rest of the evening. It had been a long time since her last society dinner party and she had forgotten how much she despised them. The conversation was often stuffy and forced, or else, if sufficient liquor was involved, chaotic and nonsensical. This evening was the former sort. The Ridgelys seemed the sort of family that might harbor interesting acquaintances, but if they did, none of those were evidenced by tonight's party. Even the kind Lord Benwillow was now snoring softly beside her, his head resting precipitously on his chest.

As for Mr. Firth and his sister, Althea quickly gleaned from listening to their conversations with others that they were the worst sort of gentry. Entitled, self-centered, uninformed and resolutely confident in their own charms. In other words, insufferable.

It had only been a matter of time until Mr. Firth, the more loquacious of the two, turned his small, watery blue eyes on Althea.

"I have many acquaintances across the city, Mr. Firth. The Earl of Maybourne is but one of them, and he was gracious enough to invite me to this estimable gathering this evening."

There. Toss out a compliment and appeal to Mr. Firth's substantial sense of his own importance, and perhaps he would lose interest.

"Not here hunting any wee ghosties are you? They've always said this house is haunted, you know."

Lord Leslie made sort of gagging sound that was quickly stifled, and Althea did not have to look at Maybourne to know he was watching her with a hard, cold stare. She was well known by certain undercurrents of London society, but most of her clients never admitted they had personally used her services. She had long ago learned that discretion as to the specifics of her work and employers was paramount, and while Maybourne was obviously happy to admit an acquaintance with her, the details of their relationship were not something Althea was going to share.

"Have they?" she asked, allowing a bit of boredom

into her tone. Just enough to cue everyone to the lack of interest she held for the topic.

Which was a lie, because if the likes of Mr. Firth had heard about Ben, she needed to know about it. As far as she knew, no one outside the household knew the home was haunted. But if Mr. Firth knew something…

"Oh yes," Miss Firth chimed in, her voice nasally and reedy all at once. She blinked her own watery, piggy eyes at Althea. "We grew up in this part of town. During the Season of course."

"We often summered at our country estate, Hogspotten, in Hampshire. Lovely place."

"So lovely," Miss Firth nodded to her brother then returned her ratlike attention to Althea, "Mother and father kept horses there you know. Finest horseflesh in Hampshire, my father used to say. And father was always right about such things."

"Always was," Mr. Firth agreed.

Althea swore she heard an impatient cough from somewhere in the direction of the ceiling. Then Charlotte, of all people, spoke up. "It sounds truly divine," the young woman interjected, in a tone of such gentility and good breeding that the Firths did not bat an eye at the redirection. "But I am dying to know, what did you hear about this house? It was empty during your youth, from what I understand."

Althea noticed Lord Leslie fidget from the corner of her eye, and she pitied the man. He was clearly anxious about the topic and it was evident the events in the parlor two days prior had shaken him far more than he let on.

Mr. Firth, for his part, lit up. "Oh yes, well, the house wasn't *wholly* empty. The absentee owner kept a few staff here to keep the place from total ruin- *skeleton staff*, you know."

Miss Firth gave a high pitched squeal of laughter while the rest of the table smiled and nodded in dutiful acknowledgment of Mr. Firth's perception of his own wit. Althea made a mental note to decline all invitations to Society dinner parties in future.

"Tell them about the boys," Miss Firth eagerly tapped her closed fan on her brother's arm.

"I'm getting there Fanny!"

"What boys?" Charlotte asked, genuinely curious. Althea was grateful the girl had as much of an interest in uncovering the secrets of Ben and his house as she did. It was far easier to let others do the talking while she observed, usually seeing far more than anyone realized.

"One night, according to the papers, a couple of neighborhood lads a bit older than myself snuck into the house. They were looking for trouble."

"Ghosts, Neal, they were looking for ghosts," Miss Firth hissed.

"Ghosts, demons, trouble, whatever they could find. In those days a lot of strange noises came from the house, and none of the staff ever admitted to it, but all us children knew there was something uncanny going on in here."

"If you keep this up, Firth, you're going to decimate my fortune. This house is worth a pretty penny on paper," Maybourne quipped drily.

Mr. Firth dipped his head. "Naturally, naturally, Lord Maybourne. Don't want to diminish your investments, of course, but this is old history now anyway. I'm sure there's nothing demonic going on nowadays."

"Demonic?" Lady Maybourne gasped. The entire table now hung on Mr. Firth's every word.

"Let Mr. Firth continue, I'm sure it's just a silly story after all." Charlotte looked down the table to her brother.

Maybourne waved a hand in permission to continue even as Lord Leslie blanched.

Mr. Firth, oblivious to his fellow guest's discomfort, obliged. "As I was saying, some local lads broke in one night. A baronet's son from next door-what's now your place, Leslie."

"Is that so?" Lord Leslie asked in a tight voice. Althea could feel the tension rippling off of him beside her. He'd hidden his dismay so well earlier, but obviously he had not anticipated the topic would arise again for the full table to hear. Althea sent a mental prayer to Ben that he stay quiet tonight and not make another scene.

Leslie was the prime contender for Charlotte's hand, and the fact that he was here tonight and hadn't been driven off already meant he might very well win it. Charlotte seemed to be slowly warming to him, and by all accounts he was wealthy, well connected, and, given his connection to the family solicitor, a known, trustworthy entity, even if Wilkes was not.

She would ask Ben later what exactly he disliked about Leslie and if there was any way he might be the answer to their problems.

She did not personally care who Charlotte married, but Althea had a job to do, and if she could do it without actually dealing with Ben and casting him from the house or whatever one did with unwanted ghosts, she would prefer to do that.

She had, she realized, no desire to cast Ben out of the house at all. She should. It might be the easiest solution, since he was still set on defying her. But...

she rather liked him, really. The thought sunk into her gut like a cold, wet thing. An inconvenient truth.

Mr. Firth loudly cleared his throat to continue his tale and Althea's attention swung back to him.

"Aye, the baronet's son it was, and two kitchen lads who followed him about like cronies. I remember seeing the three of them across the square once or twice. Older than I was, so I kept my distance, but they were always looking for trouble."

Althea half thought Lord Leslie would leave the table before any further mention of ghostly occurrences was made, but he seemed focused on Mr. Firth. As did Charlotte, who hung on every word, no doubt waiting for the part of the story in which Ben had a hand.

Curiosity gnawed at Althea, too. She had a feeling this was not a good story, for if it were a happy one, Mr. Firth and his sister would not look half so delighted.

"One night they broke in here and went creeping about, searching for the source of the strange sounds. They'd seen a man in the window a few times, a man who didn't exist, they said."

"A ghost," Charlotte breathed.

"Aye," Mr. Firth looked about the room as if it only now occurred to him the same ghastly spirit might be listening now. Althea had no doubt he was, but gratefully, Ben kept silent.

Mr. Firth continued. "The boys made it all the way up to the attic. The servants were all asleep. Not like most households, where the servants take the attic rooms- because they were the only ones in the house, the few of 'em took some of the small guest rooms lower down, so no one heard the boys up there."

"Probably mice," Lord Benwillow wheezed in a creaky voice. Althea had nearly forgotten he was there.

"MICE CAN BE VERY LOUD IN THE ATTIC," Lady Benwillow shouted across the table at her husband, not out of ire, but rather because neither of them could hear very well.

Graciously, everyone nodded in agreement with her. "I swear sometimes a mouse in the attic can sound like a veritable elephant!" Lady Maybourne smiled at her friend.

Everyone chuckled accordingly, and turned back to Mr. Firth. Soaking up the attention, Mr. Firth went on in an ever more dramatic tone. "While they were up there, something happened. And to this day, not a soul knows exactly how it all played out, but the boy who lived said a ghostly figure appeared from the darkness and terrorized them."

"The boy who... lived?" Lady Maybourne asked, her face pale.

Mr. Firth nodded darkly. "That's just it. Whatever happened that night, screaming could be heard from the street. A strange, terrible howling sound, like a tempest, and all the attic windows blew out. I myself saw the shards of glass on the street the next morning."

"I did as well, and I was only six years old at the time," Miss Firth blinked rapidly.

"What happened to the other boys?" Althea asked, unmoved. She never revealed her true feelings, especially not where the fantastical was concerned. The story was theatrical, but she was more concerned with Lord Leslie, whose face was now taut and greenish.

"Well the ghost started screaming and railing and things were flying about the room and the kitchen lad who survived said, well, pardon me, this ain't quite right for dinner, but I'm already this deep, eh? He said the *other* kitchen boy was so scared by it all he pissed himself and, the survivor wasn't sure what happened next, but the poor baronet's son-"

"Go on, Neal," Miss Firth hissed.

"The kitchen lad who pissed himself was overcome by some sort of demon, like the ghost took him over somehow, and he got this crazed look over him, and he ran and pushed the baronet's son clean out the open window. To his death."

Every lady at the table gasped except Althea. She raised her glass and took a slow, calm sip of port.

Lord Leslie was trembling now, and Charlotte was the color of their china plates.

"So the one boy was scared out of his wits and accidentally killed the other? And wouldn't that account for the glass all over the street?"

Mr. Firth emphatically shook his head. "Oh no, Maybourne. All the windows were broken- and don't say that's a simple matter of a few rocks thrown or candlesticks swung about. The kitchen lad who was possessed came for the other boy, hit him in the head so hard he passed out, and when that surviving lad woke up, the perpetrator was gone. No sign of him, or the ghost."

"So the boy fled the gallows," Lord Maybourne shrugged. "Sounds like a tragic accident of youth. Horrible, to be certain, but I don't see how ghosts have anything to do with it."

"If you'll excuse me," Lord Leslie rose abruptly, nearly upsetting his own glass of port. In a flash, he had stepped out of the room.

Charlotte caught Althea's eye and she knew they

both understood what was wrong with Lord Leslie. It was obvious, however, that Charlotte blamed Althea. As if she did not think Ben perfectly responsible for his own decisions, both recently and, more disturbingly, thirty years ago.

Chapter Nine
The Savior

At the end of dinner, Althea excused herself on account of a headache. For once, she wasn't lying. She *did* have an aching head, but it had far more to do with thoughts than any physical pounding or pain. Her mind had far too much to consider and she had indulged in far too much wine to consider it in company.

As the rest of the party, including a recently returned but still pale Lord Leslie, moved into the parlor to enjoy Charlotte's musical talents, Althea turned toward the stairs. She needed to lie down and think about Mr. Firth's story, about how she was going to accomplish her task in the few days left to her, about Ben's book.

No, that wasn't it- she shouldn't think about that book at all. It wasn't going to help, and he'd only given to her as a distraction.

A distraction she could not stop thinking about, which meant, it was working.

She needed to focus on Ben's secrets. That was the way she could convince him to-

"Mistress Althea." The Earl of Maybourne's voice was cool and commanding.

Althea paused at the foot of the stairs, swaying a little. She never drank this much, but the dinner had been so dull then gotten so tense. She'd barely eaten, and it had only been three glasses but still... "Yes, my lord?"

"Mr. Firth's sordid tale may have been in poor taste for the dinner table, but I am beginning to suspect Charlotte might be capitalizing on such rumors in the creation of her, ah, friend," he said delicately, aware that though the others were already in the parlor, this conversation was not exactly private.

"An astute thought, my lord."

"Don't humor me," he snapped, eyes flashing. He continued in a hushed voice. "Lord Leslie came to see me before the other guests arrived. He's on the verge of making her an offer, and he already knows he is my preferred brother-in-law."

"Is Mr. Wilkes aware?" Althea asked carefully.

"Leslie's uncle is the one who has convinced me of the wisdom of this match. We have a name and prestige, and Lord Leslie, though he is noble through his father's line, has only the thinnest pedigree. What he does have, however, is enough money to set us all up for life. Wilkes has shown me just a small rendering of his accounts, with Leslie's permission, and his coffers are overflowing."

"How fortuitous."

"Indeed. Besides, he is happy to accept Charlotte's rather unusual dowry."

"And what is that?"

"This house." Alarm bells rang in Althea's mind as Maybourne continued, "Leslie is happy to take it. His own town house is next door, after all, and it would not be such a burden to him as it might be to another gentleman."

"Leslie lives next door?"

"He does. Bought the place last year, for a pretty penny too."

Something about Maybourne's story, about Leslie, wasn't adding up. It all seemed too convenient, and Althea never trusted convenience. It wasn't her business who Charlotte Ridgely married just as long as she did so, but Althea did not like the idea of Leslie and, by association, Mr. Wilkes, running Ben's house.

Because that is how she thought of it now. Everywhere she went she no longer saw just the beauty or the wear, but the mind behind the design. A curious, clever mind. A mind of taste, refinement, and vision. Ben's mind.

Maybourne was still thinking about the house, too. "Tonight is not the first time I've heard stories about this house, and truthfully, I've wanted to sell the place for years but no one would buy it. Frankly, Leslie would solve all of my problems."

"You consider Charlotte a problem?" The words were out before she could stop them.

Maybourne stilled, a muscle in his sharply defined jaw twitched. "My sister knows her duty, as I know mine. It's none of your concern, but it falls on both our shoulders to clean up the mess our father left us, and that includes this damned house. Lord Leslie offers us a solution, and, judging by my conversation with him today, he needs only the slightest encouragement from Charlotte to do so. I swore to my mother I would not force Charlotte to marry without her consent, and as much as it inconveniences me, I am a man of my word."

"I understand, Lord Maybourne. I shall ensure Charlotte's mind is cleared of her fanciful notions and redirected towards her duty."

"Good," Maybourne took a step back, only now realizing how close he'd gotten to Althea. He adjusted his cravat. "She has requested to go shopping tomorrow. My mother has other obligations, so I'd like you to accompany her."

"Sh-shopping?"

"Yes," the Earl's eyes flashed icy blue. "Is that a problem? You're clearly not opposed to nice things."

His eyes moved over her outfit, which, for all its drama and dark colors, was obviously very finely made.

"It would be my pleasure, Lord Maybourne."

"Good." He turned on his heel and strode into the parlor, from which the sounds of disjointed music and out-of-tune singing already floated into the hall.

Althea took a deep breath and steadied herself. The effect of the wine was slow to fade and sleep beckoned like a siren to a sailor. She climbed the stairs and did not let relax until she reached the quiet dimness of the hallway that led to her rooms. One of the maids flitted past with an armful of linens, and Althea politely asked if hot water and a bath might be procured for her. The only thing better than going to bed would be to take a bath first.

"Of course, milady," the maid said with a curtsy.

It had always made Althea uncomfortable, being treated like one of the upper classes. She knew most people would relish the opportunity, especially if they'd come from circumstances as humble as her own. But it made her skin crawl.

"Thank you," she replied, and meant it.

Pulling her veil off, she made her way down the long hallway. She was nearly to her sitting room door when a shadow at the end of the hall moved.

"Ben?" she asked.

The shadow said nothing, but grew larger as it moved closer.

"Mr. Firth," Althea said, her instincts suddenly alert. The man had been drunk by the end of dinner, and now appeared fully foxed.

"There you are," he slurred, his ruddy face a dark enough red she could see his flushed skin in the flickering candlelight of the hall sconces. "Like my little story at dinner?"

"It is the nature of my business to take an interest in such tales, particularly if they are true."

"I swear on my own dead father that one is right as rain." He rose one unsteady hand as if swearing before a court of law. "What's worse is, that boy who survived, he was found murdered a few years later."

A chill ran down Althea's spine that had nothing to do with the draughts in the dark hallway. "Some of us find misfortune repeatedly in our lives. It is a sorry thing."

Mr. Firth shook his head. "It weren't no misfortune. My friend Baxter spoke to the policeman on duty as found the body. He'd been murdered real careful-like. Even the constable said it was the curse of this house that'd done it."

Althea pushed back the thread of unease growing

in her. The drunken man before her was far more perilous than rumors of ghostly murderers, even if ghosts, it transpired, were real. Ben was the spirit in question, wasn't he? And he would never do such a thing.

"Then I shall be particularly careful during my stay here. Thank you for the warning, Mr. Firth. Good evening to you."

Althea put her hand on the doorknob, bracing to duck quickly into her rooms, when gruff hands pulled her back and pushed her against the opposite wall.

"Mr. Firth!" she exclaimed, but the man was too far gone to care.

He pressed himself against her, reeking of port and stronger stuff he had no doubt indulged in on his own. "You might have dined with us, but you're no lady are you? Do you really talk to spirits or do you just entertain sad, lonely lords who need a little excitement?"

Althea pressed her boot heel into the toes of his left foot, but either Mr. Firth's boots were too thick or his mind too far gone for him to notice. He'd pinned one hand to the wall by her head, but she used the other dig through the folds of her skirt for the little blade she kept there, in the event of just such an occasion as this one.

"My profession is a respectable one, sir, and concerns only myself, my clients, and those of realms beyond your knowledge. If you seek carnal amusement I suggest you look elsewhere. Now unhand me."

Her fingers finally closed over the handle of her small, thin knife just as he brought his mouth down upon hers. She reached up and stabbed at the thickness of his formidable gut just as, miraculously, he was ripped off of her. A horrible, familiar howling filled the hallway as a wind rushed through so strong Althea had to cling to the wall to remain standing.

All the candles went out, but the hallway was not black. A dim, bluish light illuminated it, emanating from the ghostly figure of a tall, handsome, furious man.

"Get out, you bastard, before you meet the same end as those idiot boys you find so entertaining."

Althea thrilled to see Ben so- so *powerful*. She realized now that his anger in the blue parlor before had been largely for show. He'd been upset, yes, and trying to prove a point- but this was true fury. His translucent blue form was whole and tall and burned so hot with rage he was nearly white.

"Move, you pig," he snapped and flicked his hands. The large form of Mr. Firth was whimpering and cowering on the floor one moment, and the next had been flung into the air nearly to the ceiling. He landed on his feet, obviously held upright by the force of Ben's powers.

"Leave this house at once, and if you ever so much as look at Mistress Althea again, if you ever even dare to utter her name in anything but the highest praise, I shall find you and drag you with me into the depths of hell so dark you shall never even remember light ever once existed."

With a yowling scream, Mr. Firth flew back, stumbling into a large armoire that rattled with the force of his impact. "Y- y- yes. Yes, sir."

"Your Grace."

"Yes, Your Grace," Mr. Firth stammered, tears of fear and tendrils of drool falling dripping off his red, patchy chin. With an awkward, jerking motion he bowed to Ben, then fled down the stairs.

A moment later, the wind stopped and the candle sconces flickered back to life.

"Are you alright?" Ben asked.

Althea realized she was trembling. "Yes, I think so. Thank you."

His eyes flicked to the blade, still held in her hand. "We need to get you a better weapon."

"This one has served me well," she said, the

implication of the many times she'd had to use it settling sadly between them.

Ben nodded. "You're a brave woman."

"Bravery has nothing to do with it," she murmured.

His gaze caught hers. "Indeed. Men can be horrible creatures. I'm sorry I cannot do more."

"All of us do what we can," she said, meaning the words in so many ways. "But what's done is done, and I doubt he will be inclined to come near me ever again. Thank you for that."

"It's my pleasure," Ben replied, his voice a shade deeper than usual. Nerves flickered through Althea, not because she was standing there speaking to a ghost.

Fleetingly, she wished he were a man of flesh and blood.

Which was ridiculous.

A quiet cough broke through her thoughts. Althea turned towards the servants stairs at the end of the hallway, where Hen stood with a bucket of steaming water.

"Pardon me, miss," she said, as if nothing were amiss. "I'll be starting that bath you asked for, if you like."

"Thank you, Hen." Althea looked back to where

Ben had hovered a moment before, but he was gone. Hen scuttled past, opening the door to Althea's room with practiced ease, and entering.

"Did you see me speaking to someone just now?" Althea asked.

The maid glanced back towards the hallway. "Aye, my lady. I suppose that was His Grace you were speaking to."

"The ghost, you mean."

Hen bobbed her head. "Lord Aston. He speaks to me too, sometimes, but please don't tell no one. I- I know most of the house believe in him, but the ones he don't speak to is sometimes jealous as those of us that knows him.

The words struck Althea like a blow. No wonder Hen had been tight-lipped ever since that first night. She did know things- a lot of them. "You speak to Ben? Does Goggins know?"

The girl smirked. "Goggins knows, but he don't like it. Ben- I mean, Lord Aston, thinks it's funny to never speak to 'im. Just moves his belongings around and taps him on the shoulder sometimes. Silliness like that. Drives Goggins mad. He knows more about the house than anybody except Ben, of course. Feels he deserves more respect."

Althea moved to help her drag a large copper tub

away from the wall. It had been there the entire time, pushed beneath a side table.

"Does the Earl know about this?" Althea asked.

The maid stilled. "No," she said, nervous again, "he doesn't believe any of it. And we all decided it was best not to let on to the family, not even Miss Charlotte, though Ben talks to her all the time. He keeps our secrets, His Grace does. Values us."

"And he is right to do so." Althea stepped back and watched as the girl poured the steaming bucket of water into the tub. Perhaps her opinions of Ben were wrong. He had been born a Duke, and he was certainly untrustworthy to her personally given their opposing desires, but he had saved her from Mr. Firth and was, apparently, beloved of the household servants. Not in the way a beneficent boss would be, kind but distant, but almost a friend, if the maid's warm and familiar tone was any indication.

"If you're wondering, I couldn't see Lord Aston just now. He doesn't always appear. Sometimes I just hear him. Could you see him?"

Cool, laughing eyes and hard flesh under an open shirt flashed in Althea's mind. "I could, yes."

A wicked gleam glimmered in the maid's own green gaze. "He's probably listening, but between us gels, he's a handsome devil ain't he?"

Althea laughed, a full, genuine belly laugh that rippled up from her toes and rang through her. It felt good. When was the last time she'd laughed like that?

"Don't let him hear you saying that. I think his head is quite big enough as it is."

The maid giggled. "You may be right, Mistress. Pity he's not flesh and blood though, eh? Would make some lucky duchess a fine husband."

"The realm is certainly the worse for his bodily absence," Althea replied, not allowing herself to imagine Ben with a duchess. *Not for any particular reason,* she told herself. *Only because it was a waste of time.*

Astutely sensing her cue, the maid bobbed a curtsy. "If you'd like to prepare yourself milady, the water shall be ready for you shortly."

"Thank you, Hen. And thank you for telling me."

The maid knew what Althea meant and offered her a smile in return. A moment later, she was gone to fetch more water.

The night had gone from bad to worse. The Earl of Maybourne's dinner party had been an utter bore, which then became a real mess, when that drunken imbecile Mr. Firth decided to regale the party with that horrible story from years ago. Ben remembered that night perfectly, and frankly, he wished he didn't. The boys had been fools, half-drunk on stolen whisky and ready for trouble. Ben had done his best to scare them off, but when the scrawny one pissed himself it had incited the others to such mockery the boy had gone mad from embarrassment.

It was a horrible memory and only served to remind Ben of how helpless he was in this form, and how the living could be far more frightening than the dead. Human nature was volatile and animalistic, even in youth. One could not rely on anybody but oneself, and that was difficult when one had no corporeal form.

The story had taken a dull evening and made it disagreeable.

Then the idiot Firth had decided to take advantage of the only unprotected woman in the house, despite the fact that said lady was the evening's guest of honor. Ben shuddered to think what would have happened if he had stayed a moment longer in the shadows of the parlor listening to Charlotte's so-called singing. He'd arrived only just in time to throw Firth off Althea. That little blade of hers would likely have done the trick, too, but Ben knew sometimes such a ploy would only serve to further enrage a man.

Now Ben had another grim thought in his mind for

the night, warring with that old memory for which might put him in a more dreadful mood.

Part of him wanted to float up to the roof and stare at the moon. That usually settled his mind and put things into perspective.

Another part of him considered finding Goggins and hassling him a bit. Taps on the shoulder, flickering lights. It was an old game, but he enjoyed it. Goggins was a tough old nut and impossible to rattle. The perfect foil.

But none of those things was what Ben *really* wanted to do.

He'd briefly attended to some business belowstairs but moments later he was hovering in the shadows of Althea's sitting room. He kept himself invisible, watching Hen the chambermaid and a few footmen fill the copper tub in front of the fire with steaming hot water.

Just as the servants were finishing, a soft snick drew his attention to the bedroom door, where Althea appeared in a diaphanous black silk dressing gown.

Ben's mouth would have gone dry, if he'd had one.

As it was, he felt his essence sort of flicker. An odd sensation, and one he'd not experienced before. Even after all these years, he was still learning the nature of this form. He did not think long on it, however, because Althea was moving towards the steaming tub. The firelight danced across her pale, smooth skin, making her look for all the world like some sort of goddess of the night.

"Enjoy my lady," Henrietta curtsied, and ushered the two footmen out the door. Ben noted their faces- both lads were staring at Althea with slack jaws and Ben had half a mind to teach them some manners later.

Except the moment the door to the hall snapped shut, all thoughts emptied Ben's mind.

He was behind her, the fire before her, and Althea's body was perfectly outlined as she let the robe drop to the floor.

She was naked.

Something in Ben's chest hitched. It couldn't be his breath, he had none- but the sensation was the same, just as in life. He had not felt this way since he was a lad. He remembered the first time he'd seen a woman without her clothing as clear as crystal. It was not something a man forgot. That he'd seen countless nude female bodies since didn't matter, apparently, because Althea took him straight back to that first time nearly a century ago.

Guilt, unbidden and frankly unwanted, flashed through him. He should grant her privacy. He was no better than Firth, to stand here watching her in this moment. Yes, he ought to go to the roof now. Some crisp night air would clear his mind. Any moment now, he would leave, and never mention this, because really, it wasn't worth mentioning, and there was no point in making her feel self-conscious when now that he thought on it, he was probably going to forget the sight soon enough anyway-

"I know you're here."

Her voice was cool, husky silk against his nerves. He swallowed and said the first thing that entered his mind. "I'm sorry."

"Don't be," she whispered. "I don't mind. It's- nice, to not be alone."

"But it's not very gentlemanly of me to be here, when you're- well, you're-"

"Naked." Her head half turned towards the sound of his voice behind her and her lips hitched to one side, offering him a crooked smile he had the sudden urge to kiss straight. Which was absurd. He could no more kiss her than he could waltz into Parliament and demand his seat on the House of Lords back.

"Yes," he said, his mind feeling like molasses. "That."

Her smile deepened and Ben noticed her cheeks were unusually flushed. Whether it was from the wine she'd enjoyed at dinner- at least three glasses by his count, all from an excellent bottle of French Bordeaux he had acquired upon assuming the title- or the excitement in the hall, he did not know.

She met his gaze, hers eyes pools of obsidian promise. "You're hardly going to ruin me."

Ben flinched. The words should not have stung, but they did. He had long ago ceased mourning his lack of a body, but the sight of hers made him wish dangerous, impossible things.

As if realizing, she quickly added, "I don't mean that because of, well, the practicalities of your- of the situation. I was only thinking that a woman of my age and station is hardly beholden to the same rules as the ladies you're accustomed to."

Ben felt his cock twitch at the words. The mind was a remarkable thing. He had no body to experience such a thing, but his mind still generated the sensations. Not brought on by physical contact, but by the purest form of desire, entirely in his mind.

"Are you telling me you're not a virgin, Mistress Althea?"

"I'm telling you I'd like you to show yourself."

"As the lady wishes," Ben said, his mouth *definitely* feeling dry now. A moment later, he was lounging in the armchair beside the tub, looking up at her from the front, feigning nonchalance when in reality his body was so rock hard with tension he was worried he might blast apart and fall into the Void at any moment.

A dangerous state, then, but one he suddenly realized he was willing to risk.

Chapter Ten

The Dessert

Althea wasn't sure what had come over her. She'd sensed him the moment Hen and the footmen left, as if the space was still taut with presence. In a way, she supposed, it was.

He was sitting before her now, facing her. The tub sat between the crackling fire in the grate and the two armchairs. He was seated in one of them, leaning back, knees spread, shirt eternally open, watching her. She felt herself outlined by the flickering light, the heat at her back nothing compared to the scorching sensation of his gaze as it moved slowly over her body.

She knew what he saw. Pale, ivory skin, protected by years of moving indoors and by night. Her long, slender legs drawing up to the slight swell of her hips. Narrow for a woman, but still feminine. The thatch of midnight black curls where her thighs met. Her slim waist. Her breasts, just enough to hold in each hand, their small, pert nipples a dusky pink. The scar on her shoulder from a narrow escape long ago. The burn mark on her forearm from stumbling with a hot kettle last year. Her hair, free of its usual restraints, unbound and flowing in untamed waves down to her elbows.

As for Ben, Althea was surprised to find he was fully visible now, all the way down to his forever muddied brown leather boots.

It was not his boots that caught her eye, however, but his evident arousal.

"I didn't know that was possible. Or did you die like that?" she asked, quirking a brow.

His eyes did not leave hers, sending a thrill through her as he replied, "Neither did I, and I did not. The credit is all yours, Althea."

She swallowed, suddenly self-conscious.

Which was ridiculous. He was a *ghost*. He did not have a body, and even if he did, she was not sure what she wanted to do with him. Clearly whatever was between them had been set free by his rescuing her from Firth, a spark fanned into flame. But he was duke. Arrogant. Entitled. Commanding.

Her traitorous nipples hardened at the thought and his eyes flicked down. "Get in the water, Althea. You'll catch a chill."

Her mind rankled at the authority in his tone even as her legs- *also* traitors- obeyed. She stepped into the tub one foot at a time, aware the motion nearly bared her sex to him. He did not take his eyes from hers.

As she sank into the bath a little moan of pleasure escaped her throat. "This is heavenly," she gasped, the temperature of the water perfectly hot. There was something to be said for an artfully trained household staff, it seemed. She sank back into the water and closed her eyes, her head resting on the rim of the tub.

"It certainly is." Ben's voice was rough with desire. Althea felt her body tighten in response, delicious awareness growing between her legs.

The sensation brought her back to her senses. This was madness. Futile and impractical and... and... he might have murdered that boy all those years ago. She should ask him about it. She should get out of the tub and go to bed. Alone. She shouldn't even consider she had any other options, because she didn't- Ben was a ghost. He would always leave her alone, when it counted.

But he saved you from Mr. Firth in the hall, didn't he? The voice in her mind was as traitorous as her heart, thudding loudly, nervously in her chest.

The heat of the water seeped into her bones, making her head swim. Or was that the lingering effects of the wine from dinner?

Althea needed to regain control of the situation. Of herself. She opened her eyes. He was watching her still, like some big cat in a tree, waiting patiently for its prey.

Her voice was blessedly steady when asked,

"Where does this lead, Your Grace?"

Ben smiled in a wicked flash of white teeth, as though he had heard her thoughts. "Dessert, my darling. Would you like some?"

She sat up, water sloshing around her. "Dessert? What do you mean?"

"Baked custard and berries. I hope you like custard?"

Althea sat up, confused. "Of course. I love it. But I don't see what you-"

Without a word or the slightest effort to move from his louche position in the armchair, Ben snapped his fingers and the door to the hallway opened.

"Oh!" Althea exclaimed, moving automatically to cover her breasts.

"Don't." He was not asking, and slowly, Althea dropped her arms back into the steaming water to watch as a covered silver tray lifted off the floor just beyond her door and floated silently into her sitting room.

Her mouth fell open. "How-"

"No idea. Ever since I died I've been going at moving things around, however, and I feel it would be a shame to waste such a skill, don't you?"

Althea nodded as the tray floated straight to her. Just before it reached the tub, Ben flicked his other hand and a small side table skittered across the room to stop just beneath it. With a gentle thud, the tray settled onto the table. A moment later the silver lid removed itself to rest on the floor, revealing a dish of baked custard and berries with a small crystal goblet of port beside it.

"You did this," she said. It wasn't a question.

"I thought you could benefit from a little indulgence. It's been difficult evening."

"Yes. Charlotte's singing is atrocious."

Ben let out a sharp bark of laughter. "Poor girl. All the tutors in the world, and that is the best they could do. At least she has the face of a angel."

Althea stilled at the words. She hated that they bothered her. She hated that he was right. She *was* jealous of Charlotte Ridgely. Althea was pretty enough, in a dramatic, dark sort of way. Charlotte was like the sun. Shimmering, bright, and, yes, a little grating but generally desirable.

But did Ben desire her?

And did it matter, when he was a ghost, anyway?

Althea knew it didn't matter. *He* didn't matter, except that he needed to end whatever was between him and Charlotte so that Althea could get paid and get out of town. It was useless to care if he desired *her*. Obviously his body did, but he didn't have a body, so that was useless.

If she cared for him she was no better than Charlotte Ridgely. Worse, because she was a woman grown who should know better than to fall for some girlish fantasy.

"You don't like it."

"What?"

"The dessert. You haven't touched it."

Althea glanced at the perfect, glistening delicacy. "It isn't that."

Ben looked down at his translucent boots. "Ah. Yes. Well, if it makes you feel better, I've never done this with anyone before."

"Served them floating custard?"

He did not smile. "Let things become- allow things to feel-"

"Almost real?"

He nodded, his eyes meeting hers again with a burning intensity she felt in her core. He was telling the truth.

"There is one thing I've learned in my brief life and interminable afterlife, Althea, and that nothing lasts. We are given only what is directly before us, and there is no way to know how long it will be there. How long *we* will be here. Or when everything will change."

"What are you asking, Your Grace?"

"Call me Ben."

"What are you asking, Ben?"

He looked almost nervous. "I don't have all the answers, about me, about my curse, about any of it except," he swallowed and took a deep, intangible breath, "I know one thing. I want you, Althea. I've wanted you since that first night. It's why I didn't try harder to drive you out. Why I can't think of anything else during the day. Why Charlotte is so displeased with me."

The words washed over Althea like a wave of fire, far hotter and more dangerous than the one crackling merrily at her back.

Ben continued. "I want you, and I can never have you. Which is just as well, I'm terrible at love."

Althea's mouth went dry. "Love?"

"Yes. Don't worry, this will never come to that. I've managed to avoid it for nearly a century, I won't burden you with such sop now."

"Good. I am a professional, after all."

"And I am your work?"

She nodded, hoping he could not hear the way her heart raced. She'd felt it too of course, this tension between them. She'd tried for days now to suppress it, but he was right. There was something between them, something fierce and burning. It wasn't love. She had never loved anyone, either- not a man, not like that. Her mother had loved her father and it had ruined her life. Althea had known from birth that to love a man was to cast your fate upon a sinking ship.

Except there was no danger of it here. Not with Ben. There could never be anything between them besides whatever pleasure they could manage from their unusual situation. Althea had no idea what, exactly, they could share but she knew with sudden certainty she wanted to find out.

"One night," Ben said abruptly, as if reading her mind. "Just this once. Because life has no guarantees."

"And neither does death," Althea murmured. "I accept."

Something like relief washed over Ben as Althea took a sip of the port to calm her own nerves.

"Now what?" she asked.

This time Ben did not snap his fingers or flick his wrists. He did nothing at all, but watch her, yet the door to her bedroom opened itself all the same and out from the darkness floated a small, flat object.

The book.

Althea's heart raced.

"As a young man I traveled many places. India, Africa, the West Indies. I saw more places than anyone I'd ever met, places I could not properly describe upon my return for fear of being thought mad, so wondrous they were. Cities of white and sands of black. Palaces of gold and mountains of fire. Elephants and tigers and whales larger than the biggest ships in the world. I also learned that many places are not so… reserved as we are."

"I gathered that." She glanced at the book.

Ben laughed, the sound wrapping around Althea like a warm blanket. Somehow her bathwater had not cooled at all, but she did not dare ask if that was his doing, too.

"So you looked at it?"

"I glanced," she hedged.

Pure masculine satisfaction washed over him as Ben floated the book in front of him and began to leisurely flip through the pages. Even in the flickering shadows Althea caught glimpse of the pages as they turned. Men and women of every combination, of every color of skin and style of dress- and, mostly, undress- intertwined in positions of pleasure.

Her heart skipped a beat. "Is that where you got the book? Some far, distant land?"

"India, in fact. They've cultivated lovemaking to an art form. It's sacred there, not merely some dirty act or else a dull duty as it is in dear old England."

Althea chuckled, and took a bite of the baked

custard to calm her nerves. It was delicious. "So, what now? You're going to read to me?"

Ben's gaze scorched her as it moved across her body, wholly visible in the clear water of the tub. "Yes." His voice was low and full of sinful promise. "In a way. And I want you to lean back and imagine there is more than words between us. Use your hands, and I'll use mine. Would you like that?"

Althea felt as if her entire body were aflame at the thought. She'd been with men before who were considered adept lovers. She'd known passion and pleasure. But no physical contact had ever made her so full of need as she felt now at the promise of mere words from man who was no more than ether and light. She should ask him about Mr. Firth's story. She should confront him about Charlotte. She should go to bed and regain her sanity.

"Yes, Ben," she heard herself say, her voice barely more than a whisper. *"Please."*

Once, long ago, Ben had purchased a young stallion. A talented horseman, he had given no thought to the breeder's warnings that the horse was wild. Half mad, even. Ben had been seventeen and thought danger was nothing more than a challenge to met, a foe to be mocked.

He'd had the horse delivered to the family stables and immediately jumped on the massive, black creature. He had not bothered with a saddle or even reins, so convinced he'd been of his own prowess. The grooms leapt back in dismay and even the stable master called a warning to Ben, but it was too late.

The horse reared and took off, straight out of the gates, into the fields, and, worse, the forest beyond.

Plunging into the trees both horse and rider narrowly missed low hanging branches, protruding stumps, boulders and logs and bracken.

Ben had held on for dear life, jostling and bouncing, floating mid-air one moment and slamming into the stallion's broad, sweaty back the next, wholly unable to stop himself from meeting whatever inevitable end lay for him down the path.

That was how he felt now with Althea lying before him in the water he kept steaming with his strange, mercurial powers, the book of erotica floating midair before him, opened to a particularly acrobatic scene.

He'd found her attractive from the start. She was physically enticing, all lean lines and willowy, dark feminine grace. It was her mind, though, the sort of fierce tenacity of her that made him desire her. She was a survivor. A fighter. Full of life itself.

He wanted that.

He wanted *her*.

But he was cursed. He had no body to give her, to take her. He had only his... whatever this was that was left of him. His mind? His soul?

Not that, a voice warned in his head. This was not going to be that sort of exchange. His soul was lost long ago, and whatever was left of it wasn't meant to be seen. Known.

Loved.

That had nothing to do with it.

This was about want and need and pure, carnal pleasure. As much as he could get in this form, and as much as he could give. He hadn't been with a woman in any sense, physically or whatever this was, in eighty-five years. He was desperate for her.

He was nervous.

"Are you alright?" she asked, and he started.

"I've rarely been better," he purred. "Shall I begin?"

She said nothing, but leaned back into the steaming water and closed her eyes. Slowly, her hand moved over the length of her body beneath the water's surface, gently caressing her soft, flushed skin.

Ben nearly came just looking at her.

Which was absurd. It was all in his mind, and he hadn't been so green since he was fourteen and tupped the scullery maid, his first lover. Maggie. She'd been strong and fresh and eager.

He was stalling.

Ben flipped the pages of the book without lifting a finger then stopped, and cleared his throat. In a low voice, he began.

"A man and a woman sit facing one another on thick, soft rugs. Pillows of silk surround them, their eyes locked, breathing synched. The man runs his hand along the side of her face, the pads of his fingers, his thumb, caressing the soft outline of her."

Ben saw movement out of the corner of his eye as Althea, her own eyes still closed, ran her own long, elegant fingers across the plane of her face from temple to chin. She was so trusting and he knew, instinctively, that whatever this was between them tonight was something rare and precious. Strange, yes, and unprecedented- but he had no doubt that this strong, clever woman rarely let herself go.

It was the most beautiful thing he'd ever seen, and they were only beginning.

The stallion in his mind bucked and twisted. He should go, simply disappear and forget about this. About her. Let her fail at Maybourne's task and never darken his doorstep again.

He continued, forgetting about the book. He'd

already memorized his favorite images and physically reenacted nearly all of them before.

He let the book float softly to the floor, where it landed without a sound, and he spoke from memory. From desire.

"The woman reaches out, her hands softer than a butterfly's wings, as she runs them along his neck, his shoulders, his arms."

Ben didn't move. He didn't have to. It was all in his mind, and in his mind, he felt everything he described. And in his mind, it was Althea's hands touching him. Leaving fire in their wake as they moved across his bare, naked flesh.

The real Althea was still gently moving, caressing her own shoulders, her own arms, with the tentative eagerness of a lover. Was she imagining touching him?

God he hoped so.

"His hands slide down, his fingers running along the blades of her collarbone, they descend slowly, gently to her breasts. He envelopes them, then leans down to press his lips to one perfect pink nipple. She gasps."

Lost in the dream of his words, Althea gasped.

Ben felt his cock twitch. Eighty-five years of this existence and never once had he longed so badly for his body back.

Breathing harder, he kept himself talking, imagining his own hand moving down to gently pump his cock as he did so. "He kisses and sucks, his tongue lashing across one breast, then tenderly administering to the other. She pressed herself closer and begins to move, writhing gently in a rhythm older than time itself."

Althea shifted then, her hips undulating softly in the water. Her thighs pressed together and he could see the black triangle at their nexus moving gently in the rippling bath. He stroked himself a little faster.

He opened his mouth to go on, but to his surprise, Althea spoke first, her eyes still closed, her voice hoarse with desire. "She runs her own hands down the hard planes of his chest. Down, down until-" Althea's breath hitched, with self-awareness or lust, Ben didn't know- "she takes his manhood in her hand and pulls herself away from his attentions, drawing herself closer."

"Althea-" Ben gasped, wanting her to stop. Needing her to go on. The stallion he was on now was far wilder, far more dangerous than the one in his youth. It was careening towards an opening in the forest, a clearing- no, a cliff. The edge of the woods. The fall beyond would surely kill them both but he could not let go, he could not stop-

"She leans down and wraps her lips around him. Kissing, licking, sucking, she pumps him her hand and-"

The stallion did not slow as it broke through the line of trees and galloped over the edge of the cliff, both horse and rider in freefall.

With a guttural shout Ben climaxed, the warm, hot sensation of orgasm wracking through him so strongly he forgot it wasn't real.

Shuddering, he closed his eyes, and, cad that he was, he disappeared.

Althea knew the moment he was gone.

Her eyes flew open and her finger stopped caressing the center of her pleasure at the apex of her thighs.

He was gone, and it felt as though the air had been sucked out of the room.

Worse, the bathwater was suddenly cold.

Shivering, she rose from the tub and reached for the bit of toweling Hen had left beside it.

She did not want to think about what had just happened. She knew some women might feel shame for such a wanton display, but Althea was not one of those women. She'd been with men who liked to talk during the act before. She'd read naughty books. She'd touched herself in front of a man. What had just happened- it should not leave her shaking.

But she was trembling. Even as she burrowed under the thick coverlet of her bed a few minutes later, she could not stop shivering.

It had nothing to do with shame or cold or regret.

She'd laid herself bare to Ben in more ways than one tonight. And just like any man, once he'd taken what he wanted from her, he'd left. Hadn't he?

As long awaited sleep wrapped its tendrils around her, pulling her towards unconsciousness, Althea couldn't shake the feeling that Ben had not left for the reasons other men did. She felt as if tonight she'd reached the edge of the unknown, a precipice more dangerous and terrifying than any she'd known before. A fall from such a height could kill, she thought, and she wondered if he felt exactly the same way.

Or, perhaps, she was going mad after all.

The next morning when she awoke a piece of parchment lay facedown on the bed bedside her. Blinking back already forgotten dreams, she flipped it over.

Dine with me tonight? Your servant, B.

She threw on her dressing gown, grabbed a quill and wrote beneath the strong, swirling script:

It would be my pleasure. A.

Leaving the parchment on the bed, where he would find it if he wasn't already invisibly watching her now, Althea dressed and went down to breakfast and decided whatever the fifteenth Duke of Stafford was, he was not like other men.

And it had nothing to do with his being a ghost.

Chapter Eleven
The Bookshop

"The yellow suits me better, don't you agree?"

Althea glanced into the shop mirror, where Charlotte's reflection held up a bonnet festooned with ribbons the color of daffodils.

"I can't imagine a color that would not suit you, Miss Ridgely," the shop girl effused.

"Black," Charlotte snapped, meeting Althea's eyes in the mirror. "It's a horrid color. Makes one look as if they've just crawled out of a bog."

Althea ignored her. The jibe went over the shop girl's head, not the least because today Althea had decided to wear a dress of deep violet in lieu of her usual noir.

They had been shopping on Bond Street for three hours already and even Charlotte's maid, standing idly in the corner of the milliner's shop, was showing obvious signs of boredom. Althea was losing her own mind, a little, at the inane series of stores Charlotte insist they enter. Each one was more colorful and overflowing than the last, filled with fripperies, lace, silks, wealthy women and, naturally, gossip. Charlotte indulged in all of it with obvious glee.

If the Earl of Maybourne thought this outing would

prove a fruitful opportunity for Althea to befriend his sister, he was sorely mistaken. The man clearly underestimated his only sibling to an embarrassing degree. Charlotte had known what his ambitions were from the moment she'd been told at breakfast that Althea would be accompanying her for the day. She'd played her part well, offering only a polite and docile acceptance and expressing her hopes that Althea would enjoy the pleasures of Bond Street.

The little witch had gone on to be nothing but the very vision of lovely company ever since. Her little jibe about the color black was the sharpest barb she'd thrown thus far, her weapons of choice beings mostly painfully bland commentary and immersing herself in the most fatuous activities and conversations she could manage. She had introduced Althea to at least two dozen other women of the *ton*, and all of them were wretched company. Worse, all of them wanted to talk to Charlotte for an obscenely long time. There was no escaping, at least not quickly.

It was nearly evening now and not only had Althea not eaten since breakfast, but her feet hurt from wandering aimlessly through rows of gewgaws and not once had she managed an exchange with Charlotte more insightful than Charlotte's dour observation, "You would do well to wear less kohl."

At least none of the ladies they met wanted to speak to Althea. Either they had never heard of her and after one look decided they didn't want to know more, or they knew exactly who she was and felt compelled to stay clear. This suited Althea just fine. She only wished she'd brought a book.

Just the thought, *book*, had her blushing. She turned to closely examine a display of ribbons on a shelf so Charlotte wouldn't notice. Althea had no desire to explain where her thoughts had been all day. She could not stop thinking about the night before, about how utterly intoxicating it had been. She kept imagining what might happen tonight, then felt guilty for hoping it was something similar. Ben had said just one night, hadn't he? Perhaps he wanted to have dinner with her tonight to apologize.

Except she knew that wasn't true.

He'd been just as surprised and, and *intoxicated*, as she had.

Althea felt the color in her cheeks deepen another shade and so she turned even more to examine some intricate lace on a lower shelf.

She was a grown woman, not some ninny hammer of a girl whose head was turned at the first boy who crossed her path. She'd known several men intimately, and they'd all been lovely. Most importantly, they'd been *living*. Not ghosts. There was no future with a ghost, especially a ghost she could not trust.

Most especially a ghost who refused to cooperate with her, who she might need to expel from the house.

Except she had no idea how to do that, and, worse, she had no wish to.

The truth sunk into her belly like a sack of bricks. Heavy and immovable. She'd been fascinated by Ben from the start, not merely because he was a *real* ghost after so many years of playacting mystic, but because he was unlike anyone she'd ever met. As a person. As a soul. She hadn't wanted to get rid of him since that first night, if she were honest with herself.

Which presented a problem, especially as he was set on letting Charlotte continue to admire him.

Althea despised drama, and now she was embroiled in it. There was no good way for this to end, for any of them. No matter what everyone was going to be hurt somehow, and her only hope was to get paid and stay out of prison by the end of it.

She grimaced at the spools of frilly lavender lace and straightened. Charlotte was still cooing at herself in a mirror, so Althea looked out the window of the milliner's cozy storefront to distract herself with the cream of London society walking past. A light rain was falling, and most wealthy patrons were bundled into carriages, splashing mud as they clattered by. A few were on foot, dodging puddles and huddled under umbrellas. Some excitable young woman gave an unflatteringly squeal of delight, no doubt being shown some hideous cranial concoction of taffeta and bows, and Althea found herself longing to be out there in the rain.

Her gaze scanned the street, but paused as a familiar figure caught her eye. Lord Leslie was standing under the eaves of the shop across the street. His hat was pulled low but there was no mistaking him. Althea was an expert at observation and, following some instinct telling her not to draw Charlotte's attention to him, Althea shifted behind a display of riding bonnets to watch the man. He was up to something, she had no doubt.

Just what he was up to appeared a moment later, when a lovely lady close to Althea's age stepped out of the shop behind him. A vision of voluminous chestnut curls and a scandalously low-cut dress, she made no effort to hide herself as Leslie did. He pulled his hat further down and ushered his companion beneath a massive umbrella, clearly hoping to avoid attention.

Althea's eyes narrowed as his surreptitiously slid one hand around the woman's backside and, quite obviously, gave it a pinch.

A moment later, they had called down a hired hack and disappeared.

"I'll take these two, and the little velvet one as well," Althea heard Charlotte say, wholly oblivious to the little drama across the street.

"Does Lord Leslie have a sister?" Althea asked innocently.

Charlotte blinked. "No. He is an only child. Both his parents died tragically years ago, so really Mr. Wilkes is his only family. He didn't know until recently, though. Lord Leslie was raised abroad, I believe, and only became aware of Mr. Wilkes upon his return to the country."

Althea wasn't surprised. She'd known the chestnut-haired beauty hadn't been his sister. All the same, she'd hoped to give him the benefit of the doubt. She was not naive. Men of Lord Leslie's stations usually had a mistress or two, but it was rare to see them flaunt their sidepiece on Bond Street in the middle of the day. Even if it was raining and nobody was about. Somebody was always watching.

Althea nibbled her lip, deep in thought.

There was something about Leslie that didn't feel right. His arrogance was annoying, but not unexpected. He'd been so truly moved by the ghost story the night before she knew he at least could be humbled by fear. She felt sorry for him, somehow, just as she disliked him. Was it his desire for Charlotte, which was obviously not driven by any genuine affection? Or Ben's obvious dislike of the man? Or his connection to Wilkes, who was clearly untrustworthy?

Whatever it was, seeing him with that woman only confirmed her opinion that he was not to be trusted, either. Fortunately, she did not need to trust him. Perhaps he and Charlotte would be very happy together, living their shallow, vapid, pretty little lives, both capable of far more human feeling and accomplishment than they dared pursue, happy to live in Ben's house to the end of their days.

Guilt snagged at Althea's mind. Who was she to judge? She lied for a living and hoped to retire by the age of thirty to a life where she could ignore people altogether. How was that any better?

"Let's go," Charlotte flounced up beside her. Her maid stood behind them, arms full of packages to be placed in their carriage and sent back to the house.

"Home?" Althea asked, hopeful.

Charlotte looked at her, assessing. "Perhaps. Isn't there anywhere *you* would like to go? You haven't bought a thing today."

"I have all the worldly possessions I need."

"Poppycock," Charlotte snapped. "You might claim to deal with the spirit world but you're just as earthly as I am, and unless you're secretly a nun to boot, there has to be something you enjoy shopping for."

"Books."

The word was out before Althea could stop herself.

Charlotte's face lit up, making her even more beautiful, if that was possible. "Wonderful! I know just the place. Come with me. Thandy, give those to the footman and meet us at Simonson's."

An old, narrow building a few blocks away housed Simonson's Booksellers. Althea had heard of the place, but never been in before. Bond Street was not the part of town she did her shopping, even for books.

She hid her surprise when the man at the counter greeted Charlotte by name, but Charlotte still sensed the hidden judgment.

"I do read, you know," she murmured after casting a cheery greeting back to the shopkeeper. "I come here every time I'm in the neighborhood."

"So you did not need my suggestion?"

Charlotte cast her a sidelong glance. "Not at all. I merely desired the satisfaction."

Althea knew she was being goaded, but she asked

anyway. "What satisfaction is that, Miss Ridgely?"

"That you are precisely what you seem."

"You have no idea who I am," Althea responded evenly.

Charlotte's expression turned smug and secretive. "I know a great deal about you, Mistress Althea. Far more than you'd care to realize."

With that, Charlotte ducked between the towering stacks, leaving Althea in the center walkway of the bookshop with her own thoughts. She did not care for them. The girl was obviously playing games, trying to rattle Althea and scare her off. Althea did not want it to work, but unease rippled through her at Charlotte's words.

The coquettish Miss Ridgely was childish and often annoying, but she was also far more intelligent than she wished to let on. Althea would be a fool to underestimate her. Worse, it was possible Charlotte *did* know more about Althea than the more worldly woman realized.

Dread pooled in Althea's gut. What if Ben had been telling Charlotte about his conversations with Althea? Or… no- she could not allow herself to entertain the idea that he was telling anyone about their other intimacies. She trusted him with that much, at least.

Didn't she? When had *that* happened? Just because

she'd bared herself to him, in body and, somehow, more, did that earn him her trust? They were still at cross purposes. For all she knew he told Charlotte everything.

Althea glanced down the stacks to ensure Charlotte was still in the shop. To her slight surprise, the girl was seated in an old chair at the end of the row, one hand holding up a leather-bound tome and the other mindlessly stroking the shop cat, a small tabby. The creature seemed to know her well, which corroborated Charlotte's intimation that this shop was her favorite. It almost made Althea like her a little.

Chewing on that thought, Althea wound her way back to the front desk. "Let me know if Miss Ridgely exits the shop, will you?" she asked the shopkeeper and placed a few coins on the wood counter between them.

The man's eyes widened, but he did not take the money. "Aye, as you seem to be her chaperone this afternoon, I'll tell ye if she leaves. But she won't. More as like you'll have to convince her to go when it's time to close up."

Althea filed the words away for later and left the coins between them. She decided to allow herself a little time to relax- and research.

The next twenty minutes passed in a daze. Althea

let her eyes wander the titles of the rows and rows of books, some of them newly printed but many of them quite old. The variety of subjects was enough to keep thoughts of the night before at bay, mostly.

Every time she thought of the heat of the water, the velvet thrum of Ben's voice in her ear, the touch of soft flesh, her own, and yet guided by him-

She simply picked up another book and began reading. It was a simple matter of redirecting her thoughts. There was no point in reliving the events last night. It was useless to reflect that she'd been more intimate with a ghost than she had with any living man. Yes, she'd happily shared her body with several men over the years, and those gentlemen could claim greater knowledge of her flesh, but Ben had reached places none of those men had ever come close to touching. He'd caressed her mind, her very *soul* had felt the ministrations of his attention.

Did he feel the same way? Had he felt that intoxicating intimacy and all-encompassing pleasure, too? Was that why he'd left so suddenly- and why did she care so damned much? It defied reason- from what he'd told her he could feel nothing at all- but in that plane beyond the physical, she was certain he had been transported, too.

Wasn't she? Wasn't *he*?

A loud meow jolted her back to the present and she nearly dropped the book in her hands.

She'd been reading it upside down, anyway.

The source of the meow stepped out of the shadows at the end of the row. A large black cat with bright yellow eyes.

Althea had always liked cats. She preferred dogs, but cats seemed to gravitate to her. She'd often felt they watched her, seeing far more than she liked. This sleek fellow was no different.

"*Meow*," he said, a little more emphatically than before.

"Hello sir," Althea whispered, out of respect for the other patrons as much a desire to not be overheard speaking to a cat. "Would you like your ears scratched?"

"*Mmmeow.*"

The cat turned and sauntered around the corner, the tip of his tail twitching back and forth. After a pause, he stuck his head back around at Althea. "*Meowww.*"

Althea had not believed in ghosts for most of her life, but there had been a time when she was much more attuned to the inexplicable. Before feigning such beliefs had become her profession, she had lived in the countryside with her mother, where folk tales and superstition were commonplace. In those early years Althea had occasionally found herself led by instinct, as if a small voice or a gentle, unseen hand were guiding her. In those moments, she'd sometimes found herself escaping unforeseen danger or, once, stumbling upon a young boy about to fall in a river. She'd saved the boy's life, pulling him back to safety just as the branch he'd been climbing on snapped.

She'd set him on firm ground and watched as he'd torn off into the brambles without even a thank you.

She'd never told anyone about the boy, or about the feelings that sometimes guided her. In fact, until now she had forgotten about them herself. There was no room in Mistress Althea's life for such esoteric nonsense, despite the fact that exploring the unseen was her trade.

True belief was the domain of Jane Smith, and Jane Smith no longer existed.

So why, when Althea felt that little tug in her gut for the first time in decades, did she follow it without hesitation?

This time when the cat turned back around the corner, Althea followed.

The black cat wound through the stacks, deeper and deeper into the narrow shop. Though the building was not wide, it was far longer than Althea would have guessed. Hoping Charlotte stayed put, Althea let the cat guide her along.

A narrow doorway in the back led to a creaking staircase, so steep it was nearly a ladder. The cat pranced down it with ease, and though Althea nearly slipped twice, she followed.

The basement of the bookshop reeked of mold. The air was thick and clammy, sucking the air from Althea's lungs with its age and weight. She did not like it down here.

Still, the cat moved on. The books here were mostly stocked in towers on their sides. Some were falling apart, and others had been raided by rodents for nesting materials or whatever rodents used book pages for.

Only a few sconces lit this floor, and the cat nearly disappeared several times in the deepening shadows. Every now and then it gave another "meow" as if in encouragement.

Althea did not enjoy being condescended to by a cat, but her instincts were still pushing her along, towards wherever this cat was leading her.

Finally, the cat stopped.

The sconces flickered as if a chill breeze swirled through the room, but there was no breeze. The hairs on the back of Althea's neck prickled.

"*Meow*," the cat said, jumping on top of a tower of books as high as Althea's hip.

The cat held her stare a moment, then looked down.

Taking the hint, Althea reached for the book on which the cat sat. It leapt off just as her gloved fingers reached the thick, worn leather of the's cover.

She pulled the book from its perch, taken aback by the weight of it. Though obviously thick, it weighed much more than it appeared.

Althea held it up to the light and read the title aloud.

"*Incantations, & Other Formes of Knowing The Other Realmes.*"

The lights flickered again, nearly going out.

"Alright, alright," Althea muttered to the room as much as herself. "I understand, just lay off a bit, will you?"

The lights remained unchanged in response, and when Althea turned to leave the black cat was nowhere to be seen.

"What's that?" Charlotte asked as Althea watched the shopkeeper wrap *Incantations* in brown paper for her.

"A book on botany," Althea said easily, hoping the

topic would discourage Charlotte's curiosity.

"Botany my foot," Miss Ridgely snorted. "You got that in the basement, didn't you?"

The shopkeeper paused a moment in his work, but said nothing.

"It's a side interest of mine. A knowledge of plants can be useful in my line of work."

"Do you kill people with poison now, too? Or simply rattle off facts about weeds until the dead decide to stay where they are?"

The shopkeeper did not pause this time, but his face took on the color of the freshly printed broadsheets behind him.

Althea rolled her eyes. "My work cannot be of any interest to you, I'm sure. I thought you wanted to nothing to do with it- or me."

Charlotte gestured to her maid to gather up both Charlotte's large package and Althea's much slimmer one as the shopkeeper set it on the counter. "Thank ye, ladies. Do come again."

"Oh, I shall, Roland," Charlotte beamed. "Tell your wife I'll have some of her favorite tea cakes sent over at once. If that doesn't make her stomach settle for the babe, nothing will!"

Althea did not have time to unpack that sentiment of generosity and goodwill, because the next moment

Charlotte was ushering her out the door. "Let's go to Gunter's, shall we?"

"Won't you spoil your appetite for dinner later?"

"Pshh!" Charlotte swatted the air with her fan. "Are you a mysterious woman of the arcane Mistress Althea or simply a governess in drab clothing?"

Althea sniffed. The words hit their target. "I'm not in the business of enjoying myself, Miss Ridgely. I am here to-"

"I know, I know. You're here to make sure I never enjoy myself ever again. Because no man is as enjoyable as Benedict Aston, I assure you."

Something that felt like both guilt and jealousy jolted Althea's insides. Obviously Charlotte had no idea how well-acquainted Althea had become with Ben. Which was good, necessary, even-

For a moment she imagined Charlotte finding out and turning her back on Ben in a fit of jealousy. Would learning of his betrayal- because in her mind there was an attachment, even if such a thing did not exist for Ben- drive her away from him?

Althea did not want to risk it. Not only because such a scandal would tarnish her reputation- what sort of mystic indulged in relations with the spirits she communicated with?- but because the only thing more dangerous and unpredictable than a young woman in the throes of first love was a young woman scorned.

"Does it not trouble you that Benedict Aston is a phantom? He has no body. Surely any number of gentlemen in London could offer much he cannot."

Charlotte's perfect, pert nose wrinkled. "If you mean carnal pleasures, it's irrelevant. I'm sure if I ever wanted to indulge in those with another he would understand. Ours is not a meeting of the bodies, you see, but of the mind."

The words landed on Althea like a bucket of ice water. "What do you mean?" she asked, fighting to keep her voice even.

"He is the kindest, most thoughtful man I've never known. He always listens to me, even when I go on about the most inane things. He gives excellent advice, too. You'd imagine he would. He's one hundred and nine years old, after all."

Althea bit back her surprise. She'd had no idea his age. Strangely, she had not thought to ask. It hadn't mattered, somehow. And his attire suggested he died sometime in the last century, but he was born that long ago?

"Has he ever told you about his death?"

Charlotte shot Althea a suspicious glance. "I'm not sure I should tell you anything more about him, as you want to chase him from the house. If you do that,

I won't marry anyone. Not even Leslie. I'll just disappear forever and start a new life."

Althea reminded herself there was no sense being jealous of the young girl. Ben had made it perfectly clear that while he was occasionally amused by Charlotte, he was just as often annoyed by her. That being said, he had known Charlotte longer than Althea, and it should not surprise her that Charlotte knew things about him.

"I'm not sure I have to drive him from the house to accomplish my aims."

Charlotte's eyes narrowed. The light rain was starting again, and both ladies opened their parasols. "What then are your aims, Mistress Althea?"

"Your brother informs me your affection for Ben has blinded you to all earthly suitors. You must know the trouble your family is in, the importance of seeing you wed."

"Sold off, more like," Charlotte mumbled and Althea felt a pang of empathy for the girl. If Althea's mother had been born a slightly higher station, Althea would have suffered the same fate.

She banished the thought.

"At least your brother is letting you choose your husband. Not all young women are so fortunate."

"You don't have a husband and you seem… fine."

The last word hung awkwardly in the air between them.

"I don't need a husband, because I earn my own money. A lady of your station cannot work for money. You must simply... *have* money."

"Earning my keep on my back for some pompous old man doesn't count? Just because I'm legally his shouldn't make a difference."

Althea snorted with surprise laughter. "You're lucky no one is on the street just now to hear you. The Crown certainly does not view marriage as a form of prostitution."

Charlotte grimaced. "Maybe they should. And I'm not in love Ben just to escape marriage, you know. My brother thinks I am- he doesn't even think Ben is real. I don't know what you think, and frankly, I don't care. I am in love with Benedict Aston, and he is in love with me, and that is all that matters."

Althea hated the part of her that worried Charlotte was right, even as she knew she wasn't. She did not have the heart to tell Charlotte the truth. That was Ben's responsibility. He'd been reckless with the girl's feelings, not out of any malicious intent, but rather by being naive to how easily a young woman could fall for a handsome face and word of kindness.

"Could you marry another but carry on with Ben in

secret? You could visit Maybourne house often after the marriage and no one would suspect your affections lie elsewhere. Many, if not most, aristocratic marriages are built on a foundation of business with no real feeling."

Charlotte considered that a moment. "Possibly."

Hope fluttered in Althea's chest. Once Charlotte was married, Ben could let her down easy, slowly disengage from his friendship with her.

"But the only living man I'd consider marrying is Lord Leslie, and I'm not sure he would like it. He believes in Ben, you see, and I sense he is a jealous man."

"There is no other living man that catches your eye?"

"No," Charlotte said simply. "They're all dull and ugly, or old and fat, or handsome but stupid. Leslie at least is tolerable. If it weren't for Ben, I might even like him."

Althea tucked this information away for later consideration, because at that moment Gunter's rose up on the street before them. The rain was falling heavily now and even through the steamed-up windows Althea could see the ice shop was full with the members of the *ton* brave enough to risk the weather.

"Have you ever had an ice from Gunter's?" Charlotte asked as they made their way across Berkley Square.

"Never," Althea answered.

Charlotte's eyes widened. "Oh, you haven't lived! The lemon flavor is divine!"

"I'll have to try that first, then."

Just as they neared the entrance to the bustling shop, a large black cat streaked across their path.

"Oh!" Charlotte exclaimed, stumbling back. "What terrible luck! It went right across our path."

"Don't put such store in old wives' tales, Miss Ridgely," Althea admonished, watching the cat disappear down an alleyway. "I met that black cat at Simonson's and it was a perfectly decent creature. It must have followed us over here. I hope it gets back alright."

Charlotte's brow furrowed. "Simonson doesn't have a black cat. They only have the tabby."

Althea told herself that the chill that accompanied Charlotte's words was only the rush of air preceding them through the opening doors of Gunter's.

Chapter Twelve
The Curse

"Any progress?" The Earl of Maybourne sat behind his large, fastidiously clean desk and eyed Althea over his spectacles. The reading aids were surprising, but rendered the Earl more human. Althea liked the effect.

"Some," she hedged. The book she'd found had been far more promising than her conversation with Charlotte, but the Earl didn't need to know that. "Your sister is quite stubborn about her affections for the ghost."

"She knows it's horseshite as well as we do," the Earl snarled, more to himself than to Althea. He softened his tone. "Pardon my language."

"Pardon granted. And I share your frustration. She seems to believe I am a fraud, which makes the path of convincing her much more difficult to tread."

The Earl was pale, his face thinner than even a few days before. "If I make speak candidly, Mistress Althea, the creditors are howling at the door. Charlotte needs to marry money, and soon. I've done all that I can. I've even looked into marrying myself, but there are significant constraints on my title and none of the eligible women available to me have the sort of sum we need."

"But Lord Leslie does?"

Maybourne nodded, his hands rising to rub his temples. "His addition to the family would resolve all our late father's debts and buy me ample time to make a suitable match of my own. I only need Charlotte's agreement, and clinging to this fabrication is endangering us all."

Althea knew he included her in the statement. If she failed in this, they all failed. There was no way for her to be paid without Charlotte's marriage to someone like Leslie, and besides, if Althea failed Maybourne would likely report her to the authorities and her renumeration would be moot anyway.

"I have a plan, your lordship. It is unconventional, but I think it might be the only way forward."

"What's that?"

"Since Charlotte knows what I'm about, we cannot convince her to do anything she doesn't wish to do, like renounce her attachment to this ghost of hers."

"Which leaves us no options."

Althea lifted her lips over her teeth in what would be a smile, if her eyes were not so cold. She would not let this job ruin her. Not now. Not when she was so close to being done. She *would* complete her assignment and worry about Ben and whatever was between them later.

"To the contrary, Lord Maybourne. I suggest we hold a gathering. As intimate affair in which I shall use the most obscure and occult methods of my trade, those I learned during tutelage under the esteemed Madame Veira and honed during my years abroad in foreign courts, to hear what the spirit has to say about all this."

Maybourne was sitting back in his chair now, something between cynicism and hope warring in his aristocratic features. "Go on."

"I can induce the spirit to renounce Charlotte, leaving her with no choice but to move past her girlish affection for him. We shall all be present as witnesses. She shall have no choice but to leave the ruse behind."

"And you can do this convincingly?"

Althea did not let her confidence falter. If Ben and Charlotte could not resolve this privately should would force their hand before witnesses. She would speak to Ben once more about it, but if he refused to help her she would have to do this on her own. She was nearly out of time and her instincts told her the book she'd found at Simonson's would help, somehow. It was a little reckless and absolutely desperate, but what choice did she have?

Her smooth assurances belied nothing of her doubts to the Earl. "My reputation has been well-earned, my lord. I assure you, there shall be no doubt in anyone's mind that the spirit in this house wants nothing to do with your sister."

"And if she refutes it?"

"That will not be an option available to her. Your sister may be playing a foolish game, but I saw her in Society today and she is a smart young woman. She will not risk the appearance of true madness. She knows what is at stake, and if the ghost renounces her, she shall be hurt-" Althea knew the hurt would be genuine, but, as far as Maybourne was concerned, the hurt could just as likely stem from being thwarted- "but she shall know her duty."

Lord Maybourne was quiet a moment before adding, "And at the end, can you make it seem the ghost is gone? Well and truly gone? I don't want to risk any nonsense about a recantment."

"You wish me to rid this house of the spirit, even once he has rejected Charlotte?"

"I want this whole business over and done with, once and for all."

"I shall do my best," Althea said grimly. She had no intention of driving Ben from the house, of casting him into the Void he spoke of. She only hoped he would understand her plan and play along. All their futures depended upon it.

* * *

"Milady?"

Althea had barely left the Earl's study when Hen appeared. "Yes Henrietta?"

"I've a message for you."

"Yes?" Althea asked, intrigued.

"Aye, milady. From, er, a mutual friend."

Althea knew immediately who she meant. "A, shall we say, very *graceful* shared acquaintance?"

Hen grinned at the hidden meaning. "That's him. He would like to know if you'd care to join him for dinner tonight at eight o'clock?"

Althea enjoyed the formality of asking Hen to give her the particulars. She'd wondered if he meant to simply pop into the air at some hour 'to dine' with her, which had, upon waking, seemed odd as he could not eat. She smiled at Hen. "Let our friend know I'd like that very much."

Henrietta beamed. "I'll collect you at eight o'clock then. Just tell the family you've a headache. They're off to some snobby dinner anyway tonight."

The maid caught herself the moment the words left her mouth. "Begging your pardon. I mean, they're expected at a respectable house this evening."

"I'm sure it will be dreadfully snobby. Consider my head aching to the very devil."

Hen crossed herself at the mention of the prince of darkness, as if playing messenger for an undead Duke wasn't sufficiently blasphemous. "Eight o'clock, milady."

"I'll be ready."

Ben knew it was ridiculous to be nervous. He'd been intimate with many women and it hadn't altered a thing about his opinion of them or, heaven help him, himself.

Granted, those encounters had all been *physically* intimate. He had never been emotionally close to a woman. Or anyone, really, besides his brothers, and those relationships had been tempered by looming dread and heartbreak.

All Aston men had known their fate for generations. A longstanding and horrible family curse made it difficult to foster any real attachments with anyone. It was cruel to love when one know an untimely and usually horrible demise was certain.

Ben had always known the curse would seal his fate. He'd had no desire to fall in love, father children-especially a son- none of it. There was no point in embracing life when he'd been aware since childhood his fate was early, likely awful death. Of course death came for all, but for an Aston man it was particularly gruesome and always too soon. And that was before he'd realized the death itself was only the beginning of the curse.

Each of his forebears had been struck down in their prime, and each in some awful, ironic, dreadful way.

The curse had dictated his life, even before he had understood what it really meant. The curse did not *kill*. It destroyed. It lingered. It punished.

It trapped.

He was trapped, and had been for the better part of a century. He'd long ago railed against his fate, the cruelty of it, the idea that somewhere perhaps his long gone male ancestors persisted, just as he did, entombed between this world and the next.

He would never know, of course. He was stuck in this house. His greatest work and his forever prison.

There was simply no room for intimacy in his life, and never had been.

Which was why the prior evening's activities with Althea shook him to his very core.

That he'd thought to arrange a private dinner with her when he could not even *eat* was merely a testament his growing insanity. For, truly, he must be mad to keep up his… whatever it was… with her.

He'd befriended Charlotte Ridgely out of practicality as much as boredom. She was amusing sometimes, but largely he needed a point of contact with the owners of the house and once he'd realized her role in her brother's schemes, she'd become invaluable. The Earl himself was about as likely to talk to Ben as the local vicar. Charlotte, on the other had, was impressionable, romantic, and most importantly, bored out of her wits. She was an intelligent woman raised beneath her capabilities. She knew it, on some level. It hadn't made her terribly interesting- yet- but Ben suspected that given another decade out in the world Charlotte Ridgely would be a fascinating woman.

Unless some man quashed all the curiosity and wit out of her.

Ben was certain Lord Leslie would accomplish that, if he could. Leslie was just the sort of high-minded, line-toeing peer to believe women were no more than baubles and broodmares. But that was not the only reason Ben disliked the man. His close ties to Wilkes, whose ambitions to destroy Ben's house and therefore Ben were increasingly evident, made Leslie just as much Ben's enemy as the old solicitor.

The high, delicate chimes of a small bell rang up and into the attic. It was Ben's sign that dinner was served.

He shoved down the ghostly butterflies that had

suddenly taken flight in his stomach, and envisioned Althea's sitting room. A moment later, he was there.

She was sitting at the little table in the center of the room. A beautiful array of food was laid out before her, and a shimmering goblet filled with rich, red wine. A single blood red rose bloomed from a crystal vase at the table's center, its petals echoing the color of Althea's crimson-stained lips.

Ben floated into the middle of the room, beside the empty chair across from her.

"Sit, please," she gestured to the polished mahogany chair.

"As the lady wishes," Ben murmured, feeling suddenly like a schoolboy meeting a famed courtesan. Not that Althea was a member of the demimonde. No, it was just that she radiated an assured, sensual confidence he'd only ever seen on harlots of the highest order. Masters of their craft. She had clearly enjoyed their interlude the evening before. She was glowing and had clearly dressed to impress, but there was something more between them, a sort of magnetic thrum of energy in the room that he knew was not his doing at all.

She shifted in her seat, the only sign that she, too, might be nervous.

Which was preposterous. They were both adults

fully grown with ample experience between them, and besides, this was merely dinner.

A dinner he couldn't even eat, because he was dead.

There was no future here. There was not even the possibility of a proper fuck. This was all mere imagination and sentimentality, nothing more.

"You look stunning," he said into the taut silence.

Althea's lips twisted up at the edges and she blushed, the effect making her more beautiful than he'd ever seen her, even last night. She was so happy to see him, and, god help him, he was delighted to be with her.

The butterflies in his stomach multiplied.

"Thank you. I accompanied Charlotte to Bond Street earlier and I suppose it inspired me to try something new." She gestured to her hair, which to his shame, Ben had not even registered. It was curled more than usual and arranged in a complicated updo he had no doubt Charlotte's ladies' maid had been coopted into crafting.

"It's lovely. And the dress, did you purchase it today?"

"No, I've had this one for years, but it still suffices."

Suffice was not what the dress was doing in Ben's

opinion. The bodice was not cut particularly low, nor was the midnight blue silk notably thin, but the cut of the dress rendered all such considerations moot. It was draped and tucked to perfection, every inch of the fine, thin fabric molded to either hint at or accentuate the very best of Althea's figure. She knew it, too. Her eyes glimmered wickedly at him in the candlelight.

The butterflies plummeted, becoming a growing heaviness in his cock.

His cock, which did not really exist. Which could not actually enter the beautiful body across from his, over and over, until he brought them both to sublime, unimaginable pleasure.

"Are you alright?"

Ben blinked, and cleared his throat. "Yes, I- I just realized how awkward it was of me to invite you to dinner when I myself cannot eat."

She laughed, the sound caressing him like champagne bubbles on bare skin. "I did think it an unusual choice of activity, but then, there's nothing about our activities that is usual, is there?"

He knew she hadn't meant to allude to the night before, in the bath. But both their minds went there at once.

Her blush deepened. Good lord, she was so beautiful. Striking in general, yes, but the more alive she became the more glorious she was. Nothing like most of the women he'd known. She was like a creature of Greek myth, a nymph perhaps. A goddess of darkness and shadow, overlooked by those who sought only the day but radiant by anyone who knew the light of the moon.

Althea's black eyes met his. "Do you mind if I begin? I'm famished. Charlotte took me to Gunter's but that was hours ago, and even then, it was only ice."

Ben straightened. "Of course. Please, dine. I shall- well, what shall I do while you eat? Dance a jig? Recite Latin verse? Tell me about the time my younger brother tried to ride a pig into the village to impress the butcher's daughter but both he and the pig *and* then the butcher's daughter fell into the river? They were all fine, by the way. Just very muddy."

Althea laughed, but said, "Tell me how you died."

The candles in the room flickered as Ben's heart stuttered. Curious, he thought, it did not beat, but it could falter.

As if sensing her error, Althea's smile dropped. "I'm sorry. You don't have to, I only-"

She looked down at the still steaming meal of roast chicken and creamed potatoes before her. "When I was out with Charlotte today I realized she knows more about you than I do."

"Are you jealous?" The words were quiet but landed between them like an anvil. Althea's answer was even quieter.

"Yes."

Something that felt like hope but couldn't be bloomed in Ben's chest. He saw two paths before him. One was rational and safe. The other led to only to madness and ruin.

Already being dead, he chose the latter.

"What do you wish to know about me? Besides my death. I'll get to that, but I'd rather begin on a more pleasant topic."

Althea put a perfectly cut piece of chicken in her mouth and chewed while she thought. Ben watched her lips and wished, again, he had a body. Mostly specifically a cock, as she slowly brought the rim of her goblet to her lips and drank, wine glistening on the blood red stain of her bottom lip.

Then, deep in thought and unaware of where his treacherous, filthy mind had wandered, she licked that bottom lip.

His phantom cock jerked traitorously.

"Tell me about your family. Did you really have a brother who tried to ride a pig into the village and fell into the river?"

Grateful for a new direction for this thoughts, Ben smiled. "I did. Montague. Two years my junior and the biggest hellion of the lot."

"There were more of you?"

"I have-" Ben paused to correct himself, an old wound twinging somewhere deep inside, "*had* three brothers. My elder brother Peregrine was a god to me. He was only a year older than I was, but I followed him around so closely the household simply referred to me as his shadow."

"Did he mind?"

Ben's smile deepened, old memories rushing back to him. "Perry was happy about it, I think. Ours was a lonely childhood, and he assumed the title at too young an age. He was like a little man when I was still very much a boy. I didn't badger him too much, and I think he was grateful for the companionship."

"Did your father die young, then, for Perry to become Duke so soon?"

Ben felt the shadows cross his features. More memories, dark ones, crowded in. "My father lived long enough to father four sons then perished. It's, ah, part of the curse. All the men in my family are cursed. Most only manage one son. My father was the most prolific Duke of Stafford since the curse began. Four sons, all of us cursed just as he was."

Althea paused, fork in hand. "I don't understand. This curse that keeps you here, it isn't just yours? It's inherited?"

Ben took a long, slow breath. "I suppose I might as well tell you."

Althea sat back. "You don't have to, if it's painful."

"Well Charlotte doesn't know, not the details."

He watched with smug, purely male satisfaction as her better nature fought with her envy of Charlotte Ridgely.

Finally, she said, "You don't have to tell me."

"Ah, but I think I shall."

The look on her face was indecipherable as she said, "Alright."

Ben longed for a glass of wine of his own, to sip slowly and steady his thoughts. Instead, he merely leaned back and closed his eyes, one long dark lock of ghostly hair falling limp across his brow. He didn't bother to move it.

"I am the fifteenth Duke of Stafford. It was the eighth Duke that started the trouble. All the men of my line have been wretched. We came over with the Conqueror, apparently endeared ourselves to him with our insatiable appetites for both blood and pleasure. Before you knew it we went from knights to Dukes."

"That doesn't sound so bad."

Ben peeked open one eye. "It wasn't our efforts in battle and politics that damned us. It was the special ability of my ancestors, and, for better or worse, my former self, to have an exceedingly good time."

Althea lifted her goblet of wine and took what Ben could only describe as a *swig*. She set the vessel down with a heavy thud. "Still doesn't sound curse-worthy to me. I was born on the wrong side of the blanket and raised on the wrong side of town, by anyone's measure. A few rich men whoring and boozing hardly seems a dire sin."

"There were certainly worse men in the kingdom."

"And women, too. Don't forget we can be terrible, we just tend to hide it better."

"Fair enough," Ben demurred, wishing more than ever he had a goblet of his own to swirl as he used to during such conversations. "But even minor transgressions can be serious when the wrong person is aggravated."

"And who did the eighth Duke aggravate? Must have been a witch if she cursed him."

"She was. But worse, she was a queen."

Althea's brows rose. "*A queen* cursed you? Don't tell me Queen Mab. Ghosts and curses and witchcraft I can allow, but if this is some yarn about the fairy folk being real too…"

Ben chuckled. "As far as I know *they* are merely folk tales. Not that I'd bet on it. I've seen enough strange things in life to believe nearly anything is possible."

"I'm beginning to agree with that."

"Well, the rest of this story won't dissuade you. The queen in question was Anne Boleyn."

Althea nearly dropped her fork. "The wife of Henry VIII?"

"That one."

Althea's brow furrowed. "There have always been rumors she was a witch, with six fingers and all that, but I assumed it was all just an attempt to ruin her name."

"I can't speak to the fingers bit, but whatever else was said of her she was uncommonly skilled at witchcraft."

Ben watched as Althea considered the information, then he continued. "The eighth Duke of Stafford was a profligate lover, as was Anne. They apparently fell in together immediately behind Henry's back, which was obviously a dangerous choice to begin with."

Althea leaned back and took a bite of fresh bread slathered with salted butter. "Not a wise choice."

"It gets worse. Dear old Thomas- that was his

name, Thomas- and Anne had a great deal in common, including a penchant for jealousy. One night she left his bed, only to realize a few minutes later she'd left her favorite bejeweled hairclip in his rooms. Not only was it evidence of their affair, but also a gift from her husband- and encrusted with a king's ransom of rubies."

"Oh dear," Althea muttered, seeing where this was going.

Ben nodded in confirmation. "Though only a few minutes had passed, when she returned he was already back in bed with not one but *two* of her ladies in waiting and the footman who stoked the castle fires."

"You didn't tell me you came from a line of such ambitious men."

Ben huffed a surprised laugh. "That is one way of looking at it, and not the way Anne saw things. Worse, when he saw her standing there glowering at him, he asked her to join them. She was livid, and that night, under the light of the full moon, she cursed him and every male in his line forevermore."

"So the female children are safe?"

"There haven't been any," Ben pushed against more memories, the most painful of them all. "Not that survived into childhood, anyway."

"How dreadful. Do you know what she did? What the curse actually is? It must be on a scroll or tablet or something."

"It was a spell, a few lines long. Every man in my family knows it by heart. Would you like to hear it?"

"I think I should don't you? Unless it's bad to, you know, say it aloud."

"Oh, no, the words are meaningless unless you're a witch and have all the bits and bobs and everything she used to cast the thing."

Ben took a deep breath, then recited the words that had haunted him his entire life:

"As found is found thus bound is bound,
Unto the wicked heartless wound,
Where no thought is given forth
Forever thinking, trapped is worth
After this life before the next
All male souls of the line be hexed
Equal in sin and unknown of love's call
Shall forever be
So binds these words vexed
Trapped in limbo
Never to rest."

The moment he finished the words the fire went out and every candle in the room was extinguished by a phantom wind.

Althea gasped. "Well that did *something.*"

"Parlor tricks," Ben muttered, but he wasn't so sure. It had been along time since he'd heard the words uttered aloud, and now that he thought on it, he wasn't sure he had ever spoken them aloud himself. "As dinner here seems to be finished, would you like a private tour of the house? We have a good while before the Ridgelys return and the servants will all be minding their own affairs at this hour."

"I thought I'd seen the whole house, but if you think there's something specific you'd like to show me, I have a lot of questions about it. It is a beautiful home. The most beautiful I've ever been in."

Pride swelled in Ben's chest. "It is my second greatest accomplishment."

"What was your first?" she asked.

A voice in Ben's mind told him not to say it. Told him such revelations were too close to intimacy, too dangerous to share.

He ignored the voice.

"My daughter," he said.

Chapter Thirteen
The Sitting Room

Althea froze. "Your daughter? I thought you said-"

The look in his eyes stopped her as his words from moments ago filled her mind. *Not that survived into childhood, anyway.*

"I'm so sorry," she said, her heart aching for him. "What happened?"

They both knew he did not have to answer, but he did anyway. "She was born six months after I died. This existence was new to me and I was so angry, so utterly bitter, then she came into the world."

"What was her name?"

"Liza. She was called Liza." His eyes had settled on the fire across the room, but his gaze was distant, on the past. "From the first she was the sweetest thing I had ever known. I spent every moment with her, and when we were alone, I let her see me. Know me, if it is possible for a babe to know anything."

"They know love," Althea said quietly.

The corners of Ben's eyes shimmered and he nodded. "She was so smart and curious, far more so than her mother realized."

Something cold and heavy sank Althea's gut. She had not even thought to ask, but obviously the child had a mother. "Who was she? Your mistress?"

"My wife."

It was ridiculous to feel shock at the words. He was, or had been, a duke. Marriage was not an option for such men. Besides, the woman was long dead now, if it mattered. Which it didn't, because Ben was dead, too. Althea had even less reason to envy a dead woman than she had to envy Charlotte Ridgely. Besides, Althea was not given to envy, it was useless and unbecoming.

And yet... she needed to know. "Did you love her?" The words were out before she could stop herself.

"No." Ben's answer was sure and swift and Althea hated that it pleased her. "Ours was a marriage of political convenience, nothing more. Exactly as I wanted it."

"I see."

"That being said, I could have chosen better," Ben said, almost to himself. "Miriam was beautiful and I was young and an idiot. I did not realize she would be so volatile, and that I, being a selfish cad, should have chosen a woman with a more forgiving nature."

"You hold it against her that she was not a doormat?"

Ben chuckled. "I'm sorry if it sounds that way. No,

I was not a good person then and certainly had no understanding of women, but she was vicious. Always jealous, often violent. I did my best to protect Liza from her worst outbursts, but I did not always succeed."

There was such darkness in his words Althea did not know what to say, how to comfort a man who carried such burdens of guilt and shame. She longed to reach out and simply touch his hand, but that was impossible.

Ben took a deep breath. "Liza was two when it happened. She and Miriam were living in this house at the behest of Monty, who'd assumed the title upon my death. Miriam was throwing a party downstairs, indulging in her reputation as a beautiful, tragic widow. Every man took pity on her and she enjoyed it, enjoyed them. Which was exactly what I would have done in her place, at the time."

Althea waited, dread mounting.

"Upstairs, Liza woke in the night. I was with her as she escaped her room, looking for her nursemaids, her mother, anyone. She was crying. A nightmare, I think. I was visible to her, I know I was, but she ignored me. She needed warmth, you see, and human embrace. Neither of which could I give her. I was only a phantom, much like the nightmares she ran from."

"Oh, Ben," Althea murmured. "That's not true."

His voice grew more ragged with feeling. "It is. She ran into the hall and heard the party downstairs. She was so small, so uncoordinated, and the stairs- she-"

He could not finish, and he didn't have to. Althea guessed what had happened, even as he sobbed, reliving the memory for her. Opening this wound, for her. Althea felt tears running down her own cheeks and she longed to hold him.

After a few moments, he spoke again, still not looking at her, still lost in the flickering dance of the fire, of the past. "I was so helpless. I could have stopped it. I should have stopped it. If I'd been there, if I'd been alive- I-"

"There was nothing you could do," Althea said softly. "It isn't your fault you were cursed."

She wanted to say more, to offer greater comfort, to tell him how lucky he was to have known his daughter at all, even in half-life, but she knew there was no comfort. He'd known the worst pain imaginable, and lived with it for over eighty years, alone. She could not fathom what he had endured.

"Isn't it though?" he asked, finally turning back to her, his translucent face iridescent with tears. "The curse isn't just about dying early or being trapped. It is a lesson to each of us. Every man in my family dies because of his greatest fault. If he is reckless, he died racing. If he is unfaithful, his mistress gives him the pox. If he believes himself the best, he dies trying to prove it."

"That does not sound like a curse, Ben. It sounds like consequences."

Ben shook his head, his dark hair loose around his face. "But they are dramatic, unusual deaths. They prove a point. One of my ancestors was struck by lighting, another impaled by his own sword while drunk."

"Odd, but it happens."

"In front of the King. And he was naked."

"That is…" Althea let that picture form in her mind. "I believe you. But you cannot possibly have been so terrible to deserve this yourself."

His answering laugh was low and bitter. "I have never trusted anyone."

"I do not trust easily, either, but that is often wise. Not a flaw."

"Not the way I did it. Come, I'll show you."

He rose from the chair, hovering before her, the faint outline of his boots a few inches above the carpet. Althea stood and followed him, as he opened the door with a thought and the candles in the hall flickered to life at his whim.

"I was going to show you the house as I hoped it would be seen." His voice was cold and bitter, but Althea knew whatever he was about to share with her was just as important as what he'd told her of his daughter. "But perhaps it's better someone see it for what it truly is."

"A masterpiece?"

He shot her a look of contempt, the feeling directed not at her, but himself. "The work of a monster. A man so focused on control, on perfection, that nothing else mattered."

They continued down the hall, then down the stairs, as he went on. "I entered Oxford early, same year as Perry, but then I left early too. I knew I wanted to study architecture, to build something that would last."

"Because of the curse?"

"Yes," his voice was a growl, "We'd watched out father die in front of us, we all knew our fates, and we all dealt it it in our own way. Perry grew callous and cruel, dedicated only to hunting and whoring, distancing himself from the rest of us as we came of age. My younger brother Monty was reckless and uncontrollable, an unrepentant rake even at sixteen. The fourth, Heath, was much younger, and watched in horror as his only kin became self-indulgent monsters.

I will never know what became of him, of any of them, except Perry. He died, obviously, two years before I did. His heart gave out while fucking another man's wife."

"Is he a ghost?"

"No idea. None of us knew this was part of it, so I never thought to go to the place he died and find out."

Althea wondered if, perhaps, she could do that. If that would make things better... or worse. She would not mention it now, though. For now she would let Ben voice these memories she suspected he had not shared in decades. If ever.

"Anyway, I dropped out of Oxford as soon as I'd learned what I needed about English building. I'd gotten it into my head to see the world, to try and find a way to break the curse and maybe live a little along the way. Learn about other forms architectural. Other cultures. To be honest, other women. I was voracious for life, and I wanted it all for myself. I took everything I could, and never gave anything back."

"You were young."

Ben scoffed. "I was an idiot. My father had tried to break the curse, gathering books and artifacts of occult knowledge, but one of those antiques got him killed. I decided to go to the source- for all the reasons I just stated. I spent four years traveling, and only stopped because Perry died. As soon as I became Duke I married Miriam and decided to build a monument of my own. This house was to be only the first of many, an experiment. That's why it's so small."

Althea kept her surprise from her face. To consider this house *small* was a testament to the privilege into which Ben had been born. Privilege she should remember. They would not have been meant for each other even if he were alive. Putting the thought away for later, she followed him down the next flight of stairs, towards the ground floor.

"I did most of this myself, you know," Ben gestured at the stairwell, the house, around them. "I hired some labor, of course, but I was here every day, from dawn until dusk, working alongside them, insisting on doing the most important parts myself. I'd learned early on to do anything important yourself, not to rely on others. Others could not be trusted."

"What about your duties as Duke? Didn't you have other business to attend to? The House of Lords?"

"I didn't give a shit about any of that. I knew my days were numbered, and I wanted to leave something behind. It never occurred to me that a healthy estate and happy tenants was a legacy, too. I thought only of grandeur, of proving my will and power in the world."

They reached the entryway at the foot of the stairs. Althea felt the pain, old and long-tethered, roiling off him. "How did you die, Ben?"

Darkness flickered across his face. "I never considered the house finished, because the final piece was delayed. A custom-built chandelier I had ordered from the most exclusive glassmaker in Italy. A year after schedule, it arrived. And I insisted on installing it myself."

"Oh no."

"Yes. I was a fool. I'd let myself dissipate once I came into the title. I was only twenty-four and physically strong from the hard labor, but I was tyrant by day and a heathen by night. I was in terrible shape, drinking at all hours, bedding a different woman every evening. Miriam was rightly furious and made my life hell when she was around, as if it were much better when she wasn't. I was obsessed with the house and still devastated by Perry's death."

He was speaking quickly now, urgently, and Althea wished more than ever before that she could reach out and *touch* him.

"I gave into my worst impulses, pursuing all my favorite vices to furthest degree. I lived in shame, tightening the leash of control on myself and everyone around me so taut some of my servants fled without even asking for references. I needed to be aware of everything at all times. I couldn't stop shouting, or drinking. My mind, it- it was this constant roaring- I-"

He crumpled to the floor, kneeling as his ephemeral form hovered just above the fibers of the opulent carpet. "When the chandelier came, I wasn't relieved. I was furious. It had taken so long, and I had let myself veer so far from my original vision- the house had been a dream, a thing of beauty and wonder, and I'd let it ruin me. *I'd* ruined me. Everything became so twisted and I thought if I could just finish this one last piece, if I could only put the final touch, somehow everything would be set to rights. I could defeat the curse. I could stop living in *fear*."

Althea's heart ached for him. For the man who'd spent his life with this strange, terrible burden, losing so much at such a young age. She knew what that was like, the loss, but to know you were doomed to never escape the pain, to be lost yourself...

When Ben continued, his voice was barely a whisper. "So I refused to let the few workmen who still tolerated me assist in hanging it. I made them stand by while I rigged the ladders to hang the chandelier myself. Miriam was screaming at me, furious because I'd bedded her best friend the night before, and I was drunk. Blind drunk, and unable to trust anyone. Not for advice, not for help. For nothing. I had to finish the house myself, and the chandelier was the final piece. I wouldn't let it wait, and I don't know if it would have mattered, at that moment my every waking hour was just as terrible as that one, final moment."

"Oh, no," Althea breathed, kneeling on the floor beside him.

"I was balanced feet from the ceiling, the workmen hauling a rope to raise the chandelier to me so I could fasten it to the ceiling. One of them sneezed, *sneezed*, from the damned dust no doubt, and I lost it. I lost my bloody mind. I turned to scream at him, just as the chandelier reached my hands. I was so upset, so beside myself, I lost my balance. I reached for the chandelier but it swayed, knocking me off the ladder, and I fell."

Althea's heart hammered in her chest, but she already knew the ending of the story.

"I died instantly, at least. Broken back. One moment I was falling, shouting curses at everyone, and the next everything was black. I was in an empty space, only my screaming echoing around me, a golden light breaking through the fog, but before it cleared I felt a sort of pull, like a rope around my waist, and I was catapulted back here. A ghost."

"How awful."

"It was. I was floating over everyone as they crowded around my body. I started screaming at them again, terrified, furious, but I knew what had happened. My own pride, my damned stupid desire for control, my insistence to never trust anyone, had killed me. Just like the curse wanted."

They sat for a moment, side by side in the empty foyer, in silence, looking up at the hole in the entryway ceiling. It was still there, a symbol lost on the rest of the household, forever reminding Ben of his failures.

Althea didn't care if the family came back or the servants stumbled in. She could think only of Ben and what he'd been through, of the remarkable man he was now.

Because she knew he *was* remarkable. He was so kind now, so thoughtful and patient. The man he described in life sounded like a stranger. Death had changed him, in more ways than he seemed to realize.

She decided maybe it was time he knew her, too. "I don't trust anybody, either," she said, running a finger along the polished tiles of the floor. "My father was a marquess. He promised my mother, who was a vicar's daughter in our village, that he would marry her. But

263

he lied."

Ben glanced at her, understanding in his dusky blue eyes. "I'm sorry."

Althea nodded. She hadn't told anyone this before. Never once. "My mother had to flee, to a gentleman's house in another county, where she took on a different name and worked as a scullery maid. That's where I was born. In the countryside."

"It was beautiful, but when I was fourteen the gentleman took notice of me, and we fled again before anything could happen."

"Fourteen," Ben sighed. "So damned young. Did you understand what was happening?"

"I knew he spoke to me too much, but it wasn't until he tried to lock himself in a room with me that I understood the danger. We came to London, and met Madame Veira."

"Ah."

Althea nodded. "My mother was very superstitious and went to her for help. Madame Veira knew we needed more than palm readings and tarot. She took us in, and just in time, because my mother caught a fever a few weeks later and died. Nora raised me. She taught me how to make a living helping people hear what they needed to hear, see what they wanted to see. Like you, I learned to only rely on myself. Nora always warned me one day she would be gone, too, so I became my own woman. I did not mind the lying, the fraud, the immorality of it all, because it made people happy, and for me, it was better than the street. Better than becoming the whore my mother never wanted me to be. If it weren't for her, I would have taken that path years ago. I'm far too lazy for housework."

She smiled ruefully at the thought. It was true. She'd seen her mother break herself as a scullery maid, and Althea knew she would have taken to the life of the demimonde in a heartbeat to escape it.

"You'd have made a great man a fine mistress," Ben murmured, then hurried to add, "Or a wife."

She shook her head. "I never wanted to be a wife. I never wanted to belong to any man."

"That's why you hate the aristocracy," Ben said quietly. "Your father. And the other gentleman."

Althea did not answer. She did not have to.

Ben glanced up at the hole in the ceiling that had been the end of him, then at the floor, where Althea realized he must have fallen. Exactly where they sat now.

Calm now, he floated up to stand. "Well that wasn't exactly a tour of the house, but I hope you understand it better now."

She got to her feet. "I still think it's a masterpiece, Ben."

He swallowed hard, avoiding her gaze. "Come, there is one more thing I want to show you."

The sensation Ben was again on the horse from last night was back. Instead of an untamed stallion, however, it was now a gentle mare. He did not wish to get off it, even as he knew it would lead him to disaster just the same.

He felt raw, torn open, but his confessions to Althea. Remade by her confessions in return. They could not be more opposite in the eyes of the world, and yet he knew their wounds were mirrors.

She followed him in silence down the hall until they reached the bolted door.

"The sitting room?"

He turned to her in surprise. "You know it?"

"Goggins told me that's what it was called, before it was closed up."

"The first Earl of Maybourne to own the house didn't like it, and instead of letting him change it, I, shall we say, convinced him to leave it alone."

"You scared him out of his mind?"

Ben grinned. "Something like that. Now only I can open it, not that anyone dares."

A tip of his head and a little flash of willpower, and the locks holding the metal bindings of the door shut sprung open. With a mighty creak, the door opened. Beyond, dust-covered candles and the long-unused fireplace, void of wood, sprung to life.

"What's it like? Doing magic?" Althea asked, poised behind him in the doorway.

"It's just like thinking. I will something, and it happens. Some things don't work, but I generally can move objects and affect forces of nature, fire and wind and light. I can't mess with time or read minds or anything like that, though."

"Thank god," Althea teased.

Ben stifled the sudden, overwhelming urge to kiss her. It was impossible. It was- she caught the look in his eye, as if *she* could read minds. Blushing, she looked away, into the room beyond the door.

"Let me see this mysterious room. Goggins said the title sitting room was ironic, given it's-"

She followed Ben through the doorway and froze. "Size," she finished limply, in awe of the space.

Ben shut the door behind her, so no one would disturb them. Giving her a moment to take it all in.

The room was, of all the house, his true masterpiece. A wall of mirrors ran along one side of the massive, long chamber. Modeled after his brief time in the French court, it made the room seem even larger than it already was.

Two stories in height, equality tall windows lined the far wall. Now they looked straight into Lord Leslie's townhome mere feet away, but when Ben had built the place, he'd owned that lot, too, and had plans to transform it into a rose garden. Miriam had sold it off almost immediately and pocketed the money, before Montague had even known about it. Not that it mattered now, the windows were all boarded up anyway.

The ceiling was painted by a master from Rome, one of the few key elements of the house Ben had not personally participated in creating. A clear blue sky with swirling clouds, a faint, full moon just visible high amongst them, as sometimes happened in reality. His favorite sort of day. Full of possibility.

He had not experienced such a day in a lifetime.

"Oh, Ben. It's stunning," Althea breathed, admiring the intricately inlaid wood floor, made to look like leaves and vines. She turned towards the gilt fireplace, carved like the open mouth of an ancient god, some pan expelling fire or devouring it, it was impossible to tell. Covered in gold, the grotesque, otherworldly face flickered in the light and looked as if it moved.

Liza had been terrified of the fireplace. Ben had felt

a little guilty about that, but he loved it. It transported whoever beheld it into a world where anything was possible, whether that meant gods sprung from the earth, or else, one could simply indulge in a highly nontraditional fireplace.

Both thoughts excited him.

Then Althea's gaze reached the portrait above the fireplace, and she stilled.

"It's you." She turned to him, then back to the portrait. "And your brothers."

It wasn't a question, but then, he did not have to answer. The truth was obvious. Four young men, boys, really, all dressed in the finery of a century past, stared down at them with haughty disdain.

"That was painted when I was fifteen. I'm on the right. Perry was sixteen, in the center. He takes after our mother, with the olive skin and calculating look in his eye."

Althea smiled. "I'm sure she was beautiful."

"She was. But she abandoned us when our father died. Left Perry in charge of Monty and I. That's Monty there, on Perry's other side."

"He must take after your father. His hair is lighter, and so are his eyes."

"Very good. Yes, he does. The best looking of the lot of us, too."

Althea shot him a glance. "You're *all* very attractive. Doesn't seem fair to all be dukes *and* devastatingly handsome, does it?"

It was Ben's turn to blush. "Devastating, am I?"

Althea shrugged. "Let's say you are uncommonly bearable in appearance."

Ben chuckled. "Well, remember we're all cursed to the ruddy devil here, so don't be too envious of us."

"I'm not," Althea said simply. "Who is the little boy? Heath?"

"Yes. Our mother gave birth to him after she left us, and one day sent him to our doorstep with a note and our father's signet ring. You can see the family resemblance. We all knew he was legitimate."

"And cursed, too."

"And cursed, too."

Althea bit her lip, deep in thought. "Are they ghosts too then? All of them? Or did they break the curse?"

"I have no idea," Ben answered sadly. "I like to think Monty and Heath came to a better end, but I doubt it."

For a long moment Althea and Ben stared up at the portrait, lost in their own thoughts.

Finally, Althea spoke. "Did you kill the boy in the attic? The one Mr. Firth told us about?"

"No," Ben's answer was swift and quiet. Sad. "It's an ugly story. The boys were so deep in their cups they could barely climb the stairs. Idiots, that's all they were. Young and stupid. The little lord and his servant friends out for a lark to cause trouble. I tried to scare them off, but the smallest one, a kitchen boy, I think, pissed himself at the sight of me. The others laughed and jeers him so fiercely no one remembered I was there, and the little one went mad. I've never seen anything like it. He attacked the others, and pushed the little lord through the window."

"That's horrible."

"It was."

Althea looked back to the floor. "I'm sorry I asked."

Ben shrugged. "I'd want to know if I were you. I'd hate to be involved with a murderer and not know it."

Her head flew up. "Involved?"

"Aren't we?"

She swallowed, her eyes suddenly wary. "I need you end things with Charlotte."

"I can't do that. If she marries anyone, the house's fate is uncertain. *My* fate is uncertain. If she marries Leslie, which she almost certainly will, our fate is sealed. Wilkes wants this house demolished. To build something new, something fresh he can offer supercilious lordlings for a king's ransom. He can convince Leslie to tear down his townhouse, too, and build a palace here fit for a king. He doesn't care about craftsmanship. This place is falling apart, and he knows it. Leslie seems like he doesn't need the coin, but all men are greedy."

Ben looked up at the portrait, at the young man he had once been. "Believe me, I know. We cannot let them have it. Charlotte cannot marry."

"You will leave me destitute."

Her voice was quiet, but carried through still air.

"I cannot do it, Althea."

He saw the resolve forming in her, some inner workings of her mind. He wanted to trust her, but he knew he could not, just as she could never trust him. He didn't blame her. He knew he was horrible to deny her, but she was just as stubborn in holding her own ground.

"I can get you the money you need," he said, floating closer to her. "Do you have any idea what's in the attic of this place? The secret cubbies I hid treasures from around the world? Maybourne has no idea that this place is full of wealth. Neither does Charlotte. But it's mine. Not theirs. I can give it to you."

Althea's lip turned up ruefully. "But it *is* theirs, Ben. You do not exist."

"We can find a way, for both of us. I promise."

He mere inches away now, her face upturned and her eyes suddenly aware, desperate. For truth, for safety, for him, he did not know. All of it, perhaps.

Unable to help himself he leaned forward and-

And floated straight through her.

"Ah!" she screamed and stumbled forward, away from him. "I'm sorry, I- I'm just startled, that's all. I didn't know what would happen."

"No, no I apologize. I shouldn't have-"

"I wish you could."

Their gazes locked them, the fire from the night before flaring to life again.

"Last night you asked for just one night, Ben. Tonight, it is my turn to ask. Just one more."

He did not have to think twice. "Of course. I'll-"

Ben stopped. *He'd what?* What could he do? What could *they* do?

"I can read the book again, if you like."

"I know you weren't reading the book. That was just you, what you imagined. What you wanted."

"Your eyes were closed."

She grinned. "I peeked."

Ben chuckled. "Dear god, woman! What are we going to do? How are two people supposed to have a perfectly decent affair when they cannot even kiss?"

"You built this whole fantastic house and I- I invent realities for a living, I'm sure we can come up with something." She looked around the room as if the answer was going to pop out at her. "Your only pleasure comes from the mind, the imagination, so that should be easy."

Ben snorted. "Isn't that the hard part?"

She gave him a withering look. "Men are such basic creatures. Sex is about more than mechanics. It's about energy, life itself, two-"

"Don't say souls."

"Yes, *souls*. When it's really good."

"It can still be pretty good even if it's just mechanical." The moment the words were out of his mouth, Ben remembered something. "Althea, open that cabinet there, between the two windows."

She shot him a skeptical look but did as he asked. The tall wooden armoire did not want to open at first, but after a firm tug its hinges gave way. Inside were shelves lined with artifacts from around the world.

"Are these the treasures you'd like me to steal?"

"They're mine, so yes, take whatever you like. But no- that's not why I wanted you to open it. Look at the third shelf, yes, there. Do you know what that is?"

Althea had never seen anything like the object Ben

indicated in person, but she knew exactly what it was. "Of course. It's a dildo. But I've never seen one in silver."

"Sterling. I purchased it in France. They were all the rage amongst the ladies at court, and more than a few of the men."

A nervous thrill fluttered through Althea. "You want me to… use… that?"

"I want you to go pull the sheet off that settee and lay down on it."

Excitement coursed through Althea as she did exactly as Ben asked. She had, strangely enough, brought him to climax to the evening before. It seemed he had found a way to return the favor.

Pushing aside the part of her mind that told her this was a terrible idea in so many ways- not the least being he still refused to assist her with the Earl's assignment- she pulled the sheet covering the settee he indicated off and lay down on the soft velvet cushioning.

"Don't move," Ben commanded, sounding more ducal than ever. He floated over to the settee, hovering just above her, only his torso visible, as though he straddled her body. Althea struggled to keep her breath even, controlled. She had no idea what he was planning but the anticipation was untenable.

He raised one hand and the sound of a drawer opening somewhere in the room echoed. A moment later, a feather quill floated over the back of the settee and stopped, just where Ben's hand hovered above Althea. He lowered his hand just as the quill moved lower.

Althea closed her eyes just as the gentle brush of the feathers danced across her neck, from the base of her ear to the tender spot where her neck and shoulder met.

She moaned, already wet for him. For the impossible. Because it was not his touch, not his hand holding the feather.

But he controlled it, and he wanted to give her this. She would take it.

He teased her, stroking her with the feather along her ear, her neck, her collarbone.

"Sit up," he commanded. She obeyed and watched as another drawer, this one on a side table near the door, opened to reveal a long forgotten cravat. "I always kept spares around the house. I never knew when I might need to exercise a little… restraint."

Althea would have laughed as his meaning became clear, but her heart was pounding too fast, the sensation was too delicious as he willed the strip of linen to cover her eyes and tie itself gently behind her head.

"Now roll over," he ordered. She turned and fell onto her stomach. First, the ribbons at the back of her gown slowly undid themselves, then the ties of her corset beneath. A moment later, the expanse of her back was laid bare to him, to the feather he so deftly manipulated across her bare skin.

Her breathing grew ragged, as much from anticipation of his next move as the simple, divine pleasure of the sensations he created. There was nothing but him, his will and the feather's touch, in this moment. The blindfold shut out everything but the feeling of his ministrations and the sound of their breathing, heavy with need.

Althea fought the urge to writhe, to feel him, to press herself against him. He wasn't there. None of this was real, and yet it was more tangible pleasure than she'd ever felt in her life. But it was just the lightest touch, the simplest brush of softness on bare flesh…

Then she felt her skirts move. She did not turn, did not need to look. She knew what he planned, and heaven help her, she wanted it.

As the hem of her skirts lifted past her thighs, moving higher still, baring her to him, she felt the cool night air like another caress. She was breathing hard now, and to her satisfaction, so was he. They were both in this moment, in what it represented, together. Unable to truly consummate whatever this strange, new intimacy was between them, they could share its closest approximation.

"Do you want me to continue?" Ben asked, his voice low and ragged.

Her answer was immediate and sure. "Yes."

She felt the air itself wrap around her, raising her hips, baring her entirely to him, where she could hear him as he hovered in the air behind her prone body.

The feather was there a moment later, caressing her womanhood in light, sensual touches. Althea bit the palm of her hand to keep from crying out at the pleasure of it.

"Good girl," Ben purred, "You're ready for me?"

Althea nodded, not daring to release her hand.

The sensation changed then, the soft warmth of the feather replaced by something hard. It was not cool, like she expected. He must have warmed it somehow, to a comfortable heat.

The sterling silver dildo moved along her cleft, too unyielding to belong to a man of flesh and blood, but then, it didn't. It belonged to Ben.

Gently its tip circled her clitoris, her pleasure building and swirling around her. She moaned,

writing now. She couldn't help it. Ben's breath was
ragged behind her. He was ready, and she was, too.

The dildo shifted, positioning itself at her opening.
She moaned, wordlessly begging for release. For this.
For him.

With a gasp of his own, he pushed the silver
instrument into her, filling her to the hilt.

Althea screamed, her hand barely muffling the
sound. She knew Ben was half mad with pleasure too,
knew he was imagining himself inside her even as she
did the same. He moved the dildo out almost to the
tip, then plunged it back in again.

Althea thought she'd known pleasure before, but
just as the night before, the mind was the greatest
erotic instrument of all. They had bared themselves to
each other tonight, not in the same way they'd shared
their desires the night before, but more fully. They'd
shared their secrets. These two people who had never
trusted another soul had offered one another their
wounds, their vulnerabilities, their souls.

The thought came just as Althea's pleasure peaked,
casting her into a boundless sea of sensation. She let
go of control, let go of anything but the thought of
Ben, and she let herself fall, her body shaking,
wracked with the force of her climax. Behind her, she
heard Ben shout as he met his own.

This time he did not leave her, though. This time, when she finally stopped trembling and her breathing returned to normal, when she rolled over and pulled the blindfold from her eyes, he was still there. Beside her. Watching her in the firelight in this strange, wondrous room in the magnificent, singular house.

Their gazes locked in wordless understanding. Neither of them willing to put words to the feeling, they simply sat together, until Althea drifted to sleep.

Neither of them aware that beyond the door, Charlotte Ridgely was listening, coming to a realization of her own.

Chapter Fourteen
The Reckoning

The next morning Althea awoke well after breakfast had come and gone. Stomach growling, Althea dragged herself into her dressing gown and over to the little table in the sitting room where a thoughtful maid, probably Hen, had left a dish of scones and coffee on a tray.

She had dined with Ben here the last night, just before....

Everything else they'd shared. Everything else they'd done.

Althea massaged her temples then poured herself some coffee. It was cold, but it was her own fault she'd slept so long, returning to her own bed just before dawn. Just like it was her own fault her thoughts were a mess, and her hair was a mess, and her heart was a mess-

She didn't want to think about her heart. But everything was a mess and it was all her fault.

Last night had laid siege to her world, shattered it entirely, and rebuilt it anew. What exactly the landscape of her life, her soul, looked like now, Althea didn't know yet. But everything was different. Broken open. Terrifying- and wonderful.

She took another sip of the cold coffee and decided to examine her life later. Ben had fallen into it like a meteorite crashing to earth, and the repercussions were too far-reaching to comprehend before breakfast.

It was an important day and she would need all the sustenance she could get. Her promised week was nearly over, and she had assured the Earl of Maybourne she would conduct a summoning to finish the job. She still had no idea what she would do for it, how she could satisfy the Earl and Ben when their interests were opposites. She wasn't sure anymore what she wanted, only that she needed to finish the job one way or another, and actually casting Ben out of the house- even if she could- was no longer an option.

Something caught her attention from the corner of her eye. The book she'd purchased at Simonson's sat on the seat of one of the armchairs. She rose and brought it back to the table, where it fell open with an echoing thud.

It was massive. An ancient thing that smelled of dust and decay. Usually this sort of book was exactly the kind that excited her the most, but there was something about this particular tome that made her uneasy. As if when she read it, it was reading her in return.

Gingerly, she flipped through the pages.

* * *

An hour later, a sound at the door made her turn just as a letter appeared beneath it. Even from across the room, Althea knew the scrawling, shaky script on the envelope.

You've been far too quiet, my darling. Come see me at once. All my love, N.

Althea grinned and threw the note on the tray, dressed in her simplest gown, and was out of the house in under ten minutes. She was in Covent Garden in a flash, knocking on the former Madame Veira's door.

"You're glowing."

Nora's statement held no room for denial as she opened her door to admit Althea. The old woman's bright eyes twinkled beneath her wrinkled brows.

Althea ignored the look. "I got your letter."

Nora grinned. "You can't get off that easily, girl. You've made progress with the ghost I take it? Maybe that, and a little bit more."

Nora saw straight through Althea, as she'd always saw through everybody. It was a large part of what had made her so successful as a mystic.

Althea felt the heat rising in her cheeks. "We've gotten to know each other better."

Nora's chuckle was deliciously wicked. "About

time you let someone through that thick skin of yours."

"It's just a job. *He's* just a job. One I intend to finish tonight."

Nora set a pot of tea on the kitchen table and gestured Althea to sit. "And how do you intend to do that?"

"I found a book. It's very old, full of spells and rituals. It was hidden away in the basement of Simonson's."

"Be careful with that, girl. Such things are often hidden for a reason."

"Do you have any rituals to summon a spirit who doesn't wish to be summoned?"

Nora grimaced. "He's not cooperating then, eh? That's a pity. You can't summon a spirit who doesn't want to be summoned, not unless you're a witch."

"How does one know if one is a witch?"

Nora shot her a dark look. "You'd know. And be grateful you aren't. Neither am I, thank heavens."

"I have to try. Even if I can just get Miss Ridgely to understand what she's dealing with, that there's no future with a ghost and she cannot hold onto this girlish fantasy, that should be enough."

"And would that work on you?"

Althea flushed and took a sip of her tea. "We're not

talking about me."

"Just be careful," Nora warned, reaching into a satchel tied to her waist. She pulled out a necklace with an amulet of shimmering blue and golden stone, wrapped in twining grey metal. "Take this. If you're in trouble, it will help you."

"How?" Althea asked, taking the proffered necklace and putting it on.

"It's labradorite. My mother gave it to me, she told me it helped her find that which is lost and that which does not wish to be found. Perhaps it will assist you in summoning your spirit, or finding the answers you seek."

"Thank you, Nora." Althea held her dearest friend's wrinkled hand for a moment then took her leave. She had another visit to make before she put her nebulous plans into action.

Lord Leslie's townhouse was mere feet from the house Ben had built, but a world away in style and taste. Or, rather, lack thereof. Constructed of red brick, it was at most forty years old, and almost painfully boring.

"His lordship will be with you shortly," Leslie's butler announced, leaving Althea in a parlor on the second floor. It was done in shades of grey and baby blue and looked both cheap and tacky. Which was surprising, as Leslie dressed well and drove in a new and uncommonly expensive carriage. It was obvious he did not bother to use his ample funds on interior design.

Althea settled onto a settee near the windows, which overlooked the green square across the street.

"Mistress Althea. What a pleasant surprise." Leslie's voice was smooth and charming. Althea had not even heard him come in. He took the seat across from her. "Would you care for a refreshment? I can ring for some coffee or tea."

"No, thank you, this will be a brief visit."

He flashed his bright white teeth. "I hope there is nothing amiss?"

"Not at all, my lord. I only wished to speak to you. I know our interactions in the past have been rather unusual."

Memories of Ben's scene in the blue parlor and Mr. Firth's awful story came to mind.

"I am an open-minded man." Leslie sat back and rested one polished boot on his opposite knee. "I know why you've been spending time at Maybourne House, and frankly, I applaud your efforts."

"Ah. Wilkes told you."

Leslie's smile took on a plaster quality. "He tells me

many things, he is very well-informed man. I am fortunate to have him as my uncle."

"The Earl relies on him greatly," Althea said, threading a delicate needle. "The family is also fortunate to have his counsel."

"They certainly are. But tell me, Mistress, or may I call you Althea?"

You may not, Althea wanted to say, but it was important she be as friendly as possible. "You may."

"Excellent. Tell me Althea, have you actually met the ghost of Maybourne House?"

Althea did not want to talk to this man about Ben, but she had to see what he knew, what she was working with. "I have."

"What's he like?" Leslie's tone was casual but she felt the tension running beneath his words. He'd been understandably disturbed by the events he'd witnessed, and if he knew Charlotte harbored feelings for the ghost, he was likely anxious about courting her. Rightfully so, but that is why Althea was here.

"He is disagreeable, selfish and a total bore, frankly. Charlotte is simply using her knowledge of him to avoid marriage, which must seem mysterious and daunting to a girl her age."

"I'm sure it does, but I assure you, I would care for her if she wished to be my wife. I consider the

Ridgelys to be good friends, and though Charlotte is entertaining some unusual notions but I have no doubt she and I would suit admirably."

"So you would wed her, if she wished it?"

"I await only her consent to make an offer."

"And her dowry?" The words were out before Althea could stop herself.

Lord Leslie paused for the briefest moment, then said, "You mean the house? I don't care what comes of it, I would leave it to her. It would be *her* dowry after all and I have several homes of my own."

Althea wanted to believe him, but some deep instinct told her he was lying. *But why?*

"You know I saw you yesterday, across from the milliner's. Was raining dreadfully on and off all afternoon, wasn't it?"

Her tone was light, but he saw right through it. "Ah, yes. I'm sorry I did not notice you. I was busy attending to my cousin, who was in town for some shopping. Terrible day for it, as you say, but she lives in the country and only had a few days to spare here."

Althea knew he was lying. That would hadn't been his cousin any more than she'd been his sister. All men in the *ton* had a mistress, and if Leslie was bold enough to flaunt his, why would he hide the fact? He couldn't seriously think Althea would tell Charlotte, or, if she did, that Charlotte would care. The girl was not that naive.

"I hope your cousin can visit again when the weather is better. Under happy circumstances perhaps?"

"A wedding would be a very happy circumstance," a third voice spoke from the doorway.

"Ah! Uncle!" Leslie rose to greet Wilkes.

Althea stood, having gotten what she came for. Leslie was a cad and a liar, but he would marry Charlotte if she agreed. That was all that mattered. Althea wished for better for the girl, but such was life, and at least Leslie had funds, even if he hadn't spent them on this drab accommodation. Perhaps Charlotte could occupy herself with a remodel.

"Mistress," Wilkes bowed to Althea and kissed her hand.

"Mr. Wilkes,"she smiled, fighting the urge to pull her hand away.

Wilkes straightened and glanced from Althea to his nephew, suspicion in his narrow eyes. "I did not know the two of you were so closely acquainted."

"We're not," Althea answered swiftly. "I only came to ask Leslie a few questions pertaining to my work. It is nearly done, you see."

Wariness and something like triumph flitted across

Wilkes' face. "Excellent, excellent. We look forward to better times in Maybourne House. They have suffered greatly since the loss of the last Earl."

"So I heard."

"They are due for a stroke of good luck, wouldn't you say, Uncle?" The look Leslie gave the older man was tight, tense.

Althea wondered what sort of leash Wilkes kept on his nephew, who was a lord, but seemed unusually subservient to the solicitor.

"I wish them the very best," Wilkes smiled, and Althea did not believe him for a moment.

Ben did not know what to do. Last night had turned everything upside down. It had been the most erotic night of his life, which was saying something, but more disturbingly he felt *seen*.

Not as a ghost- he could reveal himself to anyone- but as a....a... *soul*.

He groaned and fell backwards through the floor of the attic. He settled midair in one of the guest rooms, staring at the paneled wood above. He had to convince Althea to leave the job unfinished, take some of the treasures only he knew existed, and go. He knew she was planning to leave town, and he guessed she'd return to being Jane Smith.

It was a preposterously boring name that did not fit her at all, but it was hers. Her true name. She would retire Mistress Althea and be gone forever.

He would never see her again.

Good. The voice in his mind was angry, hostile at the way she'd upended his existence. He'd survived nearly a century without feeling anything at all and now he felt *everything*. It was awful.

It was exhilarating.

A tap at the door sounded and before he could disappear, Charlotte entered the room.

'There you are," she said brightly, flouncing in as if he had not been avoiding her for two days.

"Here I am," he said, righting himself into a standing position. "I thought you were going riding in the park today."

"I already did that, silly," she purred, and warning bells rang in his head. She was in far too good a mood considering he'd barely spoken to her and Althea was still in the house. "It's late afternoon now, my assignation was in the morning."

"Your- assignation?"

"With Winifred and Anna. That's what we're calling it when we meet at the park. It's so much more romantic and exciting to have *an assignation*."

"It is. So much so I'd be careful who you mention it

to, they might get the wrong idea."

Charlotte rolled her eyes. "I'm not a fool, Ben. I only talk that way around you. Do you like it? The idea of *an assignation?*"

The warning bells were screaming in Ben's head now. She was definitely up to something.

"How are you feeling, Charlotte?"

The girl shrugged and flounced to the bed in the corner, landing on it in a pile of skirts and lace. "I feel marvelous. Don't you?"

"I'm not sure," he hedged.

"You're not sure? I would think after last night you'd be feeling marvelous."

The bells were a cacophony now, pealing wild alarm in his mind. She knew. Charlotte knew what he and Althea had done last night. How, he didn't know. Listening at the door, probably. But this was bad. Very, *very* bad.

"Well, I don't," he retorted, and it was true. He did not feel marvelous. He felt transformed. Remade. Exposed. Overjoyed. Terrified. A thousand things, but marvelous was not one of them.

Charlotte sat up and narrowed her eyes at him. "It sounded like you were enjoying yourself awfully vigorously."

"I don't know what you mean. I don't have a body,

so it's not what you think, you nitwit. It's rude, and dangerous, to listen at doors. You might get it wrong."

Charlotte tilted her head thoughtfully. "I might, but I don't think I have. I don't know how, but I know you tupped Mistress Althea."

Ben said nothing.

Charlotte smiled, and his blood ran cold. "But don't worry, I'm not upset."

"You're not?" he asked warily.

"No," she sighed. "She's clearly ensorcelled you, and that makes things much easier."

Dread was coursing through Ben now. "How so? Charlotte, what did you do?"

"I don't know whether she's a fraud or a witch, but either way, it is quite clear she is breaking the law."

"Charlotte, don't. You know the penalty for turning someone even claiming another can perform witchcraft is a year in prison. It is just as serious as someone holding themselves out as a witch."

"I know. That is why I sent the report anonymously."

Panic streaked through Ben. Althea would be arrested. She would go to prison, or worse. Even though they could no longer burn a witch at the stake, they could imprison them for claiming to perform magic for a year. A year in prison could be fatal even under the best circumstances, given the rampant disease and ironic lawlessness of those places of incarceration. Althea was beautiful, too, young and lovely and she would not stand a chance in such a place, even with her will to survive, to fight.

He had to warn her. He had to tell her.

"Ben."

He whirled on Charlotte.

She smiled.

"Why don't you let justice take its course, and come here, and tell me all the reasons I shouldn't marry Lord Leslie after all? You know, after last night, I've begun to realize what a fine catch he is. He has a very fancy coach, too. We could be at Gretna Green by Thursday, if you think on it."

Ben's panic quadrupled. She was going to marry Leslie to spite him. She was going to ruin everything. He would not be able to orchestrate Althea's rescue, because he would be dead.

Everything was falling out of control, again. He had to save Althea, but how could he, if he did not save himself?

You've always been selfish, that voice in his mind said again, soft and alluring. *Does a leopard ever change its spots? And what for, some woman you already know is a con and a born liar, just because she let you have some fun?*

She had all the fun. The fun was in your head. You could have fun in your own head any time. Stop Charlotte from wedding Leslie. That's first, everything else is later. Save yourself. Trust yourself.

Ben hated that the words rang true.

He turned to Charlotte.

"Charlotte, darling, you can't marry Leslie. I won't let you go."

Althea arrived home in the early evening and had barely reached her rooms when Hen appeared.

"Oh! There you are, Mistress!"

"What is it, Hen?"

The girl looked flushed. "You must leave tonight, Miss."

"What are you talking about? What's happened?"

"It's Miss Charlotte. She's sent a letter to the constable, turning you in for holding yourself out as a practitioner of witchcraft. They'll have it tomorrow morning at the latest."

"That's preposterous. She could easily be found guilt as well for claiming I practice it."

Hen shook her head. "She worded it real carefully, making it clear it was you who was breaking the law, and she didn't put her name to it. So even made Greg, the footman below stairs, write it in his own hand, to throw 'em off. He didn't want to, but she threatened to fire him. He's the one that told me, wants you to know. Says Ben speaks so highly of you."

Ben had been speaking highly of her to the footmen?

Pushing aside the warm feeling that evoked, Althea focused on the problem at hand. The very big problem at hand.

"Where's Ben?"

"Miss Charlotte went to find him. I- I think they're in one of the guest rooms down the hall. I heard the door shut about an hour ago."

They'd been in there an hour? Ben was obviously trying to talk her out of it, to recant.

Althea strode for the hall, reaching the door Hen indicated in moments. She paused, and listened. With any luck Charlotte was gone.

It seemed, however, Althea's luck had run out.

"Charlotte, darling," Ben purred, his voice a mockery of the warmth Althea had enjoyed only last night. "She is nothing to me. Nothing at all. Just a bit of fun. I'd let you know have your fun, you know, if you wished to stay here."

The unmistakable sound of Charlotte Ridgely giggling turned Althea's stomach. She had to be hearing this wrong. This could not be real.

"Ben, of course I'm going to stay here. I just said all that fluff about marrying Leslie so I'd know you loved me best."

Althea stepped back from the door. She'd heard enough.

The floorboard beneath her boot creaked and a moment later Ben whooshed through the closed door.

"Althea-" he took one look at her face and stopped short.

"No," she said, and turned down the hall.

"I can explain, it's not-"

But at that moment Charlotte opened the door and stepped into the hallway. "Oh dear," she said. "Well that's awkward."

"Charlotte, I-"

But whatever Ben said next, Althea never heard, because she was flying down the stairs and away from both of them.

Ben tried to push Charlotte, but in the end, he had to simply disappear mid-sentence. He reappeared in Althea's sitting room, but she was not there.

Where had she gone?

He had to explain. He knew now, with sudden, stunning clarity, that he'd made a mistake. He should have gone to warn her first and his own fate be damned. He would tell her this, beg her forgiveness and then beg her to leave, to take whatever of value he could give her and get out of London, forever.

Except she wasn't in her sitting room. Or her bedroom.

Foreboding rippled through him, as he noticed a piece of parchment on the little table where they had enjoyed dinner only the night before.

With a thought, he flipped the paper over, and read:

You've been far too quiet, my darling. Come see me at once. All my love, N.

Ben felt his world tip on its axis. He'd seen her exchanging letters in the mornings and thought nothing of it. But this- the only person in her life she'd ever mentioned knowing, trusting, was Madame Veira.

She had told him though of her lovers. He simply hadn't asked if she had one currently.

He was a fool. A goddamned fool.

Because only a fool would trust another person. Only a fool would consider loving someone else.

He could trust only himself. He could love only himself.

He disappeared and went to find Charlotte, to plead his case.

Chapter Fifteen
The Summoning

"Now? You want to do the summoning *now?*"

Maybourne blinked up at Althea from behind his spectacles. "But I had plans for dinner at White's."

"Reschedule them. We need to do this *now*. I overheard her speaking to the so-called spirit, and I think we might lose our chance if we don't act immediately, my lord."

To his credit, Maybourne did not doubt the severity of her tone. He stood at once. "What do you need, Mistress?"

"A room, any room- the rose salon, that way we are in the back of the house, away from prying eyes and ears."

"Excellent. Anything else?"

"The entire household. The more witnesses, the better."

"And you trust them?"

"Yes. I've befriended them over the course of the last week and I think they will assist us in convincing Charlotte to recant her beliefs."

Maybourne gave a curt nod, and strode from the room. Althea ran upstairs to get the book from Simonson's, and hurried to the rose salon. The necklace Nora had given her was a knowing weight against her collarbone.

How she wished Nora could be here, but Madame Veira had long since retired into obscurity. It was safer that way. Nora was far too old and fragile to face a year in prison, if she were ever turned in. It was a miracle, and a testament to the loyalty of her clients, that she never was.

Althea burst into the rose salon and began to arrange things as she would need them for the summoning. She'd performed similar rituals countless times. Old chants from medieval texts, pagan ceremonies, automatic writing, all of it had played a part in previous summonings.

But the previous summonings had been a lie.

This one was real, and this time, Althea was going to truly summon a spirit.

Then she would banish him into the Void.

Ben had tried to speak to Charlotte, but she wanted none of him. She'd seen the way he reacted to Althea and knew he'd been lying to her.

She had run out of the house, presumably to find Lord Leslie. For all Ben knew the two would be on their way to the Great North Road within the hour.

So he decided to do something he had not done in

a very, *very* long time. He would drown his sorrows.

Which was how he found himself in his hidden wine cellar. Bottles of brandy and whisky and claret, the finest wine and other, more exotic liquors, surrounded him. Even though Maybourne had discovered the stash, he'd barely put a dent in it. He did not seem to drink much.

"What a waste," Ben murmured.

"Meeeoww." The black kitchen cat had followed him down there. The creature had lived at the house a few years now, replacing the longhaired grey fellow who'd previously held of the title of mouser in chief. This new gentleman, sleek with bright yellow eyes, was Ben's favorite of the last century's kitchen cats.

All of them had been able to see him, he'd figured that out quickly, but this one seemed to actually enjoy Ben's company.

"I'm done for you know, old chap," Ben told the cat, then popped the cork out of a bottle of champagne with his mind. The fizz exploded everywhere, making the cat hiss and leap onto one of the intricate wrought iron shelves that lined the room.

"Sorry," Ben murmured.

The cat twitched its tail, in what Ben liked to imagine was understanding. Ben let out a sigh and floated into the middle of the room, the continued spray of the champagne going straight through him, and imagined he could taste it.

Soon enough even this pale echo of his life would be gone, too.

"Sit, please."

Althea had not bothered to dress in her usual costume. There was no time for feathers and lace and kohl-rimmed eyes. This was real, and she intended to be present only as herself. Mistress Althea by name, but Jane Smith, wronged woman and fearless survivor, in truth.

The assembled household staff, including Hen and Goggins and Mrs. Hooper, lined the walls of the the rose salon. Those near a chair or table took a seat.

The Earl, his mother, and an unusually flushed Charlotte, took the chairs around the little table in the center of the room where Althea sat.

"I do not think I need to explain why I've called you all here," Althea said, her voice low and powerful. "There has been a spirit in this house for as long as any of you can remember, and it is time we set it, set *him*, Benedict Aston, free."

Her voice nearly caught when she spoke his name, but Althea kept her attention focused on the goal. He had played her, just as he had played Charlotte. He was just as awful as he'd been in life. The changes she'd seen had been no more than an illusion.

A strangled sound came from Althea's right and she knew it was Hen. She'd not had time to explain to her why this needed to be done, and perhaps she never would.

Charlotte sat in silence, her face impassive.

Althea didn't like that, not one bit. But she'd decided in the half hour it took to prepare the room, that she did not care what Charlotte thought. Althea was going to expel Ben from the house, and that would be that.

Charlotte Ridgely would not be her problem.

Althea took a long, steadying breath. She was going to combine a bit of her usual theatrics with her newfound knowledge, taken from the book on the table before her. She felt the weight of the necklace Nora had given her grow, as if in answer to her will. Althea did not think she was a witch, but she couldn't be sure. She'd never worked with a real spell book, and she had no doubt that the book she'd purchased at Simonson's was as real as it got.

It contained mysteries and horrors she had never imagined, spells for things so dark and terrible she had closed it and left the room before she could continue to read. Spells to destroy, spells to kill, and worse, spells to *curse*.

There were also spells to cleanse, to start anew, to bring luck- those were the spell Althea would try next time, if she ever had a next time.

She might soon be arrested for witchcraft, she might as well earn it.

"Our collective energies are potent," she said, eyes glancing around the room. Beyond the windows, evening was falling over the small garden at the rear of the house. The light was fading rapidly.

Perfect.

"Assembled we can draw Benedict Aston out, into our presence. Together we can push him forth, into the world beyond. The world in which his soul belongs."

"You mean oblivion," Charlotte hissed.

Althea did not look at her. Did not know if this upset or, strangely, pleased the girl. She did not care.

"What you see, what you feel, may frighten you, but rest assured no harm shall come to you. For I will remain the conduit to our power, and focal point of this summoning, and the sole nexus of its impact as we channel this spirit out of Maybourne House."

Lady Mayboune's eyes were big as saucers, and she was trembling. The Earl rolled his eyes beside her and wrapped her hand in his on the table. He was clearly only here for support, for the show.

Althea prayed to the god she wasn't sure she believed in that she gave them all a show.

Ben *almost* felt drunk. Nearly. He'd popped enough corks and shattered enough bottles that the floor was flooded with liquor and still he smelled nothing. Tasted nothing. Thank god, he supposed, he'd at least been able to orgasm last night.

The thought stopped him cold.

He did not want to think about that.

About *her*.

She'd been playing him all along for a fool. She had only gotten close to him, played into his desires, to find a way to destroy him. To convince him to renounce Charlotte and destroy himself.

All that nonsense about her mother and her struggles probably hadn't even been real. She was an expert actor, and he had let himself be taken in, just like all the old biddies she tricked with her mirrors and baubles and overdone make-up.

"Never let a woman get to you," he slurred at the cat, who was now sitting atop a barrel of ale against the wall.

Ben blinked. Why was he slurring? And why was his head suddenly fuzzy? He hadn't been down here in decades but if bashing the place apart could actually get him half-cocked he should have tried it years ago.

Laughing to himself, Ben blasted open a bottle of Greek tsipouro and watched with glee as it splashed across the floor.

Althea could barely keep her hands from shaking. The room was now cast in near darkness, the only light coming from the candle before her. The air was hot and tense with the assembled bodies, everyone watching her. Waiting.

She was really doing this. She was really going to cast Ben into the Void.

She took one look at Charlotte Ridgely's passive scowl beside her and knew the answer was yes. Ben had nearly ruined this young woman's life, tricking her into loving him. Who knew what he'd said to her, really? Althea couldn't trust anything he'd ever told her, except that in life he'd been a selfish, controlling, self-interested, awful person.

Nearly a century later, he still was.

Steeling her resolve, Althea looked at the page open before her, and began to chant.

"See us, hear us, spirits here,
In this room ye shall not fear,

For what is living shall again be dead,
As what is taken is ever dear."

A candle in a sconce beside the fireplace burst to life and one of the kitchen maids screamed. Althea ignored her, her own heart beating a mad tattoo. It was working. Maybe she was a witch after all.

"See us, hear, spirits who dwell,
We summon you now, from the depths of hell,
Join us, hear us, lead our dance,
Show yourself, bring yourself, end our trance!"

Abruptly, every candle in the room erupted in flame, as did the fire in the grate. Screams and shouts sounded throughout the assembly and Lady Maybourne nearly fainted, the Earl only catching her just in time from toppling out of her seat. For his part, the Earl actually looked a little scared.

Good, thought Althea. She wasn't the only one.

Blinking at the sudden, bright light, she looked around for Ben. There was *something* in this room. She felt it. The temperature had dropped, like that first night she'd met him.

Althea scanned the frightened faces of the household. To their credit none fled the room.

Everyone was scared, nervous, but brave. Her heart swelled with pride. They could do this, she could do this.

And then she saw him.

The ghost she had summoned.

It wasn't Ben.

The cat kept looking nervously to the door.

"Don't worry. Althea's gone. Charlotte's gone. Maybourne doesn't believe I'm real and the rest of the lot love me. We're *fine.*"

Ben was definitely slurring now. He did not know how but the longer he stayed amongst the rising level of alcohol on the floor and its attendant fumes, the more intoxicated he felt. It was marvelous.

"God, I've missed this," he chuckled and turned himself into a puff of smoke. The cat's eyes went wide, and Ben laughed. "I didn't know I could do that either! Here, watch this!"

He jumped into one of the empty bottles standing on the barrel beside the cat, looking for all the world like a plume of smoke moving backwards. The cat bristled and hissed.

Ben's voice was hollow as it sounded from within the glass bottle. "I know! Imagine what a parlor trick like this could have done for me at court! Swoon, miladies, swoon away!"

Althea blinked, and felt as if time slowed, around her.

Lady Maybourne's eyes flickered open, but at half speed. Then Althea noticed everyone was moving slower, and slower, until they were still.

Everyone except the little boy standing in the corner by the door, between the now frozen Cook and one of the grooms.

"Who are you?" Althea asked, true fear running through her. Whoever this was, he was not Ben, or one of his brothers. This boy was large-boned, portly for a child, with flame red hair and freckles on a friendly, open face.

"I am Lord Edgeware's son. My name is Henry. Who- who are you?"

"My name is Jane Smith," Althea answered, feeling for the first time in a very long time that she wanted to be honest. "It is nice to meet you Henry. Do you- do you live here?"

"I don't think so," the boy shook his head. "I'm not sure. I- I used to live next door, in the red brick house. My father had it built when he married my mother. She says it is the finest house in Town."

Althea's blood ran cold. "Are you- Henry, are you

the son of a baronet?"

The boy floated closer and nodded. "That's me. Father is a baronet. One day I shall be one too. Or, at least, I think so."

He looked down at himself sadly. "I was supposed to be."

"Henry, how did you end up here? Like this?"

Althea knew the answer, or at least the essential parts, but she wanted to know what he knew. Why he was here. It couldn't be another curse.

"I stole some of father's stash of whisky. I thought it was funny. He wouldn't buy me the pony I wanted, you see, and I was mad."

He looked past the frozen household towards the windows, where the night itself had stopped. "It was wrong of me," he said sadly.

"We all make mistakes, Henry," Althea said softly. "What happened then?"

"I got my friends, the other lads in the household-mother says I shouldn't play with the help but no one else wants to play with me. Lord Harcote's son calls me a strawberry. I don't like him much."

"I'd imagine not. What did you and your friends do next?"

"We drank the whisky and decided to go to the old Stafford House. It was haunted, you know. Everybody knew it. Sometimes at night I'd hear the most awful moaning coming from the attic, and I thought maybe if I found the ghost everyone would see how brave and I was, and I could have more friends."

Althea's heart broke for the misguided little boy as she steeled herself for the end she knew the story was coming to.

"We broke in through a window in the garden."

Henry pointed to the window behind Goggins' motionless silhouette. "That one there. But they've patched it up."

Althea glanced at it. "So they have. What then?"

"We went up and up and up. The servants were asleep somewhere else, they never heard us, and we were so quiet, like mice. We got to the attic, and at first all we found was dust and real mice."

"Sounds frightening."

Genuine fear rippled across his sad, friendly face. "It wasn't, then it was. A horrible sound, like a thousand ghouls flying up out of hell came at us and everything went flying. Something hit me in the head and I cried out, but it didn't hurt me, so I ran. We all ran. Then he appeared."

"Who appeared, Henry?"

"The ghost. He was tall and his shirt was falling off and he looked like he needed bath."

Althea wanted to laugh at that description, but she was not in the mood for levity. There was no mirth in this story. Only tragedy.

"He started yelling at us, telling us to never come back and all the awful things he'd do to us if we did."

"And did he do anything awful?"

Henry shook his head. "No, Miss Smith. He didn't. Just gave us a firm dressing down, and when he was done, we went to leave."

The boy's voice wavered, as if he did not like the rest of the story. Althea knew she wouldn't, either. "But then we looked over and Robert had pissed himself. I- I know it was wrong, but we laughed. And once we started, we couldn't stop."

"Sometimes we react in strange ways when we are frightened. It's okay."

"It wasn't though. He- he was furious. The angrier he was, the funnier it was until- until-"

Henry was shaking now, his translucent form fading in and out.

"Henry, it's okay. It's okay. I know what happened. He pushed you out the window, didn't he?"

Henry sniffed and nodded. "And I've been here ever since. Sometimes I sleep for a long time, and when I wake up, everything is different. I think it's because I can stop time, somehow."

Althea made a mental note to research *that* ability. Henry was a true ghost after all, not a cursed one. Perhaps it came with different abilities. Or perhaps all spirits had their own, unique strengths.

"I try to avoid the other ghost. He- he tried to save me when I fell, but he couldn't catch me. I don't think he wants to hurt me, but he frightens me."

Althea nodded. "I understand. But he won't harm you. That's why we are here today. I tried to summon him, to send him to the next world."

The boys' eyes widened. "You can do that?"

"I- I think so. I summoned you, didn't I?"

Henry's face fell. "Not the way you think. When I'm awake I'm usually in the garden. It's hard for me to leave- that's, that's why I'm flickering. See?"

He held his arm aloft and it did, indeed, flicker.

"Like a candle," he shrugged, then sighed, looking for all the world like a bored boy of ten. "Anyway, I heard you all in here, and I thought maybe you could help me. You have that book after all."

"You know this book?"

He shook his head, his bright red hair swinging back and forth. "No. But it's real magic. I can feel it."

"But I- I am not a witch?"

"You're not," the boy said in a strange tone, glancing around the room nervously, as if suddenly aware he was surrounded by so many people. He looked at the Earl with wide eyes, and Lady Maybourne, who was staring in space, utterly overcome but frozen in time.

Althea sighed. She would not be able to expel Ben after all. She'd failed.

"I think you can help me, though," Henry continued thoughtfully. "Or maybe it's me who can help you."

"What do you mean, Henry?"

"Robert is back. He wants to complete his revenge."

"You mean the boy who pushed you?"

"Yes. I- I overheard him. I don't know when, but I know it was him. He killed Nigel years ago. He was- he was bragging about it. He never forgot that we laughed at him. He- I don't think he's right in the head. I don't think- what we did- it wasn't so bad, was it?"

Althea shook her head. "No, Henry. You were children and you were frightened. You did not mean to be cruel."

As she said the words, she knew they were true, and her heart broke for the little boy and his family.

Henry glanced over his shoulder towards the door. "Someone is coming I- I'm scared."

"Don't be scared Henry, it's al-"

Althea did not have the chance to finish her sentence because the next moment Henry was gone as the world came roaring back to life, the the door to the rose salon burst open.

"She's in here, sir!" A uniformed man called down the hall.

The household was still screaming and crying and talking animatedly. Maybourne was sitting back, blinking in consternation. His mother was strangely still, as if she remained frozen, but Charlotte was watching Althea.

Like a cat with the cream.

A moment later a constable appeared.

"Mistress Althea, you are under arrest for the violation of the Witchcraft Act of 1735. Grab her, boys."

Ben was deep in an empty brandy bottle when the sensation hit him.

Something was wrong.

Very wrong.

He poured himself out of the bottle into his usual form, only to find the cat facing the door, back arched, hissing.

"I know, I know. Something's amiss. Let me see."

Ben scanned his awareness of the house. It was harder than usual. Not because he was in the cellar, but because of the effect of the liquor. Damn, he shouldn't have let himself get like this.

Althea was in trouble. She was still here. He *felt* her. She was afraid.

"Oh no," he breathed. "She didn't make it out in time."

Without pausing to think of a plan, to think of anything, he imagined the foyer, imagine himself there, and prepared to appear in the-

But a sudden loud clang sounded and nothing happened. He opened his eyes.

He was still in the cellar.

And someone had shut the open door.

He closed his eyes and this time envisioned the blue parlor. He just had to disappear and-

And he was *still* in the cellar.

He looked to the cat, who was pacing the top of its barrel now, hissing and yowling.

"What the devil," Ben murmured, then it hit him.

Someone had locked in him.

Someone who knew was in there.

Someone who knew that iron had magical properties. Ben had always considered it an old wives' tale, that iron could tame the magic of the fairy folk

and their ilk.

Now he was part of that ilk. He still didn't want to know- and frankly he didn't care to know- if fairies were real, but he knew now with sudden, dreadful certainty that part of the old legends were true.

Iron could bind a magical being.

Or, in this case, trap a ghost in a wine cellar.

He could not leave, which meant, he could not save Althea. Perhaps Althea had been the one to lock him up... but no, he couldn't think that of her.... Could he?

I didn't matter. She could not be arrested.

He wouldn't let that happen.

He could do nothing to stop it.

Ben exploded into smoke and filled the room, the bottles quaking as he let out an ear-shattering roar of rage.

Chapter Sixteen
The Witch

"Eh, toff! Shove over!"

Althea barely regarded the skinny, pock-marked woman standing over her. Instead, she pushed herself a foot to the left, and continued sleeping.

Or, at least, trying to.

She'd gotten one of the prize places by the wall. Not a coveted corner spot, but at least a wall where she should lean against the cold, damp stone of the cell and sleep without fear of being stepped on, or worse.

Prison wasn't bad.

It was terrible.

Althea thought of Ben's description of her as a *survivor*. She'd been here a week, maybe two, there was no way to be certain, but she already knew the chances she'd last a year in this place were slim.

Just a few hours ago, or maybe it was yesterday, two women had died of a fever. Several other women were coughing now, sweating and mumbling to themselves. The more senior denizens of the cell claimed it was always like this. That, in fact, this was period of relative serenity.

Somewhere in the room a woman screamed,

sobbing and crying out for someone who was not there.

Althea shut her eyes, and thought.

There had to be something she could do. Newgate was far easier to get into than get out of, it was said. Certainly she'd been thrown in quickly. There had not even been a trial, as the constable had caught her in the act himself, he claimed. The judge had barely even looked at her before announcing her guilt.

She wasn't a witch, as no one could be punished for that anymore. But she was guilty of claiming to perform magic, in other words, fraud. Witch fraud.

The thought made her giggle.

"I'll show you what's funny," the woman on her other side, a round old lady with a thick mustache, grumbled.

Althea quieted. She had no one to blame but herself. She *was* guilty. She had held herself out, fraudulently, as someone capable of magic and occults feats. She's merely gambled that she could escape before the law caught up with her.

She'd gambled wrong, in so many ways.

Because now she was caught, and, as it turned out, magic was real. Curses and ghosts and, apparently, actual witches, all existed. Althea was not one of them. If she were, she could probably get out of this cell.

Dank and low, the room had one wall of stone and three of iron bars. Dozens of women were in Althea's, with other cells just like it as far as she could see in the dim light. The smell made her vomit the first day, but now she did not notice it.

She hoped soon she would not notice anything.

It wasn't that she wanted to give up, it was that she wasn't sure what else to do. No one would claim her, or vouch for her. The constable himself had seen her conducting a ceremony meant to summon otherworldly spirits.

Nora could not help her. Poor, dear Nora. The news would break her heart, if it ever reached her. Althea suspected it would. Mistress Althea was prominent enough in London's underworld that some would rejoice at her fall. It would make a minor column in the back of some paper, and eventually Nora would hear about it.

Nora, who could do nothing to save her. Who had herself only narrowly avoided this same fate her entire life.

Althea pushed back the tears that threatened. Again.

She could not spare the moisture.

Her only plan, if one could call it that, was to try and summon a helpful ghost. Ironic, that. But now that she knew ghosts were real, she had no doubt Newgate was full of them. If little Henry's traumatic death had left his soul trapped between this world and the next, surely some other lost souls were wandering Newgate. And, hopefully, some of them were helpful.

It would take time, though, to get their attention. Gain their trust. Get *them* to notice *her*. Because Althea was not a witch, and she could not summon them at will. She was mortal. An average human with an open, curious mind whose best chance was to catch the attention of some lonely ghost.

Hopefully one who could move objects as well as Ben. Objects like keys and doors and locks. And perhaps a ghost who could make her invisible, too.

But maybe that was asking too much.

A guard shouted a name from the door, several yards and dozens of sleeping, crying bodies away. In that far corner a group of ladies was playing cards, shouting back at the guard profanities so rude even Althea blushed.

Ben. She couldn't stop thinking about him, even when she wanted to, which was all the time. How had she gotten everything so wrong? She deserved to be here. She'd been such a fool. She was worse than Charlotte Ridgely. She'd known better and she'd still fallen in love with a ghost.

Because that is what it was.

Love.

Blind, stupid, irrational love.

She'd known it the moment they'd thrown her into the prison cart in front of Maybourne house. As it trundled off into the darkness, away from the house she might never see again, and the man who would be destroyed alongside it, she knew she loved him.

It was awful.

The guard shouted again, and some of the women near her stirred. Althea tightened her eyes and fought back the ache in her stomach that wouldn't leave. There was so little food here, and what there was she could barely consider worthy of the name.

"I know you're in here! Last call, Jane Smith!"

The woman with the pock-marked face shoved her elbow in Althea's side. "Oi, ain't that you?"

Althea's eyes fluttered open.

"Jane Smith? Alright, that's it," the guard called, turning away to address a cloaked figure beside him.

Althea shot to her feet. She had to hold onto the wall to keep from falling back down. Her legs had fallen asleep and her head swam, but she managed to shout across the cries and moans in the cell. "I'm here!"

The guard turned and waited as Althea picked her way across the cell. It took forever, and the jeers of the women followed her. Anything that happened, anything at all, earned their commentary and their ire.

"Oi, it's the chosen one!"

"There she goes! The Toff 'as a date!"

"Think yer better than us? Take your visitor and fuck off!"

"Or better yet, fuck *em!*"

Althea ignored them, focused only on reaching the barred door at the far end of the cell.

Finally, she was there. Panting and sweaty despite the frigid air, she grasped the bars with trembling hands.

"Yer Jane Smith?" the guard asked, meeting her eyes.

She held his gaze and nodded. "I am."

He looked to the hooded figure, who also gave a nod.

"Right. Yer out."

Althea barely had time to process what was happening before the gate to the cell opened, just enough to let her out. If she expected the other women to rush the door, she was mistaken. They didn't move. Didn't care at all.

But Althea's mind was racing, her heart skipping a

bit as she fought to push back the flood of thoughts filling her head. What was happening? She was free? Impossible. She was guilty. She knew she was guilty. Everyone knew she was guilty.

"Can we get her some food and water first? Perhaps a change of clothes?"

The cloaked visitor's voice was soft, familiar. A wealthy woman. Althea couldn't place it. Had one of her previous clients taken pity on her? She'd had so many powerful ones over the years, it was possible. But why they would risk revealing themselves in such a manner she couldn't guess.

But who else would come for her?

The guard eyed Althea with disdain, then led her and the hooded woman down a series of halls, away from the prisoner's cells, and into another room. This one had a bath tub filled with cold water, and a table.

"Clean up here in, then take her with you," the guard said, failing at the deference he'd clearly been ordered to give the hooded woman.

"Thank you," the woman said.

A young boy rushed in and placed some bread and cheese on the table, then darted out. The guard followed, shutting the heavy wooden door be himself with loud thud.

"Well that was unpleasant," Althea's savior said,

pulling back her hood.

"Lady Maybourne," Althea breathed.

The older woman smiled. "I'm sorry it took so long to get everything sorted out."

"I- I don't know what to say." Althea sank onto the simple wooden chair beside the table. Her whole body was trembling. With hunger or relief, she did not know.

"I'd accept a simple thank you, but under the circumstances I'd prefer you just get into that bath."

Althea shuddered with laughter, which turned to tears. Eventually she was calm enough to strip off what was left of her dress and step into the tub. She did not care that the water was cold, only that it was clean.

She leaned back and took a deep breath.

"How?" she asked.

Lady Maybourne took the chair and eyed the food with suspicion. "I knew almost immediately Charlotte turned you in. It was easy enough to get her confession, then I set about explaining things to the authorities."

"What things?"

"That we were mounting a play, a diversion for the household, many of whom cling to the old ways. I said my daughter was young and naive and had misunderstood that you are nothing but an actress and it was all a performance at my behest. Charles backed up my version of things and even Charlotte was forced to recant. Albeit, I'm ashamed to say, reluctantly."

"She is young."

"She is foolish. I love my daughter dearly, but I hope she grows up into the person she has the potential to be. The person she is currently is not one I am proud of."

Althea had nothing to say to that. The dowager countess was clearly sharper and more observant than she seemed.

"But why save me?"

"Because you might be a fraud, Althea, but you are a good person and you have a good heart. I saw the way you spoke to that boy. You did not flinch, you merely offered him kindness even as every moment you stayed in our house brought you closer to this."

Lady Maybourne gestured to the damp, dark walls of Newgate and it took Althea a moment to register what she'd said.

"You- you saw Henry?"

The Countess said nothing, but her eyes sparkled in the dim light.

"How? I thought everyone was frozen. He said- I

mean, I saw-"

"You saw what I wanted you to believe, which is that I was stuck in time as everyone else. But I was not, Althea, because I am not like everyone else."

Althea sat up in the tub. "What do you mean?"

Lady Maybourne eyed the shut door for a moment, as if listening for anyone outside. Satisfied, she spoke. "Here, wash your hair and scrub that filth off and I will explain. I think we owe each other some honesty, at last."

"But I haven't any soap."

Lady Maybourne held out her hand and blew on it. To Althea's amazement, a bar of soap appeared. The Countess extended it to her.

"You're a- a witch?"

Lady Maybourne bowed her head. "Not a very powerful one, I'm afraid. I'm limited to parlor tricks and, on rare days, minor visions."

"I don't understand. I thought witches were, well, everyone makes you sound-"

"Awful? Dangerous? Wicked?" The countess laughed, the sound like chimes tinkling in the breeze. "Hardly. I suppose some are, but that's true of any group."

"If you're a witch, why didn't you get rid of Ben?"

"Because I like him. He doesn't know it. No one

knows what I am. My children never inherited the gift, as far as I can tell, and mine is so small it wasn't worth making a fuss about."

Lady Mayborne shrugged and eyed the bread and cheese again, the waggled her fingers at it. In its place was a tray of roast beef and apple tarts.

Althea's mouth watered and she began scrubbing in earnest.

"I'm also not powerful enough to summon ghosts, or banish them. But as I said, I do have the odd vision from time to time, and several months ago I had one."

"What was it?" Althea asked, soap dripping down her face from her lathered hair. Her life had reached a point of disbelief that she had no qualms about learning Lady Maybourne was secretly a witch all along. An actress in her own right, playing a flighty mother to serve her own ends. Ends which had apparently included Althea.

"It wasn't much, but you were in it. I was speaking to you in the foyer. You'd just saved us, all of us, and the house, too."

"But I haven't. I've ruined everything."

"Hardly, my girl. Fate never takes the paths we see coming, even if we know the ultimate destination."

Althea rinsed her hair and began scrubbing the grime from her body. Neither she nor Lady

Maybourne blinked an eye at her nakedness. Such things were immaterial when one was being sprung from Newgate by a secret witch.

"Has Charlotte married Lord Leslie?"

Lady Maybourne let out a long suffering sigh that told Althea just how much she despised the match. "Thank god, no. My daughter is not Lady Robert Leslie yet and with any luck she will never be. That is why you must come back."

The words rang a bell in Althea's mind, but she couldn't place it.

"And what of Ben?"

Lady Maybourne's eyes grew wary. Althea's heart dropped. "No one has seen him since you left," she said quietly. "I'm sorry. We do not know where he went. Not even Charlotte can find him."

That wasn't right. That couldn't be right. Althea wasn't a witch and she had not even gotten to try the banishing spell, anyway. He had to be in the house. She could not allow any alternative.

"Perhaps Henry can find him?" she asked.

"I haven't seen him, either. I think perhaps he fell back into one of his sleeps. Poor, dear, boy. I'm not sure he fully understands what has happened him. What a dreadful tragedy."

The bells in Althea's head rang louder, and

memories flooded back. "What did you call Lord Leslie?"

"What do you mean?"

"You said his full name, just now. That Charlotte is not yet-"

"Lord Robert Leslie."

The bells pealed so loudly Althea could barely think straight. "Oh no," she breathed.

"What is it?" Lady Maybourne asked, sitting up straight.

"Henry was right. The boy who killed him has come back to finish his revenge. He was mad after all. It's- oh it all makes sense now. I don't know how Wilkes is involved, but- you said Wilkes did not know he had a nephew until recently?"

"Yes, when Lord Leslie purchased the townhome next door and- oh, my dear girl. He's Robert."

Althea nodded. "Lord Leslie is the boy who killed Henry. He's come back for the house. He's come back for Ben."

"Oh no."

"Lady Maybourne, we have to stop him."

"Oh this explains so much. Wilkes' strange behavior, the fires-"

"Fires?"

"Last year someone tried to set house ablaze

several times. I was able to stop it before anyone noticed, but just barely. I never saw who was responsible."

"Leslie was trying to destroy the house, or he got Wilkes to do it. Either way, we have to keep him from Charlotte. We have to get him to confess to killing Henry and the other boy. He's mad."

Lady Maybourne was pale as a ghost herself. "The owners of the house next door. They were relatives of Henry's, his brother's children. They were found shot by a highwayman last year. That is how the house came up for sale-"

"We have to stop Leslie. None of us is safe until he is locked up."

"Or worse," Lady Maybourne murmured, a vicious look entering her doe-like blue eyes. Althea decided she liked the woman. She had spirit.

"First, Althea, you must eat. You're nothing but bones. Come." She conjured a towel from thin air to wrap around Althea as she rose from the water, and Althea did not bother to question it. She would have the rest of her life to comprehend the mysteries hidden in plain sight. For now, she needed to focus on saving Ben.

"How long have I been here?"

"A little over a week. My masquerade ball is this

evening. I shouldn't have come here myself, but the judge sent word you'd been released and I couldn't let you rot in here another minute. I had to see you, to explain everything."

"You have no idea how grateful I am."

"If you want to repay me, save my family." The Countess' eyes were alight as they met Althea's. "But first, I have a question."

"Anything. What is it?"

"Do you own a mask?"

The cat, at least, was enjoying himself. Mice seemed capable of coming and going despite the locked door and, Ben was surprised to learn, cats could drink a lot of liquor without being the worse for wear. At least, this cat could.

Ben wished he could say the same for himself.

He'd figured out the intoxicated feeling that enveloped him in the cellar had nothing to do with the alcohol and everything to do with the iron. It stifled magic, twisted it, and, given that he was little more than a lot of magic and a whisp of soul, it had him completely fuddled.

He was sick of the feeling. Now he was hiding in various bottles just to try and escape it, but he had little luck. All the shelves were lined with iron and the door was covered with a filigree of the stuff.

The wrought iron had seemed so elegant when he's installed it. Oh, the best laid plans and all that...

Ben turned himself back into a puff of smoke and funneled himself into an empty port bottle.

Port.

Althea had enjoyed his port, hadn't she? If he could, he'd buy her the finest port, every night for the rest of their-

Ben stopped. That way lay madness, indeed. He reminded himself he did not like Althea, not at all. And there was no 'rest of' anything. He was dead, and she was a cold, traitorous, liar.

He oozed back out of the bottle and into his usual form.

Ben had no idea how long he'd been trapped in here. Surely only a day or two. Maybourne didn't call for a bottle of the good stuff every night, but it was often enough that Ben had begun to resent his overreach on Ben's hard-won collection of fine spirits.

"Fine spirits," he mumbled to the cat, who was asleep on an upper shelf.

It had been a long time since Ben was this alone without distractions and only his thoughts- the cat didn't count- for company.

"Shabby time for it, too," he mumbled to himself,

then turned to the cat. "Never trust anybody, do you understand? Never. They will stab you in the back, every time. You give someone an inch, they take a mile. And your heart."

Ben closed his eyes.

"And then they smash it under their perfect, heeled boot."

He sighed.

"Which conceals their very shapely ankle. Slender, like the rest of them, and pale, but so very soft."

He groaned in frustration and fought the urge to break another bottle. He'd already destroyed a fortune's worth of liquor. He wondered why Maybourne had not tried to sell some of it off. After all, it was the only stash of treasure the Earl had found so far and it was worth a hefty sum. Especially the French stuff. From what Ben had gathered, that was hard to come by these days.

Pity they'd been fighting the French. Again. He'd always liked the French.

The women, especially. And the butter.

His mouth watered, mentally. A memory of decadence, nothing more.

Just like him.

He chuckled and the cat peeked open one eye, as if to say *excuse me, I'm sleeping here.*

"You're always sleeping," Ben mumbled. "Lucky bastard."

The cat closed his eye, but Ben could have sworn it rolled a little first.

It was ironic that he, Ben, and the cat, too, he supposed, were imprisoned when somewhere far off in the city Althea was, too. Likely Newgate. Ben shuddered. The thought made him want to wretch, but that was pointless, just like everything else in his non-life.

Perhaps the Void would not be so bad, after all.

In the Void he would not feel like his heart had been ripped from his chest and carried off.

To Newgate.

In the Void he would not have to remember anything. Not French butter, not cats, not the taste of brandy, not Althea's husky, delicious laugh. Not the millions of ways he had failed everyone in his life. His father. His mother. Perry and Monty and even little Heath. Miriam, who he never should have married. Liza-

A searing pain, like a knife in his heart, ran through his chest. Even after all these years he felt the pain of her loss as if it had just happened.

And now he had failed Althea, too.

It didn't matter that she'd lied to him. Well, it *did*,

but she did not deserve a year in Newgate for that. Few people survived a year in Newgate, and if they did, it was at a cost he would never wish anyone to pay. Especially not Althea.

He should have gotten her out of this mess. He should have *done* something.

But there was nothing he could do.

He had no control over anything, no power. He was nothing but smoke and sour memories.

Perhaps the Void would be better than this after all.

Chapter Seventeen
The Ball

"Oh, miss," Hen breathed, stepping back from Lady Maybourne's dressing table. "You look-"

"Stunning," Lady Maybourne finished for her. "Thank you, Henrietta. You've done wonders. I think perhaps you've been wasted all this time. You are a natural ladies' maid."

Hen beamed at her employer. "My lady, thank you. You are too kind."

"Hardly," the Countess smiled. "Now go and keep an eye on things, will you? If you see Lord Leslie or Wilkes, keep them in your sights, but do not let them see you. If they do anything odd, inform us immediately."

Hen bounced a curtsy and hurried from the room.

Althea took a deep breath and looked in the mirror. She had never been to a ball before. Never had to dress like one of the aristocrats she worked for, in the finest fashions and most decadent styles.

She hated the awareness that came over her as she looked in Lady Maybourne's dressing table mirror, but she felt *good*.

Really, unusually good.

"It suits you," Lady Maybourne said quietly, as if

reading Althea's mind. She didn't think the older woman could, but the Countess had seen a lot of life and obviously understood how unusual this was for Althea. "I'm so pleased we could make such quick work of it, too. But I am sorry about the wig."

"Don't be, I've always wondered what life would be like as a blonde. I'm afraid it's going to be considerably more exciting than I would have guessed."

"With any luck things will go smoothly."

Althea smiled grimly. "I do not believe in luck, Lady Maybourne. Did Mrs. Hooper complete her task?"

Hen answered. "Aye, Niles says he did it himself. Everything is ready, Mistress."

Althea took a deep breath, picked up the mask from the table, and put it on. The soft crimson ribbons fell down the back of her neck, gently tickling the tender skin there.

Like a feather.

She pushed the thought away.

She pushed *every* thought away, except for the one that mattered: they had to stop Leslie.

Lady's Maybourne caught Althea's gaze in the mirror, pale blue meeting warm black.

"Are you ready, Jane?"

Althea gave her a grim, determined smile. "Let's dance."

There was a party going on upstairs. Ben could sense it even with his addled abilities. Could it already be time for Lady Maybourne's Masquerade? That meant he had been in here for a week.

At least the Earl had decided not to raid the cellar for the good stuff for his mother's party.

He would not be pleased when he saw the state of the place. Half the bottles were either empty or shattered on the floor. Ben would have to ensure none of the staff were held responsible for that. Perhaps they could say it was an earthquake. Did earthquakes strike English wine cellars, exclusively?

Ben giggled. God, his head hurt. Everything hurt. He felt weak and useless and utterly miserable. Even the cat was done with their confinement. He'd been sulking and hissing at everything for hours.

A rattle at the door had both of them jumping back. The cat hissed again and Ben prepared himself for whoever would enter. If he'd been locked in here on purpose…

The lanky, slightly stooped silhouette of Goggins appeared in the doorway, holding a candelabra.

"What the hell-" the old butler began, then stopped

short at the sight of Ben. His eyes widened. "It's you."

"Good evening, Goggins. It is evening, isn't it? Or are we throwing morning masquerades now?"

To his credit, Goggins was not afraid of him. His eyes narrowed. "You've been very busy recently. And I don't just mean this." The butler gestured to the disaster inside the cellar. "Though his lordship won't be pleased when he finds out."

"I imagine not, but as I put the lot of it here, I think it's my right to do whatever I wish with it."

"You are a duke, aren't you?" Goggins mumbled, and Ben knew it wasn't a compliment. "What are you doing down here, anyway? A lot has happened this past week. Half the household's been looking for you."

Ben feigned nonchalance. "Have they?"

"Aye. Lady Maybourne set us all on the task. Seemed mighty keen to see where you went after they hauled poor Mistress Althea away."

Well that confirmed it. She was in some dank cell somewhere by now.

Ben knew he should be happy about it. She was guilty, after all. But instead his heart ached. He could not leave the house. How could he rescue her?

Because whatever she'd done to him, she did not deserve Newgate. She deserved-

Ben ignored the first thoughts that came to mind, thoughts of happiness and family and *love*.

And decided she simply deserved… something other than prison.

"Why did Lady Maybourne want me? I thought she was terrified of me, poor thing."

Goggins shrugged and watched as the cat, who had been carefully making his way out of the room, darted past him and into the hallway beyond. At least one of them was happy now.

"She didn't say. But Lord Leslie made an offer to Miss Ridgely, and she accepted. The Earl intends to announce the betrothal tonight at midnight."

"And why should I care?"

Goggins shrugged, gingerly stepped into the cellar past the shards of glass and sticky puddles of residue, and selected one of the finer bottle of bordeaux still intact. "I really couldn't say, Your Grace. Enjoy your evening."

And with that, Goggins exited the cellar, leaving the door wide open.

It was surprisingly easy to blend in. Most of the guests had already arrived by the time Althea reached the ballroom on the second floor. She'd glanced in her first full day at the house, but it had been dusty and empty then. Little more than a large open space with windows overlooking the street below.

Now it was radiant.

Filled with stands of twinkling candles and members of the *ton* dressed in their finest, most whimsical attire, the ballroom of Maybourne house was transportive. Althea should have guessed.

Because it wasn't the occupants or the music of the string quartet in the little balcony above that made the room come alive, it was the light.

The tall candelabras on the floor were merely practical. The sconces not the walls were divine. Thin sheets of filigreed bronze with little shapes of moons and stars cut out between the latticework of metal, the candles within the sconces cast a dancing, otherworldly light across the room. These lined the walls, while on the ceiling the constellations had been painted in detail on an inky blue sky. How had she not noticed before? The stars sparked and twinkled in the firelight cast up from below, each tiny star above composed of a fleck of golden leaf.

Althea's breath hitched at the sight.

"Lady Smith!" Lady Maybourne appeared from the throng, looking for all the world like a hostess greeting a tardy guest. No one knew they had seen one another mere ten minutes before upstairs.

Althea curtsied, grateful for the sturdy ties on the mask the Countess had given her. "Lady Maybourne, it is an honor to attend this evening. What a crush! And the house is positively resplendent."

The Countess' eyes sparkled behind her demi-mask. It was made to look like the curving rays of a setting sun, and paired perfectly with her high-necked gown of pale pink run through with golden threads. "It is a beautiful room, isn't it? Pity I can only take credit for illuminating it. But come dear, let me escort you to the punch bowl."

As they wound their way to the side of the room, Althea's eyes raked the assembly, working to identify key players despite their costumes. A tall, lean figure who could only be the Earl of Maybourne was dancing. A man in a wolf's mask who looked very much like Lord Leslie was by the wall, deep in conversation with a portly older man with a thick mustache and a demi-mask shaped like a pumpkin. Althea did not see Charlotte, but a throng of young people in the far corner seemed a likely position.

The Countess leaned towards her as they sidled through the crowd. "Wilkes is in Charles' study. I suggest you begin there. I shall give the proper notice and be ready for midnight. Send the signal if we need to change course."

"Excellent, I shall."

They reached a table holding up a massive silver punchbowl. Althea took a glass for herself, and another for her hostess.

"Oh, you are too kind!" Lady Maybourne tittered loudly. Under her breath she added, "Good luck," and turned to visit with an collection of other guests on her right.

A moment later Althea was off, casting the contents of her glass into a potted plant by the door, she ducked back into the hallway. It was the work of a minute to reach the Earl's study.

Inside Wilkes was standing over the Earl's desk, maskless, flipping through a ledger. He started when Althea entered the room, leaving the door slightly ajar behind her.

"Madame, apologies," he murmured, taking a step away from the ledger. Althea did not need to know what he was eyeing to know it was none of his business. *How had the family not realized sooner their solicitor was a snake?*

Althea wondered if perhaps Wilkes had a bigger role in the previous Earl's financial failings than anyone knew.

That was a topic for another time, however.

"Good evening." Althea smiled at him and floated

across the room, her gown of beaded crimson silk gently brushing her against her bare legs beneath. She had never worn anything so fine, so decadent.

Tonight was a first for many things.

Truth being perhaps the most important, and the most dangerous.

"Do sit down," she waved her hand at the Earl's chair. Wilkes did not hesitate to sit in it.

He gave her a lecherous look, his beady eyes roving across her figure. She knew what he saw. The dress of bloodied silk, beaded to look like flames rising from her hem to her thighs, where the color shifted subtly, to a brighter, hotter crimson. Golden threads outlined the scandalously low bodice. The sleeves were tight and spare, barely clasping her shoulders. Not the puffed sleeves so popular with virtuous young women.

She was not dressed like a virtuous young woman.

She was dressed like sin incarnate.

The idea had been Hen's. The young woman had stated immediately that the best disguise was not merely a giant mask, but a new person entirely. A woman who flaunted herself, a creature not of darkness and eccentricity, but of power and light.

A flame.

The dress had been urgently brought over from

London's finest dressmaker. A costume destined originally for the theater, tonight it was Althea's.

She did not want to know what the gown had cost the Countess, even just to borrow for the night.

The mask, at least, had been free. The Countess had pulled it from a heavy wooden box deep in her armoire and explained that she had worn it on just such a night, a masquerade long ago, when she had met her now deceased husband.

It was a romantic story, and the mask itself was breathtaking. Althea had never asked what the Countess' background was, but her family must have been rich at Croesus. The mask was a full mask, with a slight indent along one side to highlight her high, sharp cheekbones. Painted golden at the center, the color morphed through orange and cherry red until finally it was nearly black at the edges. Flames were painted atop this, dancing and licking the high points of the face, the tip of each tendril graced with a single, miniature ruby. It was the most beautiful object Althea had ever seen, and as she'd donned it in Lady Maybourne's dressing room, Althea had felt like someone else.

A woman of fire and light. A goddess.

They'd also thrown a wig of cascading blonde curls piled high atop her head. *That* definitely made her feel like someone she was not.

But the desired effected was achieved. Jane Smith looked nothing like the notorious Mistress Althea.

Wilkes, her first true test, did not seem to know her at all. In fact, he seemed to think he was the lucky recipient of a visit from a noble lady looking for a secret rendezvous while the rest of the party was busy. Alarmingly, he also seemed to think he'd been chosen to deliver this theoretical good time.

"You're a pretty one, ain't ye?" he purred, his aristocratic airs slipping.

With relief, Althea heard a little bell sound down the hallway outside. That was her signal. It was time for the first phase of the evening.

"Mr. Wilkes, isn't it?"

Concern flashed across the man's face. His accent improved by several social ranks. "Have we met before? Surely I'd not forget such a creature as yourself."

"Our acquaintance is irrelevant, I'm afraid. I am here on a matter of business."

Wilkes *definitely* looked uncomfortable now. "And what is that?"

"How long have you known Lord Robert Leslie?"

Wilkes' eyes darted to the door. He already knew where this was going, and coward that he was, wanted no part of it. "A year, if that. I barely know him to be honest."

"And yet he is your nephew?"

Wilkes shifted in the Earl's desk chair. "I don't see how my familiar affairs are-"

"Mr. Wilkes," Althea spoke more loudly. She'd heard a scuffling sound near the door. *Good.* "Lord Leslie is currently under investigation for fraud, embezzlement, and several counts of murder. Do you have any information that would be of use to the authorities or not?"

Wilkes blinked several times, as if he had not heard her correctly. Then he stood. "Ah, yes, an investigation. Leslie, he's- he is a bad man. Terrible man, really. If you'd let me go to my office in the city I'd be happy to gather several documents I think would be of interest-"

"No." Althea's voice was sharp. "We need to know tonight. Answer my questions and you'll be set free of the matter. I have several associates listening in currently and two of them outside the windows behind you, pistols pointed at your person. If you do not wish to answer, we will have you taken to a more… inspiring setting."

Wilkes swallowed, a sheen of sweat breaking out over his brow. "I'll do my best to answer, Miss-"

"My name is not relevant here. Only your information. Tell us, is Leslie your nephew?"

"No."

"Is he as wealthy as he claims?"

"N-no. He doesn't have hardly a penny. Spent it all on the house and coach and, and his finery. To fit in."

"And why did he do that?"

"I- I don't know."

"Our other accommodations are highly conducive to productive conversation, Mr. Wilkes, I assure-"

"He has a list!"

"A list?"

Wilkes glanced nervously towards the windows, but they revealed only darkness. Which was, Althea knew, all that lay behind them. But Wilkes did not know that.

"He is a most vindictive man. He remembers every slight, every insult. Covets that which others have and- and does whatever he needs to in order to achieve his own ends. Or...."

"Or what, Mr. Wilkes?"

"Revenge."

"Revenge for what, Mr. Wilkes?"

"That I do not know, Madame. He never told me. Only that he has a long list. I've seen it. Most of the names are crossed off, but he has a few left."

"And he asked you to help him?"

Wilkes swallowed again, a bead of sweat sliding down the side of his face. "It was not a request."

Althea's voice was firm, unyielding. She had the confirmation of her theory, but she wanted one last bit of truth from Wilkes. "How did he convince you, then?"

Wilkes said nothing, but glanced again towards the windows. Another shuffling sound came from the door to the hall. She was losing time, and she still had not found Ben. No one had. Midnight was approaching, and she had to ensure everything was in place before then.

She took a chance.

"Did he learn of your embezzlement?"

Wilkes blanched. Althea felt triumph surge inside her. She was right. She could take down more than just Leslie tonight.

"I do not know what you've heard, but I deal honestly with my clients."

"You mean Leslie did not discover your petty thefts and your creative bookkeeping? He did not watch you from just outside these very windows, which face his own house so clearly, as you stole from the Earl of Maybourne."

The look on Wilkes face told her she hit her target.

Wilkes leapt up. *"You bitch,"* he hissed and lunged for her.

At that moment the door to the hallway burst open and the Earl of Maybourne strode inside. He was wearing a mask like a golden lion, but his ice blue eyes were unmistakable. And, just now, they were livid. Several footmen and Goggins rushed in at the Earl's heels.

Wilkes staggered back and realized he had been tricked. Before anyone could reach him, he spun on his heel and jumped out one of the open windows behind the desk. A loud thud and pained cry confirmed he was still alive. Althea suspected he had forgotten the study was on the second floor.

Not that it mattered to her.

The footmen turned and ran out of the room, shouting to get others to meet them in the garden, where they could capture Wilkes, who was likely not moving quickly after the fall.

Maybourne paused long enough to take Althea's hand. "I do not know who you are, my lady, but I owe you a great debt."

"Consider it a gift," Althea said, and meant it. She did not care about the money any longer. She should never have cared- there were other ways to survive, other jobs. Her refusal to listen to Ben and put her greed aside had nearly cost her everything.

Maybourne looked as if he wished to say more, but at that moment Wilkes gave another yelp below the window. The Earl spun on his heel and ran from the room.

"Very well done, Mistress," Goggins said once the room was empty. She was not surprised he, at least, recognized her. "Ben will be delighted to hear of this."

Althea stilled. "Have you seen him, Goggins? Do you know where he is?"

Goggins nodded. "I saw him only minutes ago. He'd been trapped in the wine cellar."

Relief washed over Althea so powerful she let out a strangled sob. "Is he alright?"

"He was a bit worse for wear, but I think you'll find your ambitions this evening are in alignment."

A maelstrom of emotions battled in Althea's mind, her heart, but she did not have time to sort them out now. Ben was a selfish, horrible cad and she could not trust him, but she also knew she could not let Leslie destroy him. If she didn't stop Leslie tonight, before he saw his demise coming, she might not get another chance. Leslie was a dangerous man, and like a wild beast, would be more dangerous when cornered.

"Thank you, Goggins. Where is he now?"

"I'm not certain but I'd hazard a guess he is

looking for Miss Ridgely."

Of course, Althea thought. He would try to convince her not to go through with the betrothal. It was all he could do, short of bringing the furniture down on Leslie's head.

Which, if he had to, he very well might. He'd shown a real aptitude for violent objects that day in the blue parlor.

"Where is Charlotte?"

"I'd imagine she is either dancing or freshening up. She chose an ensemble this evening with rather a lot of powder."

Althea laughed, and threw her arms around the old butler. "Thank you Goggins, thank you."

As she stepped back, Goggins did not flinch. He merely straightened the sleeves of his jacket and said, "Yes, m'am."

Charlotte was in her rooms, powdering her cheeks. Ben was not surprised to find her there, nor was he surprised that she had chosen a masquerade ensemble with the least amount of mask possible.

Dressed as a shepherdess, but all in soft pinks and blues, her mask was little more than a filigreed plaster eyepatch with an opening large enough for anyone to see her lovely, big, blue eyes. She obviously wanted everyone to know exactly who she was, and decide she was absolutely lovely.

Ben found the costume both gaudy and an affront to the spirit of the event, but then, there were more important topics to confront her about.

He appeared directly behind her.

She jumped, and seeing his reflection in her dressing mirror, screamed.

"Hush, woman! Good god, you want everyone to come running?"

Charlotte whirled on him. "Only if it means you go away again."

Suspicion flared in Ben's mind. "Did you lock me in the wine cellar?"

Her brow wrinkled with genuine confusion. "No. Is that- is that where you've been all this time?"

"Don't worry about it. I need to talk to you."

She shrugged and sat down again to continuing re-applying her make-up. "I can't imagine why. Everything is quite settled now. I've come to my senses and realized how utterly hen-brained I was to be in love with *you*, when you're dead. And now I am going to marry Lord Leslie, who is both alive and rich."

Ben floated to her side and glared down at her. "You can't marry Leslie."

"I can and I will. Tonight, in fact."

Ben froze. "Excuse me?"

Charlotte looked up at him with an angelic smile and batted her long, thick eyelashes. "We decided it would be a surprise. Even mother and Charles don't know. Wilkes got us a special license. Instead of a betrothal party, this is our wedding party."

Ben staggered back.

"No."

Charlotte shrugged. "Yes."

The door to Charlotte's bedroom burst open at that moment and both of them whirled towards it.

"Who are you?" Charlotte asked, but Ben knew.

Althea.

Except, she wasn't Althea.

She was blonde, but that was not what made her… different. The thoughtful, cynical creature he knew had been replaced by a sinuous, fiery Valkyrie. Just as he had once imagined, she wore red, but the effect was not merely pleasing. It was devastating. He wanted to pull her into his arms and rip off her silly wig and that fantastical mask and bury his head in her hair and then kiss her senseless.

But he could do nothing but stare at her. Helpless, as always.

"You may call me Lady Smith," Althea said, her

eyes ablaze as they moved from Ben to Charlotte and back.

Ben knew how this looked. Althea already thought he'd lied to her, that he was secretly in love with Charlotte all along- or, worse, that he'd been so heartless that he had played both women's affections for his own amusement and gain. Either way, it did not look good.

"Well, Lady Smith, this my private bedroom. If you're looking for the privy, I suggest you go-"

"I am not looking for the privy." Althea took a step closer and Charlotte snapped her mouth shut in outrage. "I am looking for *you*."

The words were addressed to Charlotte, and Ben hated the way that fact... hurt.

Which was ridiculous. Althea owed him nothing. In fact, she'd lied to him, too. He would be more than happy to never speak to her again, now that he knew she was, miraculously, out of prison.

Safe.

Alive.

Near him.

Damn it all.

With a huff of frustration, he floated between the two women. "Come now, *Lady Jane*," he said, his eyes meeting Althea's to inform her that he knew exactly who she was. "There is no need to take this tone. I'm sure whatever you have to discuss with Miss Ridgely can be done in a civilized-"

"Wait a moment!" Charlotte screeched, standing and knocking over the stool she had been sitting on. "You're not afraid of him- you're not even surprised he's here. Charlotte peered through Ben's translucent form, then, finding that ineffectual, over his shoulder, at Althea. "*It's you,*" she hissed.

Althea watched her with stony regard. "You cannot marry Lord Leslie, Charlotte. He is a liar, a thief, and a murderer."

Charlotte staggered back and let out a bark of laughter. "Oh that's rich! Coming from *you*, of all people."

Althea took a step towards her, not even looking at Ben. He hated it. Hated the way she ignored him.

"He is not a well, man, Charlotte. He only wishes you to marry you so that he can destroy this house and Ben with it."

Charlotte laughed. "That doesn't even make sense! He is a proper gentleman. Have you seen his friends? His clothes? *His carriage*? He is young and wealthy and has no use for this house or Ben."

Althea eyes were earnest beneath her glorious mask. "Charlotte, please listen to me. None of you are safe as long as Leslie is free. You are nothing but a pawn to him."

Charlotte's laugh took on a bitter, slightly hysterical note. "Aren't I a pawn to everyone? Isn't that my greatest feature? Poor, insipid Miss Ridgely. So pretty, so shallow. All she's good for is getting money back into the family coffers."

Althea flinched. "It does not have to be like that. There are other ways, Charlotte."

"Oh, like what, lying and cheating for money? Where did that get you?"

Ben cleared his throat. "I don't think you're going to make progress here, Althea."

Both women turned on him. "She's back to being Althea, is she?"

"Stay out of this!"

Ben floated back to look at both of them. The two women could not be more different. "Ladies, enough. Charlotte, Althea is right. Leslie is a villain. You cannot marry him."

Charlotte's dainty mouth snapped shut and she looked from Ben to Althea and back. After a moment, she gave a haughty sniff. "You two deserve each other. I hope you both rot in hell, or wherever Leslie sends you. He's a good man and better yet, he's a *living* man."

She snatched up her reticule and stormed out the door, leaving Ben and Althea alone, staring at one another helplessly.

Chapter Eighteen
The Fraud

"You don't love her?" Althea asked.

Ben knew the words cost her. He shook his head slowly. "No. I don't."

She nodded, her expression unreadable behind her mask.

"Do you have a lover?" The words escaped before he could stop them.

Her head snapped up. "Is that supposed to be a joke?"

"What? No. I- I saw the letter in your room. I mean my room. I mean- it was on the table. I've seen you writing them, and I wondered-"

Althea's head tilted back and she let out a long laugh. "Oh no! No, Ben, don't tell me-" She lifted her mask to wipe away a tear. "You thought N. was my lover?"

Ben felt sheepish. Suddenly, profoundly, an idiot. "Yes."

Althea took a step toward him, then caught herself. "N. is Nora, better known to the world as Madame Veira."

Relief flooded Ben and filled him to the brim. He floated back, letting the information settle in. "So you did not betray me?"

Althea's expression turned rueful. "Not exactly. I was going to try and banish you to the Void, because I caught you seducing Charlotte again. But no, I have no other lover."

Other lover. Ben knew there were more important words in her sentence, but those two were the only ones that hit him like a punch to the gut. They were lovers. Of course they were, after what they'd done. What they'd shared. But to hear her say it...

"I understand if you hate me about the Void bit. Turns out I'm not a witch after all, so I couldn't do it anyway, but I was just so angry with you, and-"

Ben raised a hand to quiet her. "Althea, it's fine. I forgive you. I was an idiot for not turning Charlotte away sooner. I was a selfish cad for just trying to save my own skin."

He paused and looked down.

"I don't even have skin."

Althea giggled, seeming even more like a new woman. Whoever she was, Ben wanted to know her, too. He wanted to know every version of her, past, present, and future.

Don't.

The voice in his mind was stern with warning. There was no future for them. There couldn't be. But there was right now, tonight, and there was a job to finish. Then she would be safe, and so would he, because Leslie would be stopped... and Althea would be gone.

"We have to do something about Leslie."

Althea straightened. "I know. Lady Maybourne and I have a plan."

Ben blinked. "You and, excuse me, *Lady Maybourne?*"

"I'll explain later. What time is it?"

Ben glanced to the clock on the wall. "Half an hour until midnight."

Althea nodded. "We're running out of time. We have to hurry. The Earl is going to announce Charlotte's betrothal to Leslie at midnight and Wilkes just confessed to assisting him. If Leslie does not reveal himself and his crimes tonight it will be so much harder to stop him."

"Impossible even."

Althea's eyes shot to his. "What do you mean?"

"They aren't getting engaged midnight. They're getting married. A surprise for the family. Not even the Earl knows."

Ben knew Althea's face paled beneath her bejeweled mask. "Then we have to go, now."

"What's the plan?"

"Follow me, and I'll explain."

The attic was dark and and stale and smelled of dust. Even the air felt thick with it, with age and silence, as if neither wanted to move nor allow anyone to move through it.

Althea bit back a cough and held the single candle she carried higher.

She had never been up here, and as she inched along the thin, narrow floorboards, she knew why. Ben had claimed only the chandelier remained for the house to be finished, but this was an area of the house that still felt half-formed. Boards and construction materials sat in stacks and piles on the floor. Crates were piled high, and stained sheets covered countless strange, indecipherable objects. This room was the repository of anything unwanted in the house, and had been since it was built. No wonder the Earl did not know what was kept up here.

There was darkness here, too. Something darker than the absence of light that pressed in wherever Althea's single candle did not touch. She thought of those boys all those years ago, of poor Henry and the young Leslie's madness. For it had been madness. Children could be cruel, but to be driven to murder, and this calculated scheme for total revenge, it was not the work of a healthy mind. Wilkes' confession implied there were others, as well. A list of anyone who had wronged Leslie, a testament to his vengeance.

With a sudden chill Althea realized if she did not complete her task this evening her name would be added to that list.

He had to be stopped, and she had to do it.

The air around her grew lighter, a pale, silvery blue. She paused and turned around, careful not to disrupt the piles of junk on either side of her.

Ben's face was grim. "He's on his way. The message worked."

"Good."

"Althea, why don't you let me handle this? I can get him to confess as well as you can, and it won't be safe for you here. He's a dangerous man. And this room- can't you feel it? Ever since Henry died there has been an evil here."

Althea glanced over her shoulder at the narrow strip of moonlight that came through accumulated bric-a-brac. A large, round window presided over the far side of the attic, looking over the back of the house. The window Henry had been pushed out of. Glass shards, coated in thick dust, still covered the floor, though the window had been mostly covered with planks of wood by some subsequent Earl of Maybourne.

She turned back to Ben. "It has to be me. You would upset him too much. He would never trust you."

"If he is upset, he is more likely to make a mistake."

"*Trust me*, Ben. Please? I have lied and playacted my entire life, always on the edge of disaster, always courting danger. And nothing bad will happen. You will be here, and the others know what we're about. Once he's confessed, we're done."

Ben regarded her with stony defiance as a muscle in his jaw twitched.

"I know you want to do everything yourself, and I don't blame you for it. I would not trust me, either, after what we've been through. But I'm asking you to take a leap of faith. Let me do this. Let me help you."

"You don't understand. It is too dangerous. He is too dangerous, this room- it's, it isn't safe up here, Althea, it's falling apart. Be reasonable. I won't let anything happen to you. I-"

Whatever Ben was about to say was cut off by a creaking on the narrow stairway that led into the attic.

"He's coming," Althea breathed. "Go. Now. You know the plan, just *trust me*."

Ben's eyes flashed in defiance, but he disappeared, like a candle blowing out.

Althea took a steadying breath and raised her own candle higher so only her face was visible, floating in the darkness.

A heavy thud told her Leslie had arrived.

"Good evening, my lord. I'm pleased you could spare a moment for our little rendezvous."

Ben hated this. Ben hated every blasted second of this. Leslie was at the top of the stairs, eyeing Althea with wary assessment. His face was mostly covered by the snarling likeness of a great, white wolf. His light grey jacket and white brocade vest made him look ghostly in the darkness. The mask made him look rabid. Vicious. Dangerous.

Every instinct Ben had told him this was a bad idea.

But he could do nothing to stop it.

Well, you could... His mind flashed an image of Ben using his ghostly powers to break off a sharp piece of wood and run Leslie through with it.

Except that would not solve anything, because Althea would be blamed, and seeing as she only just got out of prison for fraud he doubted she wanted to return for murder.

So he hung back amidst the piles of construction materials and priceless artifacts no one had bothered to uncover for decades, stayed invisible, and waited.

"You're not the individual I was told to meet here," Leslie said quietly, stepping gingerly into the attic like a wild animal fearing a trap.

He was right to be afraid. It *was* a trap. But Althea knew her part, knew she would have to use every bit of her cleverness and illusion to obtain Leslie's confession.

"You really believed the footman when he said poor little Henry was here? Hard to imagine you are so sentimental, Leslie."

Lord Leslie's eyes narrowed. Their masked faces were lit only by the candles each held, the rest of the dark, cavernous space cast in deep shadow.

"I did not come up here for sentiment. I came to see who was threatening me."

"Threatening you?" Althea's voice was arch, calm.

"Yes, using this place and that name to summon me on this happy evening, I consider that a threat. I must be downstairs in ten minutes to announce my betrothal, so let's not waste time. Who are you?"

Althea took a step backwards, deeper into the attic, in the direction of the front of the house. She'd already assessed which part was directly above the foyer. The servants had done her bidding well. If she could get Leslie to admit his crimes directly above the hole in the floor where Ben's chandelier had been intended to hang, the funnel Althea had fashioned to amplify the sound would take whatever was said and deliver it to those assembled below.

It was a trick she'd used in her summonings, a way to evoke the presence of spirits when there were none.

Or so Althea had thought.

Tonight the trick was not meant to conjure evil, but to end it.

She had only to draw Leslie close to that hole in the floorboards, and with Ben's help she would do whatever she must to inspire his confession.

Leslie took a step after her. Good.

"*Who are you?*" he snarled.

She was only a few feet from the opening now. A small amount of light, filtered by the funnel she'd had the servants carefully reach down and affix to it below, marked the spot.

She paused, and removed first her wig, and then her mask.

"*You.*" Leslie's growl was guttural and furious. "You think to blackmail me? The Earl not paying you enough? Or did he decide he did not need to reward a criminal?"

"You would know the rewards of criminality better than I would, Leslie. I've seen your carriage. Costs more than your uncle would make in a year."

"My wealth and my family are none of your concern."

Good, Althea thought. He did not know anything had happened to Wilkes. If he had, he would have let on. Or, more likely, he would have fled himself.

She took another step back, the beadwork at the hem of her gown hissing along the rough wooden floorboards. "You mention blackmail, but that is not what I seek."

Leslie took a step forward, his wolf's mask snarling silently down at her. He was a tall man, taller than Althea had realized. A flash of nerves ran through her. Some of the servants would be waiting at the base of the attic stairs, just in case she needed help. It would be fine. *She* would be fine.

"What do you seek then, *Mistress Althea?*" Leslie spoke her name as if it were a curse.

It was beginning to feel that way. But she could not let him know she was afraid. He needed to see what she wanted him to see. What *he* wanted to see.

"An alliance," she said.

Leslie stopped short. "An alliance? What sort of

alliance?"

"I will capture Ben for you if you promise not to marry Charlotte Ridgely."

Leslie paused, calculating. "Why?"

"Because I know who you are and what you've done, and she deserves better, frankly."

Leslie snorted. "Does she? I thought the two of you were getting on about as well as a fox and a hen."

"Am I the fox?"

"That remains to be seen."

Althea straightened. "I am a businesswoman, my lord. My reputation with the Ridgelys and their peers is the lifeblood of my business. This is especially so after my recent... misunderstanding with the authorities. I will not be hired to see Charlotte wed to a living man only to have that living man be *you*.

"I'm touched. And insulted," Leslie pressed a hand to his chest in a mock bow. "But Charlotte is the one who sent you to Newgate, surely you cannot feel so charitably towards her?"

"She is young and foolish, but she is not a bad person."

Leslie stilled. "And I am?"

"I know what you did here, in this very room, thirty years ago, and I know what you've done since."

A sound, primal and dark, issued from Leslie's

throat, rendering his strange mask even more lifelike. Althea's stomach quivered, but she held fast. She was getting close. If Lady Maybourne had done her part everyone should be assembled below, quiet, waiting. Listening.

"You know *nothing*."

"I am a mystic, my lord. I know far more than you give me credit for. I spoke to Henry, the boy you murdered thirty years ago. He confirmed everything."

"I don't believe you."

Damn it. Althea decided it was time for phase two.

"Don't believe me? I *can* summon spirits, you know. Will them to me, extract from them the information I or my clients seek. Would you care for a demonstration?"

To her surprise, Leslie kneeled, set his own candlestick on the floor beside him, straightened, and shrugged. "I don't appreciate games, but this party has been dull. So why not? Amuse me."

Althea bristled at his tone, but she had no choice. She reached into her bodice and pulled the necklace Nora had given her over her head. It's stone amulet glittered in the candlelight. Labradorite, wrapped in lead. Both, Althea had read in the book from Simonson's, held acute magical properties. One could summon spirits, the other could bind them.

At least in theory. Althea knew it was unlikely she could eek such powers from the thing, that only a true witch could use it as it was meant to be used, but Leslie did not know that.

She held it aloft in one hand as she raised her candlestick in the other.

"What the devil is that?" Leslie asked, ripping off his mask to get a better look at the stone in Althea's hand. But she ignored him.

"Hear me, oh spirits of this house!" Her voice was strong and powerful. Commanding. "You harbor in your midst he who built you, he who is bound forever unto this place, cursed in fear, so show him to me, bring him forth, bring him here!"

There was a roaring sound, like wind descending, and then with a pop, Ben appeared.

"How dare you?" he demanded, then looked at Leslie. "What is he doing here?"

Althea did not answer, but kept her gaze locked on Ben. He'd told her what he'd been up to in the wine cellar all week, and they'd decided to use his newfound skill.

She narrowed her eyes, flame and amulet still held aloft. "Silence!"

Ben rounded on her. "Don't *silence* me, woman! I built this house! It's *mine*. And I don't much like you in it- or him. In fact, I'm done with this nonsense. You can't just summon me here like I'm some kitchen boy. I am lord here. *You* get out. Now!"

Althea's chest heaved with forceful breaths as she summoned her strength, eyes focused on Ben. She transferred the necklace to the same hand that held her candlestick, reached between her breasts, and removed a perfume bottle the size of her palm.

"What the-" Ben started, but Althea cut him off. Her voice was hollow, empty, as if she were only a vessel as unseen powers spoke through her.

"I bind thee, spirit, bind thee unto my powers as you once were bound unto this house. Cursed forever ye shall be, but now you are mine eternally!"

Althea's arm jutted out, pointing the mouth of the bottle at Ben.

With a very convincing shriek of horror and dismay, Ben slowly dissolved himself little by little into smoke as he funneled himself into the perfume bottle. Once fully inside, Althea popped the cork in.

"There," she said, turning to Leslie. "Do you still think I'm a liar?"

Leslie hadn't moved.

A chill ran through Althea. There was a look in his eyes that told her she had made a grave miscalculation. Her mind raced to determine what it was. He'd been so close to admitting his wrongdoing, even now with what they had on him, he could be ostracized… she only wanted to convince him to ally with her, to see her as someone he could trust enough to be honest. Even for a moment. Even if he only admitted to murdering Henry it would be enough to put him away forever…

Leslie raised his slender, pale hands and slowly clapped, walking closer to her with every contact.

Smack.

Smack.

Smack.

Althea lowered the candle she held back to its normal height, and glanced nervously towards the door.

Smack.

Leslie was only a few feet from her now, so close to the hole in the floor. Anything he said now would be perfectly audible below.

Althea's heart raced.

"Very dramatic, Mistress Althea," Leslie purred, his eyes glinting in the candlelight. "I'm sure those sorts of theatrics work wonders on old ladies and small children."

Althea said nothing. Her mind was racing. He wasn't falling for it, for any of it. She just needed him to confess.

"I, however, am neither."

"No, you're not," she said. "You are a liar. A thief. And a murderer of innocents. Aren't you?"

Leslie's lips turned up. "Oh, I am."

That was a confession. Not thorough, but enough to have him locked up and interrogated properly. Althea knew her heart should soar with triumph, but as she beheld the look on Leslie's face she found it was sinking like a stone.

His smile was vicious, feral. Evil. "But I am so much more than that, you little fool. Now give me that pretty little necklace of yours."

Althea glanced at the necklace Nora had given her, still gripped tightly in the fingers that held up her candlestick. "No. It was a gift. And I think we are done here, my lord." She opened her mouth to shout to the servants at the foot of the stairs, but no sound came out. She felt as if the air were being sucked out of her lungs.

She looked at Leslie, who stood before her with one hand raised high before her shocked face. He was mumbling something under his breath, something strange and terrible and-

He stopped and her lungs opened again. Coughing, Althea gasped, "You're- you're- you know magic?"

Leslie's smile was smug. "Of course I do. I'm a witch."

Althea's racing heart stopped. "Oh good god, not you, too."

The opaque blue glass of the perfume bottle was annoyingly thick. Ben couldn't hear very well from inside, but he knew things were going poorly. Althea should have gotten Leslie's confession by now, and it sounded like Leslie just admitted to being a witch. Which couldn't be right, but then, it was obviously something was wrong.

He knew this was not going to go according to plan.

If only they'd consulted him earlier.

He could have thought of something far more foolproof, far less dangerous.

Why she'd listened to Lady Maybourne's counsel he still didn't know, they the woman was clearly a kindly, harebrained...

Althea dropped the bottle and suddenly Ben's world exploded.

In a flash, he was back to his usual form.

A moment later he was enraged- and terrified.

Leslie was standing mere feet from Althea pointing

a small pistol straight at her heart. Both of them were only a short distance from that damned hole in the floor she said she'd rigged up to broadcast this little meeting. But if everyone at the ball downstairs was listening, why had no one come up to help? Was Althea really going to let herself get murdered just to prove Leslie was a murderer?

"Put down your pistol at once, sir," Ben commanded Leslie in his most frightening, ghoulish voice.

Leslie barely glanced at him. "No, thank you. Why don't you run along now and scare somebody else?"

Althea shot Ben a warning glance.

He ignored it. "I said, put your pistol down. If you shoot her everyone will know you're a murderer."

Althea, desperation in her black eyes, looked to Leslie. "They already do, Leslie. They're all in the entry hall directly below us now. They've heard everything. So why don't you put the pistol down and-"

Leslie gave a low, dark chuckle. "You're both idiots. I knew you'd try to trap me into a confession. Either that or you, Mistress Althea, were really as unscrupulous as they say and wanted to squeeze me for coin. I came up here anyway. And do you know why?"

Althea and Ben looked at one another. Leslie's pistol was still pointed at Althea's heart, and at this range, even with the darkness of the attic, a shot would be fatal.

Ben's mind raced. He had to *do* something. He refused to stand by helpless for a second time as death came for someone he loved-

Loved.

Oh lord. He loved Althea. Even though he couldn't trust her. Even though she- well, she hadn't lied to him. He'd been her only lover. And she'd only tried to cast him into the Void because she thought he'd wronged her.

They'd both been fools.

And now- damn it all to hell, he *loved* her.

He could not let her die, not like this. Not for another fifty years. Or more. Or ever.

He had to do something.

Chapter Nineteen
The Host

Althea's heart was hammering so hard she could barely hold onto the candlestick. She'd already dropped the bottle, but that was mostly to get Ben's attention. She'd surmised he could not hear what was going on, and she definitely needed his help.

She needed everybody's help.

Where were the others?

Her eyes glanced to the stairwell.

Leslie rolled his eyes. "No one is coming because I rendered the stairway impassable. Simple blocking charm. Now focus, my dear. I was telling you why I came up here even though I knew it was a trap."

Althea didn't want to indulge Leslie but the longer she kept him talking, the better chance she and Ben had to figure out a plan. "Why?"

"For the same reason I killed those boys. And the next door neighbors. And everybody else."

Althea's brow furrowed. She didn't need to ask. She didn't want to ask.

Leslie gave her the answer anyway. "Because power isn't money, Mistress Althea. It isn't status. It isn't a war ship or a membership at White's. *Life* is power. And some of us are lucky enough to know how to extract it."

"You mean you killed all those people to steal their life force?"

Ben threw his hands up in the air. "Althea don't listen to this, the man is mad. He's clearly lost his-"

Leslie shot out a hand and blasted Ben backwards across the room.

Althea shrieked, but could do nothing. Ben had no body, and she had a pistol pointed at her heart.

"I was an orphan, did you know that?" Leslie asked, his voice soft and bitter. "Of course not. You see, the Crown made it illegal to kill witches nearly a century ago, but that didn't stop the common folk. They still found ways to persecute my kind. My mother was falsely accused of theft, and in a terrible tragedy was strangled before she reached gaol. No one would admit what happened, but I knew. I was six, and I left, before they could get me, too. But not before I'd taken my mother's spell books, buried beneath the floorboards of our tiny, rat-infested cottage."

Althea waited for Ben to stir, but he was hovering motionless, a few inches from the floor by the big, half-boarded window. And Leslie was still talking.

"They were very old, the books. Complicated. Dangerous. For two years I read them, memorizing them, and then I burned them."

"Smart of you," Althea mumbled, watching Ben from the corner of her eye. He still hadn't moved.

"I know," Leslie smiled, looking truly mad. "By then I'd come to London, and found that even for a smart young lad there was no way up in the world. Only sideways and down. I didn't like that."

"None of us do."

"You've done surprisingly well for yourself," Leslie allowed, "but we're not talking about you. I am talking about *me*. You wanted my confession, I will give it to you. It's a little experiment. If I unburden my soul a bit, perhaps I can siphon off more of yours. Life force, or *souls* if you will, strengthen my magic. At a cost to my own soul, of course, should I die- murder is terrible for that- but then if you capture enough of other people's lives you can extend yours indefinitely, according to my dear mother's books. So far, they've been correct."

True fear ran through Althea. She had to get out of here. She had to get *Ben* out of here.

"You are a monster."

"And you're not? How many hearts have you saved that should be broken? How many purses have you emptied that should be full? I may take souls but you act as if they mean nothing, Mistress Althea. You use them for your own gain, how are we any different?"

Althea's chest rose and fell. "I do not think I have the power the decree life and death, Leslie. I merely help interpret it. We are not the same."

"Aren't we? You despise your clients. It's obvious. I share your contempt for the upper classes. Privilege for those who luck into it, never those that earn it. I've found a way to take what I deserve. Can you honestly tell me you have not done the same?"

Althea said nothing.

"I thought so," Leslie sniffed. "As I was saying, I found employment with the Baronet next door and befriended the other boys my age. His son was a sad, lonely thing and followed us around even though he was our superior in the eyes of the world. It was a simple thing to get them drunk and convince them to come here. I'd suspected there was a ghost in the house, but I wasn't afraid of it. It was the perfect bait for bored little boys, and I knew I was far more dangerous than any ghost."

"So you did it all on purpose."

"Yes, Althea. Every. Single. One."

"But why did you come back?"

Leslie shrugged. "Consider me sentimental. That, and I knew this damned attic was filled with more valuables than the Regent's palace. I'd scouted the house before I brought the boys here, but as a child I hadn't realized what all this was. Later, when I did, the Maybournes owned the place and it was impossible to get in."

"So you aren't trying to destroy the house?"

"Of course not. I'm trying to own it."

Althea's mind raced. "You didn't try to burn it down? Lady Maybourne said-"

Leslie chuckled. "That was Wilkes. Trying to undermine me without my knowing it. He didn't know the value was up here. He thought it was the house itself and if he damaged the place he could buy it out from under Maybourne and sell it back to me for higher. As if I wouldn't have killed him first."

Althea swallowed and willed Ben to move. Nothing.

"So now what? Everyone downstairs can hear you. You can't kill me and get away with it."

"Not without a proper distraction. I was going to set fire to the house and rappel out that stupid window with whatever valuables I could carry. It felt poetic, having pushed Henry out of it and all."

"You're really horrible," Althea grimaced. "I mean truly abhorrent."

Leslie leveled a flat look at her. "Aren't we all? But it doesn't matter, because I have a new plan. A much better plan."

Althea's blood ran cold. "What do you mean?"

Leslie gestured to her hand with the muzzle of his pistol. "Give me that necklace."

Althea knew it was stupid to refuse, but if he wanted it that badly, her instincts told her to keep it from him. "No."

"You don't even know what it is, do you?"

"Labradorite."

"Yes, and?"

"And iron."

Leslie sighed. "In your possession, yes, that's it. Because you have no gifts, it will do nothing for you. For *me*, however…"

He eyed the stone dangling beneath her fingers with pure hunger. "Give it to me."

"*No.*"

He straightedges his arm, the pistol dead set on her heart. "I will not ask again."

Ben felt like the entire house had fallen on him. Crushed, that was the feeling. And it was awful.

Consciousness returned to him slowly. Something about Leslie and the attic, and he was a witch? Yes, that was it. And Althea, something about Althea being-

Ben floated upright.

He must not have been out long, because Leslie still stood before Althea, his pistol pointed at her heart.

"I will not give it to you," Althea said in a low, steady voice.

"Then I will take it," Leslie snapped and pulled the trigger.

Instantly, Ben disappeared and reappeared in front of Althea, putting himself between the bullet and her chest. She shouted and fell to the side as the bullet passed straight through him and into her shoulder.

She cried out, landing hard on the floor as the candle she'd held went out.

Ben shouted, and spun towards Leslie, who ignored him as well as the sudden darkness around them. He merely walked over to Althea and snatched something from her hands.

And put it over his head.

A necklace.

Ben didn't care why. He cared for nothing but Althea. He kneeled beside her, cursing his existence. He wanted to hold her, care for her, bind her wound. It wasn't fatal- it couldn't be, he would not allow it- but there was so much blood already.

He conjured a gust of wind to lift her head.

Her eyes fluttered open. "Ben? You're alive? Well, I mean... ow, my shoulder hurts."

"You've been shot. Leslie shot you."

She tried to sit up, but fell down again with a cry of pain.

"Don't move, darling. I'll get us out of this."

"No, you won't," Leslie said quietly, standing over them. "I'll be escorting you somewhere else, I'm afraid. And I don't think you'll like it very much."

Ben straightened, hovering protectively over Althea. He used another gust of wind to silently raise several of the crates behind Leslie. He'd bring them down on his-

With a hiss, Leslie spun around and waves an arm at the crates. They blasted into splinters. "*Enough*," he hissed. "I'm going to create my distraction, kill the two of you, and get the hell out of here. With two souls as powerful as yours bolstering my power, I should be set for some time."

"How are you going to distract everyone when they can hear everything you're saying?"

"I shall have to create something that cannot be ignored. You might appreciate this, with your little air tricks. I shall bring a storm upon this house, such as none can withstand."

Before Ben could say or do anything to stop him,

Leslie ripped the stone amulet from the cord at his neck and held it aloft, and began chanting in a low, urgent voice.

Althea tried to sit up again. "What's he saying?" she whispered.

"I don't know. It's not any language I've ever heard."

Faster and faster Leslie spoke and the house shuddered.

"Ben, we need to get out of here. Everyone needs to get out of here. Disappear. Warn them." Her voice was barely audible now over the howling in the air.

Ben took one look at her, the woman he loved, struggling to sit up as her blood died her dress a deeper crimson. "No, Althea. They heard enough. They'll go. And I won't leave you."

"Ben you must-"

"No," he said again, as the house shuddered a second time. The sound of howling winds echoing a long way off, getting closer. As if a maelstrom were descending upon the house. "I won't go anywhere without you. We have to get you to safety."

He glanced towards the stairwell. It was too far, the path through all this treasure too narrow. Leslie would stop them. There was no way out.

Leslie's voice grew louder, and the howling of the

wind strengthened. It sounded like screams now, hundreds, no- thousands of voices, taken by the wind, twisted, amplified, cast out. The house shuddered a third time.

Ben felt helpless. Again. Perhaps he should try and disappear, but for what? He could not carry a weapon back up with him. He could not fight Leslie, whose own supernatural gifts were clearly superior to his own.

He sent his own small pocket of air to bolster Althea, to help her sit up.

It was all he could do.

Althea was livid. She was furious about getting shot. She was angry about her plan to stop him going completely sideways. And she was positively beside herself that she could do nothing to help Ben.

If Leslie brought this whole house down- which seemed increasingly likely, as the whole place groaned and shook under the power of whatever spell he was casting- Ben would go with it.

She could not let that happen.

She also couldn't sit up.

Then, suddenly, everything was still.

Dread filled Althea as she turned to the place where Leslie stood, facing the boarded up window.

Except there it was no longer a window of glass and wood. It was a window of writhing, screaming darkness.

Althea's blood turned to ice.

"Ben," she whispered. "What is that?"

She knew the answer before he spoke. Knew it in some deep, primal place in her soul.

"The Void," Ben breathed. "He didn't conjure a storm. He conjured a doorway into the Void."

A sense of cold emptiness, of *nothingness*, so profound Althea's every fibre screamed to flee, emanated from that gaping wound in the world.

Leslie staggered back, looking at the stone in his hand. "It was supposed to be a storm. I- I don't know what happened."

He turned to Althea and Ben. "But perhaps it's easier this way."

He rushed at Althea and grabbed her ankles. Fiery bolts of agony ran through her body, exploding in her shoulder. She screamed and thrashed, trying to dislodge him.

Ben flung object after object, anything he could find at Leslie's exposed back, but Leslie was able to fend off every attack. He'd been right about the power he'd gained from killing all those innocents. He was unstoppable.

But Ben kept fighting, kept trying to save her, as Leslie dragged Althea closer to the quivering, pulsing portal of nothing across the room.

When Leslie half-turned to blast apart a pianoforte Ben had launched at his head, Althea freed one booted foot and kicked. Her heel made contact, crashing into Leslie's nose with a sickening crunch. He cried out and let go of her. She scrambled back, supporting herself on one elbow.

As she did so, she realized no one was coming to save them.

No one could make it past Leslie's defenses.

No one could stop him.

No one could save her, and not even she could save Ben.

Except...

She'd been a fraud her entire career. Now that's she stumbled into the reality of forces beyond this world, she knew with certainty she'd never come close to them before. All those years that she had pretended to communicate with the dead, she'd been speaking to empty air. She was not a witch. She had no supernatural powers whatsoever.

She had only her wits, her instincts, and a will to survive.

All three now told her exactly what to do.

* * *

Ben's powers were flickering. It rarely happened, but he knew he could burn out. Every attack he launched at Leslie took more of his energy. Every new onslaught was weaker than the last. He was running out of time.

Worse, he was running out of hope.

At least Althea had landed that excellent blow to Leslie's thin, arrogant nose.

Seizing the opportunity, Ben doubled his attack while Leslie was down. Every object he could find, every golden candlestick and ancient Roman bust he'd hoarded up here for decades now came flying, battering Leslie with all the force Ben could muster.

Even hunched and in pain, Leslie easily kept up.

Ben roared with frustration, watching as his swings grew shorter. His blows grew softer. His powers lessened.

Away to his right Althea was hunched in the shadows, praying.

Praying? He hadn't thought her a religious woman, so that couldn't be right.

But if ever there was a time to find God, this was it. Ben would not judge her for it. If anything he was envious, as he knew there was little any higher power could do for him now.

* * *

"Spirits of this house, come to me. Come here. Help us, please. Help Ben. Henry, sweet Henry, awaken. Please come and aid us. Stop Leslie. Stop this madness. Anyone, please. *Please.*"

Never once, in all the years Althea had earned a small fortune for summoning spirits, had she actually *tried*.

Really tried. She'd pretended to mean it, of course. Her heartbroken clients expected as much. Those poor souls who no doubt prayed every night for the sakes of their lost loved ones.

And she'd taken advantage of them for it.

Now, for the very first time in her life, Mistress Althea truly asked for contact with the spirit world. Not just asked, but begged.

For their help.

As the final words of Althea's plea left her lips, she swallowed them on a sob. Tears were streaming down her face, ruining her once perfect make-up. The ball seemed a lifetime away. All that existed now was Leslie's madness and Ben bravely, fruitlessly, trying to stop him.

Then the air stilled and turned to ice.

Even the strange vortex to the Void paused, as if listening.

But there was no sound as the spirits appeared.

Henry was first, popping into existence beside Althea. He looked down at her. "Oh dear, Miss Smith. That doesn't look good."

Althea smiled through her tears. She didn't know what the little boy could do, but he'd listened. He'd come to help. "No, Henry. It's quite painful."

"I imagine so."

Leslie and Ben had stopped fighting, and it was Leslie who found his voice first. "Henry?"

The ghost of the little boy looked over at the man who'd killed him with such ferocity Althea sat back. "You're going to pay for this, Robert."

Leslie gathered himself enough to stand and wipe the blood from his nose with the back of his hand. "I doubt it. You see how helpless the Duke here is, you think you can do any better?"

Henry shook his head. "No, but they can."

In a flash the room was full of soft blue light as dozens of ghosts burst into being, lighting the darkness and filling the room. A lord in armor and a peasant woman with the pox stood beside a man with a broad nose wearing nothing but animals hides. Behind them what appeared to be three Roman centurions hovered, scowling at Lord Leslie with fury in their ancient eyes.

Everywhere Althea looked there were ghosts from every era in history she knew of. Men, women, too many children, all watching Lord Leslie with loathing.

"Where- where did you come from?" he asked, sounding for the first time all evening a little afraid.

"She summoned us," Henry said, pointing to Althea.

"And you thought I was a fraud," she said, grinning at Henry. The little boy grinned back.

"This is- this is impossible. How are there so many of you?"

The knight floated forward and answered in a low voice. "We are all the souls who died on or near this place and never found our peace. We've had little to do these eons but consider our plight. The nature of good and evil."

A little girl in a grubby tunic floated forward. "And you, sir, are evil."

Leslie staggered back. "I- I'm not. Being clever is hardly a sin. I can help you, you know. I know spells that could bring you back to life, return you to your bodies- well, not *your* bodies, but good fresh un-rotten ones. Would you like that?"

The host of the dead said nothing.

Leslie wiped the blood from his broken nose again. "Very well. Perhaps we can come up with another arrangement."

"I don't think that's fair to him," the knight said, tossing his head at Henry.

"H- Henry? You know it was an accident don't you? I never meant-"

"We heard everything you said, Robert," Henry said in a cold, surprisingly adult voice. "And we didn't like it."

Leslie turned to Althea. "Mistress, send them back. You brought them here, they will listen to you-"

"No," the pox-faced woman snapped. "We won't. And you're boring us now, so let's get on with it."

"Get on with what?" Leslie asked, but his words were drowned out by the army of ghosts descending upon him, each with different abilities and powers, combined rendering even Leslie incapable of defense.

Althea closed her eyes as translucent bodies flowed past her, around her, through her. She did not know where Ben was in the melee, but she hoped he stayed clear of it.

Lord Leslie's screams rent the air and the hole to the Void resumed its howling.

The ghosts were dragging Leslie towards that hole. His pleading was frantic, and Althea covered her ears against the terrible roaring of the ghosts that drowned it out.

After a moment she peeked, just in time to see Leslie held aloft by the powers of the ghosts, suspended in the air before the tear in the universe his own powers had made.

Henry floated before him and said something Althea could not hear.

Leslie's face blanched as Henry took a deep breath, puffed out his cheeks and, with all the force his small frame could muster he blew Leslie into the waiting blackness.

Leslie disappeared instantly, sucked into nothingness.

Henry called out in triumph as his spirit grew brighter, until he was little more than a white ball of light. Then, he was gone. His business finished, he moved on. The ghosts cheered and roared their delight, fading to nothing within moments, gone to whatever otherworldly feast they might throw themselves. The doorway to the Void shuddered, as if still swallowing Leslie.

The house trembled.

Then the void snapped closed with a resounding snap.

For a moment, nothing moved. Silence reigned.

"Oh," Ben said from beside Althea. "Well that's good."

Then a crack appeared where the hole had been, at the attic window, and grew bigger.

"That's not," Althea said. "Quick, move!"

Except Ben did not need to move. He had no body.

It was Althea who needed to flee as the floor split open and the house slowly tore itself in two.

Ben watched helplessly as a seam rent down the center of his house. He knew it wasn't just the attic. He could hear lumber and tile and and plaster splintering all the way down to the basement. Whatever power Leslie had used to open that window into the Void, falling into it himself seemed to cause its power to cave in on itself. The good news was it meant the hole was closed and no one else would be sucked in.

The bad news was Ben's house had not been designed to handle that sort of cosmic force. Bad rainstorms, yes. The occasional blizzard, sure. But a vortex into the liminal space between life and death?

No, Ben had not learned anything about *that* at Oxford.

"Althea, run to the stairwell! Get to the side of the house! The middle is-"

He was cut off by her scream as the floor beneath her feet gave way. She'd stepped at the weak spot above the foyer many stories below. The spot where he'd meant to hang his chandelier, to reinforce it for the heavy crystal. The spot that had been dismantled and abandoned after his death, considered too full of bad luck for any subsequent workmen.

The house was already buckling, and just Althea's weight was enough to collapse that part.

They tumbled down, barely catching onto the edge of the floorboards as they separated. Fortunately, her portion held, even as the other side of the house inched away from her, splitting in half, crumbling beneath them.

Ben flew to the edge, sending out every bit of power he had left to hold her up.

Beneath her, far below on the beautiful marble floor of the foyer, he saw whoever remained of the party guests fleeing the house. A loud crack told him the grand staircase just out of sight was cracking.

Goggins ran by, looked up, and kept running.

"Ben, help me," Althea breathed, her eyes wild. She could barely move her left shoulder, and her right hand was slipping, her fine silk gloves making the task twice as difficult.

"I'm here darling, I'll save you," Ben said, but he didn't mean it. He couldn't. What could he do? This was just like Liza all over again.

He felt his power flicker and Althea slid back an inch. She screamed. "Ben! Can you push me up?"

He tried. Nothing happened. "I'm drained Althea, I can't I-"

"Soften my fall then. I'll let go, and it's okay if it's not a soft landing, but you can keep me alive can't you?"

Ben could barely bring himself to meet her eyes.

She saw the truth in them, and tears filled her own.

"I don't know what to do," he said. "My whole life I tried to fix things. I wanted to keep things safe. Keep the people I love safe. And now I don't know how to save you."

A tear ran down her beautiful face. "The people you love, Ben?"

"Yes. Yes, Althea I love you."

His power flickered, harder this time. She slid another inch, her boot sliding off her foot and landing on the marble below. Around them windows shattered and wood buckled as the house disintegrated. Any moment now the floor of the attic would give way entirely.

"Althea!" A voice called, and Ben looked down.

"It's Goggins and Maybourne. They've got a quilt and a bunch of cushions beneath it."

"To catch me?" Althea asked, unable to see for

herself without losing her hold.

"It won't work. It's too far."

Ben's power flickered again, and Althea shouted, struggling to maintain her hold. She was only maintaining contact with the splintered wood by her fingertips, and her gloves were sliding off. "Ben, drop your power. Let me go."

"What?"

"Let them catch me. The house is going to collapse soon and we all need to get out. Please Ben, just trust me. Trust them. *Let me go.*"

The words were the most terrifying Ben had ever heard.

"No, Althea, I can't."

"You have to, Ben. Please. *Trust me.*"

Such feeling wracked Ben at the words that his power shuddered and she fell, losing all contact with the edge of the floor. He caught her only just in time, keeping her suspended in the air just below him, as the dregs of his power ran out.

Althea raised her black eyes to his, and to Ben's surprise he did not see fear in them. Only love. "I love you, Ben," she said.

The words struck him like a bolt of lightning through his heart, into the core of his very soul. The truth of them shattering his fears.

The house groaned and he felt the attic sinking in on itself, the floors below bending under their own weight.

He had to trust her. He had to trust Goggins and the Earl. He had to *trust* that she would be okay, even though he could do nothing for her, except let her go.

So he did.

Chapter Twenty
The Duke

The last thing Althea saw before she fell was Ben's face, a warm smile breaking over his handsome features. He trusted her. He *loved* her.

And she loved him.

She'd nearly lied- she nearly hadn't told him at all. She was accustomed to hiding the truth, masking it unless it suited her.

She was terrified to tell him, terrified to give him that power over her.

But she'd done it anyway. Because a truth like that *had* to be shared.

And it felt wonderful to share it.

She landed on the padding Goggins and the Earl had laid out with a hard thud, the quilt they held between them softening the blow as she slammed into the cushions beneath. For a moment, she could not breathe as all the air rushed from her lungs.

Gasping, she did not struggle as the Earl of Maybourne scooped her up in his arms and carried her out of the house.

The night air felt cold and real. Althea had the sensation she was waking up from a dream. But as the Earl set her down on the soft grass of the little garden at Cavendish Square, and Althea looked across the street, she knew it had been no dream. The house was collapsing, engulfed now in flames as its many gorgeous sconces fell and shattered.

Many of the guests remained, watching the spectacle. Somewhere in the distance the sounds of men coming to help put out the flames reached Althea's ears, but the Earl beside her stood motionless. Simply watching as it all burned down.

The thought struck Althea like a lighting bolt.

It was all burning down. The house would be gone. *Ben* would be gone.

She staggered to her feet, biting back a cry of pain in her shoulder.

Lady Maybourne appeared at her side. "Althea dear, sit down, please. Doctor Cossington has been called. He must see to your-"

"No!" Althea cried, lurching away. "Ben's in there! We cannot let it burn!"

"Darling, Ben is already dead. It's- it's too late."

Althea saw the truth in Lady Maybourne's eyes but she refused to accept it. He was dead, yes, but he could not be gone. She could not lose him.

She staggered towards the wall of flame.

"Ben!" She shouted. "Ben!"

With a mighty crack and a roar of fire another

massive chunk of the house fell. Althea stumbled back, the heat nearly unbearable. Suddenly men were everywhere with buckets and horses crying as they drew fire engines and men appeared with pumps and hoses and water and-

And none of it mattered, she realized.

They could not save the house. The fire was too big, too fierce.

It was gone.

Ben was gone.

Ben felt like hell.

He opened his eyes.

He was *in* hell, more like. Around him everything was on fire. Smoke burned his lungs and smoke filled his nostrils. It smelled nothing like the old pipe tobacco he once loved. This smoke smelled angry, hostile- composed of things not meant to burn.

Which was odd, he thought. *It shouldn't smell like anything.*

He struggled to his feet, half-crawling away from the old fourposter he'd fallen in. It had then fallen, and then kept the worst of debris from landing on him.

It was a miracle, he thought, as he stumbled into the back garden, away from the flames. The fall

should have killed him. Somehow, though, he'd lived.

Several men charged in from the mews.

"Clear the way sir! Fire brigade coming through!"

Ben stepped to the side to let them pass. The smell of wool and sweat washed over him.

Not wanting to be a bother, he made his way to the back alley behind the mews and decided to walk around the block to watch the proceedings from the relative comfort of the Square.

Althea could not stop crying. Even when urgent voices and strong hands urged her to get up, to move out of the middle of the street, she ignored them.

Finally, someone- probably Maybourne again- lifted her bodily and hauled her back to the grass.

She cried there, too.

The pain was unbearable. After everything they'd been through, and he was just- gone? Ben couldn't be gone. The world could not simply continue without him in it. It was unthinkable.

It was impossible.

"Althea," someone beside her hissed.

She looked up and into the tear-stained face of Charlotte Ridgely.

"What is it?" she asked, not particularly wanting to talk to Charlotte Ridgely just now.

"Althea I'm sorry. I'm so sorry for what I did. I- I wasn't thinking. I didn't know. And-"

"And what?"

"And I think I really might be mad."

Althea wasn't sure how to politely respond to that, so she said, "It's fine, Charlotte. I forgive you. We all make stupid choices sometimes."

"No, I mean, I really think I might be mad." She pointed through the trees to the edge of Cavendish Square, where a man was standing in his nightclothes watching the excitement.

No, those weren't nightclothes.

They were just very revealing clothes.

A thrum of energy ran through Althea, followed by sadness. In profile, lit by the flames, the man looked like Ben.

"You're not mad, Charlotte, that fellow does look like Ben. You're just in shock, we all are."

Charlotte's wide blue eyes met Althea's. "Althea I- I think that *is* Ben."

The words did not make sense at first. It seemed impossible. No, that wasn't it- it *was* impossible.

Then the man turned and faced her, and, somehow, it wasn't.

"Ben?" she breathed, getting awkwardly to her feet. Someone had put her arm in a sling, but it still hurt like hell.

She just suddenly didn't care.

The man took a halting step towards her, as if unsure of something. Then he looked down at himself and back at her.

Althea ran, tears streaming down her face, and did not stop until she slammed into Ben's broad chest, where she was immediately enveloped in his arms.

"How?" they both said at the same time.

"It's impossible," Althea sputtered through her tears, which had, somehow increased.

"I- I broke the curse. One moment I was fading, I couldn't hold you- and I- I let you go, and then I woke up, like this."

"You trusted me, Ben. You let them catch me. You chose to act not from fear, but from love."

The words were out before she could think them through, but she knew they were true. So did he.

"Love broke the curse after all," Ben murmured, pushing Althea's hair back from her tear-stained face. "Old Anne Boleyn had a vicious sense of humor."

Althea laughed. "You don't think she loved your ancestor Thomas do you?"

"I have no idea. I hope not, but then, maybe she thought it was important for him to know what it was."

"And do *you* know what love is, Benedict Lionel Aston?"

Ben smiled down at Althea, the flames of his burning masterpiece sparkling in his eyes. "I do."

Two Weeks Later

Althea had never stayed at a hotel before, but she'd now been at the Clarendon a fortnight. She as not certain she wished to leave. The rooms were comfortable, the beds even more so, the French cuisine delectable and the service excellent. She had only to relax and recuperate and her every whim was cared for.

She felt like a traitor to her class for enjoying such privilege, but then, she reminded herself, she had been shot and only narrowly escaped both a burning building and a doorway into the space been life and death itself.

She deserved a break.

So did Ben, who was still reeling at the return of his body. His life.

They'd both been in shock the first few days, when Lady Maybourne had shuffled them into the hotel along with her surgeon, who had made quick work of Althea's arm. The bullet had come out easily enough, and with sufficient laudanum Althea had barely noticed.

More accurately, she'd not had a clear head for a week, as the drugs for her arm rendered her woozy at best. She'd already weaned herself away from them though, not enjoying the sluggish feeling of them. The pain had gone down, too. Enough, according to the doctor, for the patient to consummate her marriage.

Because the moment her head had cleared a week ago, Ben had asked for her hand, and using a genuine special license courtesy of the Earl- the one Wilkes had obtained for Charlotte and Leslie had been a fake- Althea and Ben had married in their cozy hotel room. She'd been in bed, still under strict orders from the surgeon, but Lady Mayboune and the Earl and even Charlotte had come to bear witness. Goggins and Hen were there too, and, best of all, Nora.

It had been the happiest day of Althea's life.

Now, a week later, she hoped to overturn that record.

"Are you certain? The surgeon said it was very important you're sufficiently healed."

Althea rolled her eyes. "We'll just have to be careful. This time."

A muscle feathered in Ben's jaw. She knew he wanted this as badly as she did. "Please, Ben. Life is too short to deny ourselves such happiness."

He sauntered up to the bed where she lay, bolstered by a stack of feather pillows, and slid his cravat slowly off his neck.

"Are you going to blindfold me again?"

"Not this time. This time I want you to see every single thing I do to you. With my own flesh."

An excited thrill ran through her.

Someone knocked at the door.

Ben groaned. "Who is it?"

"Lady Maybourne! Let me in, I'll be brief."

Althea nodded to go ahead, and Ben opened the door. Lady Maybourne bustled in. "Oh, am I interrupting something?"

"Nearly," Ben growled under his breath as Althea answered, "Not at all, Countess. Please come in."

Lady Maybourne curtsied to Ben and alighted in the seat beside the bed. "They've been sorting the wreckage of the house. Much of the house is gone, but a lot of pieces are intact. Most of what was in the attic, in fact, as it fell on top."

"The fire didn't destroy it all?"

"No, those marvelous firemen arrived just in the nick of time. The houses on either side of us were barely singed. It's a minor miracle, everyone is talking about it."

"Has the Earl seen what's left?"

"You mean, does he now realize he was sitting on a fortune in the attic this entire time?"

Ben didn't answer.

Lady Maybourne smiled. "Yes, he does. And he's decided you should have it all. It is, after all, yours, Your Grace."

Ben's face went blank with shock. "He can't. He'll be bankrupt. He should have it."

"You can take it up with him."

"I shall. We should split it in half, at least."

Relief washed over Lady Maybourne's placed features. "That is very generous of you, Your Grace. I know Charles is pursuing some renumeration from Mr. Wilkes' as well, though whether we can get back any of what he stole from us remains to be seen."

"Well half of mine is yours, Countess. And please stop calling my Your Grace. I'm not a duke anymore. My title expired decades ago and I'm not going to try to explain to the King where I've been all this time."

"His brothers passed away," Althea informed the Countess, "and none of them left an heir. The line- and the title has died out."

Lady Maybourne scoffed. "The title maybe, but not the line. You're back now, Lord Stafford, and dare I say better than ever. Death has a way of improving one."

Ben laughed, but Althea realized she'd not talked to the older woman privately since that horrible night. "Countess, how many witches are there in England?"

Lady Maybourne stilled, then looked around as if to ensure no one else could hear them. Then she said, "I have no idea. Not many. I've only met two in my whole life, and we tend to sense each other. I'm still ashamed I didn't catch on to Lord Leslie sooner."

"You had no idea what he was?"

"None. But I think he was so far gone my own powers could not recognize him at all. Like ships in the night."

Ben's brow furrowed. "What do you mean gone?"

"My mother told me there is light magic and dark magic, just as we have night and day, you know, opposites. Balance. Few witches go too far to the darkness, because it often kills them. But it can happen, and I think that's what happened to Lord Leslie. Obviously, it has killed him now, but he survived a long time without anyone being the wiser."

"I don't suppose you know why that doorway in the Void opened when he was trying to conjure something else entirely?"

Lady Maybourne thought on that a moment. "I've considered it, and I can't say for certain, but I do know dark magic only knows dark things. He opened the

Void. There was so much death in him, his soul was drained and black, but also powerful, with all those lives he'd taken, it sort of inverted on itself and that was all he could conjure. The worst form of nothing, the opposite of life- not death, but oblivion."

Althea shrugged. "Makes sense to me. As much as any of it. Personally, I think I'm done with magic and ghosts and witches. No offense, Countess."

"None taken. You've had more than your fair share. As I say, I've only met two myself."

Ben gave Althea a wry smile. "But you really can't complain, wife. You did spend your entire career claiming you could speak to exactly such creatures."

Althea said, "Point taken" at the same moment Lady Maybourne cried, "Creatures! You've had a proper body for a fortnight and now you're better than the rest of us."

Ben chuckled and nodded at a package protruding from Lady Maybourne's satchel. "That's not a wedding present is it?"

"No. It's not. I think it belongs to you, Althea."

She pulled the brown-paper wrapped parcel from her bag and set it on Althea's lap. The brown paper fell away easily under Althea's hands, revealing the book she'd bought at Simonson's.

It was entirely unscathed.

A chill ran down Althea's spine.

"I think perhaps you should keep it, Lady Maybourne," she said. "It is a powerful item, and I am done with such things."

Lady Maybourne glanced nervously at the book. "If you insist. But if you ever need it, do not hesitate. Such objects often choose their owner, and not the other way around."

"Consider it a gift," Althea said, settling back into the bed as the Countess said her thank-you and farewells and snuck out.

Leaving Ben and Althea alone.

Finally.

Ben could not believe it. He was a alive. Better yet, so was Althea. They'd done it. They'd broken his curse, they'd stopped Leslie, they'd found a way to be together.

And, surgeon's orders be damned, they were going to be together in every position possible.

Not today, however. Not until Althea's shoulder was fully healed. This afternoon was better suited to gentle lovemaking. He had the rest of his life to ravish his bride, and he fully intended to do so.

But first, he wanted to go slowly. To cherish her. To love every inch of her, with every inch of him.

He pulled his shirt off and laid down on the bed beside her, facing her. "If your shoulder hurts, we stop. Deal?"

She said nothing.

"Althea."

"What? I'm trying to be honest from now on. I'm not going to lie to you," she laughed. "How about if my shoulder hurts more than whatever you're doing feels good, *then* we stop."

Ben gritted his teeth. This woman would be the end of him.

"Were you always this stubborn?"

"Yes. Were you always this handsome?"

Ben snorted. "Yes. Now lay back, there's something there, on the corner of your mouth."

She did as he asked, a smile curling the corners of her lips. But that wasn't what he meant, and she knew it. "You better lick it off."

"If you insist," he said and took her mouth with his. The gentle kiss immediately turned hungry, ravenous. They'd been so good about letting her recover. Ben felt like a starving man forced to sit by while a banquet took place before him, but now, it was his.

She was his.

Lips and tongues and teeth met in a dance older

than time itself. Althea moaned and arched toward him, but he gently pushed her down. For her shoulder, he told himself.

She allowed it, reveling in the feel of the pressure of his body against hers. He loved it, too. He loved every sensation, every taste, every smell. He'd forgotten what a wonder it was to have a body. It was far more intoxicating than the ability to summon wind or cast objects about the room.

Life itself pulsed through him, singing in his blood, and, increasingly, gathering in his cock.

God, he was happy to have that back.

Althea lifted her good hand and pulled him closer. "Ben," she sighed, her breath hot against his ear as his lips moved across her jawline and down her neck.

"Althea," he purred, then paused. "Or are you Jane now that you've retired?"

"Call me whatever you want, you bastard, just don't stop."

Ben chuckled and resumed his dedicated ministrations to the soft flesh at the base of her neck.

By the time his mouth had paid proper homage to her shoulders, her breasts, her hands, her belly, her thighs, and finally, her womanhood, his cock was practically screaming for release.

"Ben, please," Althea begged, lost in pleasure.

She'd come twice already from his tongue and if her shoulder pained her, she certainly did not notice.

Still, Ben was careful as he shifted his weight to rise above her, settling himself between her thighs. Anticipation coursed through him, as though he were coming home after long journey. In a way, he supposed, he was.

Althea moaned beneath him, writhing, pleading for him. Finally, it was time. He did not have to hold back a moment longer, and thank god, because he didn't think he could.

She was slick and hot and ready for him and Ben pushed in, slowly, only an inch, then surged in to the hilt. Fully seated inside her, they both cried out in ecstasy.

When Ben opened his eyes, Althea was crying. "Darling, are you alright?"

She smiled up at him, looking like an angel. "I can honestly say I've never been better."

Ben laughed and gently moved his hips, testing the sensation. Frissons of pleasure radiated along his body. "Neither have I, darling, neither have I."

Althea raised her hips up to push herself against him, draw him deeper into her body. "I love you, Benedict Lionel Aston."

"And I love you Althea- Jane- whoever you are."

They both laughed until Ben started to move again, a pulsing, demanding rhythm. Althea met him stroke for stroke, until both of them were covered in sweat, their breathing ragged. Faster and harder Ben pumped into her, reveling in the feel of her, of his cock, of their joining. It was ecstasy. He was in heaven. He'd died, then come back to life, and now, somehow, he was in heaven.

Althea seemed to agree as at that moment she cried out, "Oh god!" and he felt her body shudder, her innermost muscles pulling him, milking him, as his cries joined hers and he let himself fall down, down, down... into oblivion.

He landed in her arms.

Epilogue

Eighteen Months Later, Selwood Forest

Happiness was much easier to enjoy than Althea had imagined. Most of her life she hadn't trusted her good fortune, largely because she so rarely experienced it. Anything positive in her life she had earned, or her mother had, and it was always at great cost. Worse, it rarely lasted.

Or so Althea had thought.

Now, she knew, she'd gotten happiness all wrong.

She took a deep breath of the bracing morning air. It was her favorite part of the day, these brisk dawn walks. They never did them in London, but here at the little country house she'd purchased for them, it was now tradition.

Except this morning, when she was alone, because the baby had woken up fussy and Ben had taken it upon himself to comfort him. Peregrine Montague Heath Aston. Named for all his uncles, little Perry was three months old and had already redefined the limits of happiness for both Althea and Ben.

She loved to watch her husband and son together, knowing how much it meant to Ben to care for the child. To hold him. To have it all be *real*.

Nora was a saint, too. She cared for the babe whenever Althea asked, and sometimes when she didn't, instead anticipating the little family's needs with her characteristic intuition.

They'd been here at the country house for six months now and it had been the best six months of Althea's life. Ben's too, she knew. Nestled on the edge of a large clearing in a sloping, wooded dell, the cottage was a sanctuary of peace and life. Flowers and clover covered the soft green grass beneath the trees. Deer and rabbits and the occasional fox made themselves comfortable in the shade.

It was the opposite of London. More beautiful even than their house in London, which Ben was having updated while they were here. Nothing major, only some cleaning and repairs, with alterations to one of the bedrooms for Perry. When they returned the house would finally be finished, exactly as Ben wanted it to be.

Althea sighed.

Who knew it was possible to be this happy?

The sound of wheels rattling on the drive made her turn. A carriage was visible through the trees, trundling towards the house.

That was odd. They never had visitors at this early hour.

She went inside to tell the cook to prepare some breakfast. She was famished, and she imagined anyone on the road this early in the day might be, too.

The rattling came to a halt and a moment later Althea heard a knock at the front door.

Straightening her skirts, she shooed the maid away and opened the door herself.

She froze.

"Good morning. Is this the residence of Mr. Benedict Aston?"

A man stood there, framed by the glowing light of dawn behind him. Even in the shadowy light of the doorway Althea could make out his handsome, familiar features.

A tousled mane of dark hair, pulled back into an easy queue. Totally out of fashion. Totally familiar to her.

The nose, strong but slightly bent. High cheekbones. A haughty, teasing glint in his clear blue eyes.

His skin, slightly olive. Just like his father's.

"One moment please," Althea gasped and slammed the door in the man's face.

Ben could not move. Perry had fallen asleep ten minutes ago, but Ben could not pull himself away from the crib. Every rise and fall of Perry's tiny chest filled him with hope, with happiness, with- with *life*. Ben loved his son more than anything, besides Althea, of course.

He felt guilty sometimes, as if he had betrayed Liza. But he knew that was ridiculous. He knew that his love for Althea and Perry would never mean his love for Liza diminished. There was room enough in his heart for all of them, and more.

Perry's tiny hand clenched and unclenched in sleep. Ben felt like a soppish old grandmother, the way the sight made his chest swell.

He couldn't wait to teach his son to ride, to fence, to hunt and- and *everything*.

The door to the nursery opened and Althea peeked her head in. Her face was flushed and Ben knew immediately that something was wrong.

"What is it? What's the matter?"

"There is someone at the door."

Ben blinked. "At this hour? That's strange. Who is it?"

Althea's mouth opened wordlessly then shut.

"Althea, who is at the door?"

"Ben, it's Perry."

Ben decided it was time for his morning cup of coffee, after all. One for Althea, too. "Nonsense. Perry is right here, darling."

He gestured to the sleeping babe, but his wife merely shook her head.

"No, Ben. It's your brother."

A Note From The Author

A medium who doesn't believe in ghosts falling in love with one? The idea for Benedict's tale came to me almost the moment I considered what the second Ghost Duke's story should be. It felt natural to pair him with someone who did not believe in ghosts, and only more exciting if she was someone who made her living from just such beliefs. The narrative tensions were obvious and tantalizing...

Then came the reality.

My research for this book quickly revealed a glaring challenge. My original concept for Althea was that she should be a medium, and the crux of her love story with Ben- the breaking point, as it were- should be a seance. Visions of a round table and any number of references from Disneyland's *The Haunted Mansion* danced through my head.

But seances- and mediums- as we know them did not exist in 1810. These were a Victorian fabrication, and a largely American one at that. It would be decades before the sort of ghostly interaction I'd originally envisioned would be historically plausible.

The occult has always been with us, however, and I felt certain there must be *something* to draw on for a commercial occultist in 1810 London. It turns out, I was correct. *Solomon's Secret Arts: The Occult in the Age of Enlightment* (Yale University Press, 2013) by Paul Kleber Monod saved my tail and provided a fascinating and invaluable overview of the occult in this unusual period of English history. As advances in science, technology, and the elevation of 'reason' took over the Western world, any interest in arcane or magical beliefs was relegated to the shadows. It did not, however, disappear. Belief in and fear of magic has, after all, been with humanity since our very beginning. Figures such as Althea have never disappeared but there have been numerous times (the Enlightenment and Regency being one of them), that such figures would need to practice their arts covertly.

One reason is England's Witchcraft Act 1735, which plays a key role in this book. The act made it illegal to claim any human being had magical powers or was guilty of practicing witchcraft. The penalty was a year in prison. Much better than burning at the stake, but still serious business. The last person to be imprisoned under the act was Helen Duncan in 1943. She was caught conducting a fake seance and detained for fears that she would reveal military secrets, as she'd 'contacted' the spirit of a sailor from the HMS Barham, whose sinking had not been revealed publicly. She spent nine months in prison.

As for historical accuracy in other areas, much of Althea and Ben's romance is fantasy, but I am happy to report that sterling silver dildos really were all the rage in 18th century France.

On that happy note, I thank you for reading *Romancing the Ghost Duke*. It has been sheer delight to bring this story to life, and I cannot wait to share with you what's in story for Ben and Perry's other two brothers...

Montague's story is on its way, coming September 2024: *The Ghost Duke and I*. Pre-order is live on Amazon now, if you want to be sure to get it as soon as it's released! Monty is the bad boy of the brothers, so you know it's going to be good. *(HINT: He's haunting a remote inn on the way to Gretna Green, she has secrets- and a fiancee, they're trapped at the inn by a violent snowstorm... with a man who wants to destroy them all... and danger, swashbuckling, and spooky spicy romance ensue!)*

If you'd like to find out more, or be notified about new released, please find me on social media- or, just hit the follow button on Amazon.

Thank you for reading.

- Cynthia

* * *

IG: cynthiahuntromance
FB: Cynthia Hunt Romance
TT: cynthiahunt.romance

Made in the USA
Columbia, SC
13 August 2024

40410844R00259